SNAKESKIN SHAMISEN

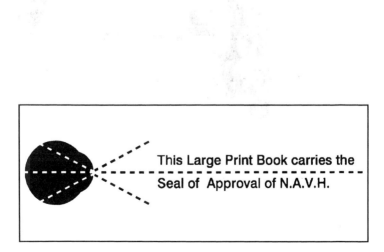

This Large Print Book carries the
Seal of Approval of N.A.V.H.

SNAKESKIN SHAMISEN

NAOMI HIRAHARA

WHEELER PUBLISHING
An imprint of Thomson Gale, a part of The Thomson Corporation

THOMSON

GALE

Detroit • New York • San Francisco • New Haven, Conn. • Waterville, Maine • London

LIBRARY OF CONGRESS CATALOGING-IN-PUBLICATION DATA

Hirahara, Naomi, 1962–
   Snakeskin shamisen / by Naomi Hirahara.
     p. cm. — (A Mas Arai mystery #3.)
   ISBN-13: 978-1-59722-397-3 (lg. print : pbk. : alk. paper)
   ISBN-10: 1-59722-397-2 (lg. print : pbk. : alk. paper) 1. Murder —
Investigation — Fiction. 2. Japanese Americans — California — Los Angeles
— Fiction. 3. Gardeners — Fiction. 4. Gamblers — Fiction. 5. Large type
books. I. Title.
PS3608.I76S63 2007
813'.6—dc22
                                     2006037907

Published in 2007 by arrangement with The Bantam Dell Publishing Group, a division of Random House, Inc.

Printed in the United States of America on permanent paper
10 9 8 7 6 5 4 3 2 1

For Wes

ACKNOWLEDGMENTS

Resources from the Okinawa Association of America in Gardena were instrumental in providing the background on the history of Okinawan Americans. They included *History of the Okinawans in North America,* produced by the Okinawa Club of America and translated by Ben Kobashigawa; *Okinawa: The History of an Island People* by George H. Kerr; *Okinawan Diaspora* and *Reflections on the Okinawan Experience,* both edited by Ronald Y. Nakasone; *Okinawa Dreams OK* by Tony Barrell and Rick Tanaka; and finally *Keys to Okinawa Culture,* produced by the Okinawa Prefectural Government.

OAA's librarian, Jane Kuniyoshi, was kind enough to direct me to appropriate books and videos. Any inadvertent errors in the interpretation of this material are completely mine.

The Brand Library in Glendale was a

wonderful source of Okinawan and Japanese music, including the CD *Rough Guide to Okinawa.*

Thanks also to writer Gary Phillips for turning me on to the Southern California Library for Social Studies and Research, where records of the Los Angeles Committee for Protection of Foreign Born document the struggles of certain Okinawan Americans during a troubled period of this country's history.

Again, the following individuals greatly aided in clarifying and distilling plot lines: über-agent Sonia Pabley, editor extraordinaire Shannon Jamieson Vazquez, copyeditor Anne Winthrop Esposito, and all other sharp-eyed readers at Bantam Dell.

Finally, I acknowledge my husband Wes and his extended family, who inspired me to write about Okinawan Americans in the first place.

"Once we meet and talk, we are brothers and sisters."

— Okinawan proverb

"The nail that sticks up will be hammered down."

— Japanese proverb

CHAPTER ONE

Mas Arai didn't think much of slot machines, not to mention one with a fake can of Spam mounted on top of it. Mas was a poker and blackjack man, and he had been for most of his seventy-odd years. Slots were for suckers. For heavy *hakujin* women in oversized T-shirts and silly earrings. And as far as he was concerned, Spam was strictly for eating — a fat, shimmering slice resting on a rectangle of sticky rice and tied together with a band of nori, dried seaweed. That's how most of the Japanese he knew in L.A. ate it.

His late wife, Chizuko, hadn't been a fan. She was straight from Japan, while Mas had bounced back and forth from row crops in his native California to the rice fields of Hiroshima. Chizuko had disapproved of Spam, and instead attempted to push *natto* — fermented soybeans, sticky as melted glue and rancid smelling as a baby's behind —

onto their unsuspecting neighbors. Only Mrs. Jones, a large black woman with a middle as wide as one of the tires on Mas's Ford gardening truck, had taken up Chizuko's offer. After she'd opened her mouth wide, placing the web of *natto* on her tongue and swallowing the sticky and stinky beans, Mas had half-expected her to rise from their kitchen table and head for the bathroom. But instead she'd smiled sweetly as if holding on to a secret. "Like okra," she'd said. "Only chewier."

Mas was more of a Spam man, with some limits, of course. Spam was perfectly acceptable at potlucks of the Americanized Japanese, in particular the second generation, the Nisei, and their children, the Sansei. Mas could live with Spam being served at the coffee shop of the California Club, a favorite casino choice of Nisei families, Hawaii-born gamblers, and gardeners like Mas. Hell, he would be first in line to order Spam, eggs, and rice for breakfast or a couple of Spam sushi, referred to as Spam *musubi,* as a midnight snack. But once he left the confines of the coffee shop, he just wanted to fix his eyes on the clean surface of green felt tables.

Yet to get to those dollar blackjack and poker games, Mas always had to make his way through rows of slot machines. In recent years, it had only gotten worse. Instead of the standard slots, with cherries and 7s, these new machines joined the video age and took their themes from old television and game shows. Others looked more like children's games, with jumping frogs and Chinese takeout boxes and silly cartoon sounds. Too much noise. Mas just gritted down on his dentures and shook his head as he passed by.

But when he first laid eyes on a Spam slot machine, he knew that the gaming industry had gone one step too far. First it was that ridiculous lit-up giant Spam can positioned on top of the machine like an askew crown. Then there were the multiple video images of people eating and serving Spam, and then Spam itself. What did any of that have to do with gambling?

Those thoughts returned to Mas as he sat in his fake leather easy chair in his own living room after a meal of rotisserie chicken from the local discount warehouse store. He was reading the L.A. Japanese daily newspaper, *The Rafu Shimpo,* as he did every evening, when he saw it — a quarter-page photo of a Spam slot machine on page three. And that wasn't the worst of it: two Sansei men were clutching the slot machine as if it were a Vegas showgirl. They had leis around their necks and glassy looks on their faces. Drunk as skunks, thought Mas. He adjusted his reading glasses. One of the men in the photo, a guy with long graying hair pulled back in a ponytail, looked familiar. No, couldn't be. Mas turned on the light beside the easy chair, pounding excess dust from the lampshade. There was no doubt now; it was his best lawyer friend — well, only lawyer friend — G. I. Hasuike. Beside him was a thick-chested Sansei man in a tight T-shirt. He had a mustache and sideburns. He looked like any other Japanese American man of a certain era. The type to hang out in smoky bowling alleys and pool halls. In the man's left hand was a cardboard rectangle, a giant check from the casino. Mas carefully counted the zeros. Five of them, all behind a number 5.

"Sonafugun," Mas muttered. Half a million dollars. He read the caption underneath the photo. "Randy Yamashiro, left, celebrates winning $500,000 in the Spam Slot Machine Sweepstakes at the California Club casino in Las Vegas with friend George Hasuike." Mas groaned. Now every Japanese fool, every single *aho,* would be making their way to the California Club for a try on the Spam slot machine. Any child, or even a

14

monkey, could stuff coins into a slot. It didn't require the guts and smarts necessary for card games. It wasn't fair and it wasn't respectable. But then again, $500,000 could buy its share of respect.

There was a brief story underneath the photo and caption:

Randy Yamashiro, a resident of Hawaii, credits George Hasuike as his "good-luck charm." Yamashiro, who is visiting the mainland from Oahu, announced that he will be holding a luncheon in Torrance, CA, in Hasuike's honor later this week. The two men were in Las Vegas for a reunion of Asian American Vietnam War veterans.

Mas knew that he should be impressed with Yamashiro's generosity, but instead it made him sick. Going to rub our noses into it, thought Mas. The last thing he would do was go to any meal paid for by a winner of a game based on a food product.

Mas's best friend, Haruo Mukai, of course, was of another opinion. Haruo, like Mas, had escaped from the ravages of the Bomb in 1945. Mas returned to America, his birthplace, physically intact, whereas Haruo had left his dead eye behind in Hiroshima. Haruo's good eye was as good as,

15

if not better than, a pair of Mas's eyeballs; he saw things that Mas had a hard time seeing. Like their obligation to go to that luncheon. Haruo had received a personal invitation — Mas would have, too, if he'd bothered to get an answering machine.

"We gotsu a go, Mas," Haruo insisted over the phone. It was close to eight, the time Haruo usually went to bed before working the graveyard shift at the flower market in downtown Los Angeles.

"I don't have to do nutin'," Mas replied. Sitting at home seemed like a more appealing option.

"*Osewaninatta.* G. I. the one who help youzu out wiz a ton of legal problems, rememba?"

Like a typical Japanese, Mas thought, Haruo would pull out that card. *Osewaninatta,* Japanese would say to each other. I am in your debt. You've helped me out, and I owe you, big-time.

"Get you, Mari, out of more jams than you can count," Haruo kept going.

Mari was Mas's daughter in New York City, and Mas didn't appreciate Haruo using her as part of his argument.

"Yah, yah, yah," Mas said quickly, not wanting to be reminded of past troubles. *"Orai, orai."*

16

Mas ended the call soon after that. He immediately regretted agreeing to go to the party. It was fall, a time to reassess and rescue scorched lawns and dried-out plants on his gardening route. It was a season to restrategize, not to wander twenty miles south to the coastal suburb of Torrance.

Haruo had invited Mas to go with him and his girlfriend of two years, Spoon Hayakawa. Spoon's real name was Sutama, but Mas guessed that it could have been worse — being called "Fork," "Knife," or "Chopstick," for example. Shaped like a gourd, she had long salt-and-pepper frizzy hair, which she held back with a stretchy headband. She was also a Nisei, and being an all-American gave her an easy sense of humor. Mas and Haruo, on the other hand, were Kibei Nisei, which meant born in the U.S. but raised in Japan. This duality resulted in men and women who were either sweet or sour. Haruo was sickeningly sweet, the type to hold hands with his girlfriend even when he was pushing seventy-two. That was hard to take for Mas, the classic sour, so he declined Haruo's offer. Another invitation came from other family friends, Tug and Lil Yamada. Again, Mas passed, making up a story about needing to deliver some plants to a customer on his way to the

17

restaurant. The last thing Mas wanted to be was a third wheel. Indeed, if he had to go, Mas would go alone.

A lot of times, Mas noticed, when you looked forward to something — like the start of the horse race season at Santa Anita Racetrack on the day after Christmas — time went slow. Each gardening job before the twenty-sixth of December seemed tedious, because it was the very thing that stood between Mas and his favorite holiday activity. But when you weren't that excited, it was entirely different. So cutting trees, shaving hedges, clipping rosebushes — they all seemed to merge together, and then finally it was Saturday and Mas was parking his truck in a gravel parking lot in Torrance.

Torrance had an Orange County feel to it — new land, large, pristine boulevards, and only a few bunches of trees in the business parks. Aside from its main high school building and the old retail section by the defunct train depot, nothing seemed to predate 1950. There had once been strawberry fields and flower farms, but then progress came, wiping out the farms and bringing in tract homes, super-sized malls, and corporate buildings, all shiny and reflective like structures to be launched into space.

Since the 1990s, Torrance had become king of the Japanese American communities, beating out its northern neighbor Gardena, which had held the throne since post-World War II. As the Sansei left their fathers' jobs as gardeners and producemen to become dentists, lawyers, and doctors, and made more money, they headed south to Torrance. It was like a hole in a dam — soon Japanese American families and businesses poured into the lowlands and then climbed up the Santa Monica Mountains into the Palos Verdes Peninsula.

G. I.'s party was being held at a Hawaiian restaurant called Mahalo. It must have been an International House of Pancakes in a previous life, because it had the same gingerbread-house sloped roof and concrete-block columns. But instead of being painted baby blue, the building was a tan color, perhaps to simulate Hawaii's sand, even though Mahalo stood along a huge six-lane boulevard filled with whizzing cars.

Mas was late because his 1956 blue-green Ford truck had been giving him problems. It had been stolen a few years ago, stripped of its guts like a cleaned-out trout. But the thieves hadn't been able to open the mouth of the machine, the hood, which had been dented and scarred when Mas's daughter, then six, and her friends had jumped on it like a trampoline. Ironically that past pummeling was the one thing that ultimately saved the engine, since no one but Mas knew how to open the damaged hood.

With the engine still operational, Mas had simply improvised on the truck's gutted interior. He found an old neon yellow Chevy driver's seat at the junkyard and jammed it into place. As it was a little too wide, Mas had to saw off part of the passenger's-side cushion and seal it with some black duct tape. Haruo had located an old dashboard from a 1970 Ford pickup, giving the truck the clashing look of two disparate decades. An old mug glued onto the driver's-side door with rubber cement had served as an adequate ashtray back when Mas had smoked. He'd kicked the habit a couple of years ago, so the mug was now filled with old Bic pens and a free promotional flashlight from a Clippers basketball game. Mas locked the car with a screwdriver (who would steal his truck anyway, especially with new Toyota Camrys, Infinitis, and Honda minivans all parked in nice, straight rows?). Lately, the dependable engine had been sputtering out, a flame growing fainter over time. Mas knew that one day he would have to finally retire the Ford, but today was not the day.

He walked to the restaurant and opened the heavy wood door. Inside, it was cool and dark; Mas blinked a few times to get his bearings. He could make out a counter filled with macadamia cookies, bean cakes, and other pastries. Up above were fake palm fronds and strings of leis made from mini conch shells.

"Aloha," said an Asian woman in her twenties, her cheeks as smooth and brown as the Hawaiian sweet bread on display. Her hair was long and straight, and she wore a yellow Hawaiian shirt with a pattern of white hibiscus flowers.

"Yah. Lookin' for G. I.," Mas said.

"Huh?"

"The party in the back, Tiffany." Another waiter, his hair standing straight up like the teeth of a comb, jabbed an elbow in Tiffany's side.

"Oh, please come this way." Tiffany led Mas down the stairs into a large open room with bare wood beams draped with more fake palm fronds. The youngster then returned to her post at the hostess table, while Mas stayed on the bottom stair, surveying the crowd. There were people logjammed at

21

the buffet line, scooping steaming noodles and meat out of metal trays and onto white plates. Families, including harried Sansei mothers and old ladies with their grandchildren, sat at round tables. A bar to the side with an overhead television tuned to a college football game attracted a couple of men with apparently no social skills. A stage in front held microphones on stands. And in the back were a bunch of Sansei men in polo shirts and long-sleeved button-down shirts. Two of them were wearing white carnation leis: G. I., the man of the hour, and his friend Randy, the jackpot winner. Mas's plan had been to say hello and then good-bye, but the smell of soy sauce, ginger, and bacon made him reconsider. He was here anyway; couldn't hurt to get in an early dinner.

A Sansei man in a windbreaker apparently observed Mas's change of mind.

"You a friend of G. I.?" He had a raspy voice, like a coil of wire being unraveled.

Mas nodded.

"Well, come in, come in. Have some food, beer." The man extended the Sapporo beer in his right hand toward the buffet line. "I'm Jiro. Another buddy from 'Nam."

Mas introduced himself and stepped down so that he was on the same ground level as

Jiro. The man was about Mas's height, a little over five feet tall, and his face was marked by a spray of freckles, splatters of different sizes and shapes. When he closed his mouth, his lips both puckered out as if he were waiting for a kiss that would never come.

Mas looked back at G. I. and his entourage. Jiro followed his gaze. "Bunch of lawyers," he said, pressing the opening of the beer bottle to his lips. "I tell him, where are all the good-lookin' single women? He say all the good ones married. You believe that, Mas?"

Mas didn't know if all the good ones were married or not, but one thing was sure — no good ones would gravitate toward this man.

"Now that G. I.'s back with Juanita, he's no longer looking."

Juanita? That was the first time Mas had heard that name. Sounded like someone from Mexico or South America. Mas was curious. He had never met a lady friend of G. I.'s.

"All the ones our age have *daikon ashi* — you know, those white-radish legs. I like mine hot, with legs that don't quit. Now, these young Buddhahead girls have them." Jiro gestured toward Tiffany and the rest of the waitresses with the hibiscus shirts. "Too young for me. I was born at the wrong time." Jiro pursed his lips again.

No sense in having regrets about when one was born, thought Mas. No person had control of that. Mas could have had his own lists of "if only, if only." If only my friends and I weren't in Hiroshima in 1945, they would still be alive today. If only I was a different skin color and born a different time, maybe I'd be an automobile designer and not a no-good gardener. But those "if onlys" wouldn't change his past, present, or future. It was better to just swallow your fate, the plain fact of your existence, than to be a *nakibiso,* a crybaby, mewing constantly like an abandoned kitten. Inevitably, people around you get sick of the noise and start thinking of ways to get rid of you rather than to help you.

Mas himself started to think of ways to escape from this pitiful man. "I go eat," he announced, and Jiro didn't put up a fight. He seemed to understand that hunger was a desire that could not be postponed.

Mas picked up a white ceramic dish and a pair of disposable wooden chopsticks. He tore the paper sleeve off the chopsticks and stuffed the paper in his jeans pocket. He knew all about these *johin* types, fancy-schmancy women who folded this throw-away paper into a chrysanthemum-shaped chopstick holder. But this was a no-nonsense buffet where nobody cared about presentation or looks. The whole point was food, and lots of it. Hugging the plate to his chest, Mas snapped the chopsticks at the seam and rubbed the *hashi* against each other to shave off any splinters. Biting his lips, he was now ready to partake and to partake big.

The only problem was the old *hakujin* man in front of him. He was at the Chinese chicken salad station, carefully maneuvering the tongs so as to avoid any wonton strips. *Bakamitai,* thought Mas, like a fool. Mas didn't have time for such nonsense and dug his chopsticks — at least he was *johin* enough to use the back side of them — into a corner of the pan, lifting out lettuce, mandarin orange slivers, and, yes, plenty of wonton strips onto his plate. The leaves of the lettuce glistened in a dressing smelling of sugar and sesame oil.

"Mas? Mas Arai?" The man with the tongs had temporarily halted his mission and looked down. Mas nearly dropped his chop-sticks.

"Mista Parker." As soon as Mas said it, he wished he could take it back. When he had known Edwin Parker, he had only been a mister, but Mas had read that he was now a judge. Had been, actually, for twenty years.

"Good to see you, Mas. It's been a long, long time. You look the same."

Parker, for the most part, hadn't changed either. He still had most of his thick hair, only it was now yellowish white instead of copper brown. He stood erect and wore his blue polo shirt as if he were in a suit and tie. The Parkers had lived in Pasadena in a white Southern-style house with an expansive wooden porch bordered by an insect-infested gardenia bush.

"You live in same place?"

"Yes." Judge Parker nodded.

There was an awkward silence then. The Parkers had let Mas go because they felt that he didn't use enough color in his landscaping. What was wrong with green? Mas thought. Couldn't these city folks see the different shades — from the waxy deep green of the gardenia leaves to the bright green of young palms to the blue green of certain pine trees? There was beauty in all those different hues. Were they so blind that they needed brash reds and silly pinks?

But Mas had taken his last check from the Parkers without complaint. The Parkers had always been on the *urusai* side, the type to

26

always call Mas about a leaky sprinkler or dying ficus. His business was still going strong at the time, and who needed an *urusai* two-bit lawyer and his wife to spoil things?

"Whatchu —" Mas began, and stopped himself. Who cared why Judge Parker was there? None of my business, Mas told himself.

But the judge read Mas's mind. "I'm on the board of the Japanese American Bar Association. G. I.'s the president, of course."

So Judge Parker was running in the same circles as G. I. What a strange world this was. Mas didn't know what a *hakujin* judge would have to do with a Japanese legal group, but then again there would be merits in brushing elbows with the many high-profile Japanese judges these days. G. I. had told Mas that many had gotten into law because of camp — the American World War II detention camps that had held their parents, aunts, and uncles in barren deserts and swamplands simply for having Japanese names. Now these judges were meting out justice, but instead of preserving civil rights, their decisions dealt with sports stars and car designers.

"And you know G. I. . . . ?" Judge Parker asked.

Mas waited. What could he say? That G. I. had once bailed a friend out and also found a criminal lawyer to represent Mas's daughter? That didn't sound too good, so Mas instead offered, "Friend of a friend." That much was true. Mas didn't want to keep making small talk, because what good did it do either of them? Judge Parker must have been feeling the same way. "Well, good to see you, Mas. You take care of yourself," he said, taking his wontonless salad into the crowd of people.

Finally alone, Mas went down the buffet line. There was no need for more salad, because lettuce took up too much room on the plate. A healthy spoonful of sesame chicken, globs of crunchy fried dough dipped in a sweet syrup and sprinkled with roasted sesame seeds. Then *chashu,* slices of roasted pork, the soft middle the color of worn shoe leather, but the outside a bright reddish pink like a harlot's painted rouge. A pile of kalua pig, shredded like dried-up grass. Tofu salad, cubes of diced bean curd with diced tomatoes, green onion, and bean sprouts, soaking in a dressing of *shoyu* — or soy sauce, as the *hakujin* liked to call it — ginger, and rice vinegar. The obligatory bacon-fried rice and chow mein, soft noodles in a tangle of snap peas, carrots, and chicken. And last of all, a line of Spam *musubi* organized like soldiers marching to war.

Mas's plate was so full that his Spam *musubi* rested on top of an ocean of chow mein. He headed first toward the bar, but lawyers had taken up all the seats. He didn't want to sit at any of the round tables, because he didn't want to make conversation with any old ladies or hear the whining of small children. He finally opted for the corner of the stage. It was abandoned; obviously the entertainment was over or yet to start for a while. Balanced on a stand beside the microphones was a Japanese instrument shaped like a banjo, the kind that geisha and old men in kimono plucked while sitting on their knees. A *shamisen.* Usually the box of the instrument was covered with white animal skin, but this one had the skin of a snake instead, shiny and taut.

Leaning against the edge of the stage, Mas placed his overflowing plate a few inches away from the *shamisen.* He decided to tackle his food in layers and first took hold of the Spam *musubi.* The taste and texture of the soy sauce-dipped Spam, salty and thick and juicy, merged perfectly with the bland gentleness of the sticky rice.

"It's Okinawan." A Sansei woman stood

next to Mas. She wore a couple of colorful woven fabric bracelets around her tanned wrists.

Mas raised the half-eaten *musubi.*

She shook her head no and pointed to the musical instrument. "The *shamisen,* I mean. I think it's called a *sanshin* in Okinawan. My grandfather used to play one."

Why would I care? Mas wondered.

"Juanita Gushiken. I'm G. I.'s girlfriend." She held out her hand.

Mas stuffed the whole *musubi* into his mouth and wiped the grease onto his jeans. Couldn't the girl see that he was busy eating? Mas wondered as he quickly gripped her callused hand.

"And you're Mas Arai, the detective gardener," she went on.

Mas swallowed a lump of the Spam *musubi.* Detective? What kind of stories was G. I. spreading? "Detective" had a bad connotation in Mas's mind. It was okay for television shows, but not in real life. Detectives stuck their noses in other people's business, and worst of all, they took money for it.

"That's what G. I. calls you," Juanita went on. "He said that you probably could beat my butt. I'm a PI myself. You know, a private investigator. G. I. and I met on a slip-and-fall case. The insurance company hired me to spy on his client. Of course, my client won the case. One thing about G. I., he's not a sore loser."

Mas had a hard time making sense out of Juanita Gushiken. He didn't know where she came from, but Gushiken was a one-of-a-kind name. An Okinawan name that went with the snakeskin *shamisen*. Mas didn't know much about Okinawa, other than it was a string of islands right below the main southern smudge of Japan. Okinawans were Japanese by citizenship, but there were some distinctions. Okinawans were known as being hairy and big boned. Peace lovers, yet the ones who had developed karate. Pork eaters who lived forever, or at least longer than any other humans in the world. Mas knew his share of Okinawan gardeners, but most of them kept to themselves, just like Mas stuck to other Hiroshima people, like Haruo.

Mas took a better look at Juanita. Although she did have a full head of jet-black hair cut bluntly at her chin, she didn't look particularly hairy, aside from her eyebrows, furry like freshwater lures. One sign of her Okinawa roots right there, thought Mas. Her body wasn't squat but lean. She wore a sleeveless top, which showcased her muscles. Mas figured that Juanita was at least forty years old but in a body most thirty-year-olds could only dream of. The kind of body that Jiro chased around in the little imagination that he had.

G. I. and his entourage had circulated throughout the room and back to the stage.

"Mas," G. I. said, "you've met Juanita."

G. I. looked happy, the happiest Mas had ever seen him. The scars on his cheeks, remnants of a teenage skin condition, were barely noticeable in the dim light. He had trimmed his ponytail so that it didn't look like a horse's tail anymore. In lieu of a watch, he had the same woven bracelets as Juanita around his wrist. In addition to the white lei, he had on a white shirt; in fact, his whole body seemed lit up as if he and not his friend had won the half million dollars.

G. I. put his arm around a man next to him. "This is the jackpot winner, my good buddy Randy Yamashiro. Randy, this is Mas, Mas Arai. The gardener I was telling you about."

"Hey." Instead of extending his hand, Randy merely nodded his head toward Mas. Mas blinked his eyes in return. Mas didn't care for shaking anybody's hand, and apparently this Randy felt the same way. For

Mas, it dated back to Chizuko's preoccupation with the dirt underneath his fingernails. He was trained to hide them, and certainly not show them off to strangers.

Randy was barrel-chested, sturdy as a bag of fertilizer. His eyes looked a bit puffy, as if someone had banged his eye sockets a couple of times — a sign of hard living and one too many beers, Mas thought. Randy had an unlit cigarette in his lips. Mas couldn't help but feel a pang of envy; he wouldn't have minded a Marlboro just about now. Randy seemed to read a recovering addict's mind.

"At Vegas I got used to smoking indoors," he said, removing the cigarette from his mouth.

"Mas kicked the habit a couple of years ago," G. I. explained. "Got to live long for his grandson."

Mas grunted, and Randy reciprocated with a grunt of his own.

Mas sensed that Randy was a quiet man, nothing much like his photo in *The Rafu Shimpo.* Mas had a notion that men from Hawaii were always smiley and full of laughter. But it was obvious that laughter had left Randy Yamashiro long ago.

"Saw youzu pic-cha in the newspaypah," said Mas.

"Yeah," Randy said, looking embarrassed. "The casino PR chick wrote all that stuff and had our picture taken."

"C'mon," said G. I. "Don't be so Japanese. Five hundred grand! That's a big deal."

Randy returned his cigarette to his mouth and shrugged his shoulders.

Mas didn't know what to say to the sullen winner. "Youzu see Haruo or Tug?" he asked G. I. instead.

"They left already. They didn't want to stay too late, I guess."

In a way, Mas was relieved. He could take only small batches of people at a time, and today he had already met enough strangers to last him the rest of the year.

"Excuse me, gentlemen," interrupted a tall man carrying a camera. He wore a safari vest and red-framed glasses. "May I get you all together for a group photograph?"

Mas narrowed his eyes. Didn't look Japanese, but then who said he had to be? Mas remembered that the photographer's byline in *The Rafu Shimpo* had a Latino name. They were all touched by Latinos in California and the rest of the Southwest. Since Mas had worked the lettuce and tomato harvesting circuit when he first returned to the U.S., he should have been used to the mix of cultures, but it always seemed to catch him off guard.

"Sure, sure," G. I. responded, but the rest of the group weren't as eager.

"And the musicians in the back —" The photographer addressed the two men who had begun setting up sheets of music on stands. They must have been a father-and-son team; they had the same long, sad-dog faces, except the older one's hair was a brilliant silver as bright as a full moon. They both wore matching black kimono and *hakama,* long, flowing pants. They waved their hands in front of their faces, a sign that they wanted to refrain from the photo opportunity.

The group pushed Mas, the shortest in the bunch, forward. Then Mas felt someone new at his side. The freckle-faced man, Jiro. From the corner of his eye, Mas spied Juanita rolling her eyes. She didn't think much of G. I. and Randy's Vietnam War comrade; that was clear. G. I. whispered something in her ear — maybe telling her to behave?

"Say cheese," said the photographer, and Mas mouthed "Chee-su" as the flash went off. He didn't think he was smiling; he might have been clenching his teeth, in fact.

The father-and-son musician team waited patiently as the group dispersed to make room for their performance. Mas headed for the bar. The televised football game had finished, and all bar stools were open now. "Sapporo," he told the bartender, and the beer bottle was twisted open, letting out a mist like the smoke from a lit cigarette. The bottle was nice and cold, and Mas enjoyed letting the bitterness dance on his tongue. This party was not half-bad, he thought to himself.

Another man in his seventies perched on a stool beside Mas. He hunched over as if he didn't want anyone to see his face. He, too, had heavy bags under his eyes — didn't anyone sleep at night anymore? Mas wondered. The man ordered sake on the rocks and barely acknowledged Mas, which was fine with him.

An emcee was saying something, and then the music began. The two men sat in chairs, their *shamisen* in their laps, while a Japanese woman and a *hakujin* man dressed in a short kimono jacket called a *happi* coat stood in front of a microphone. Mas didn't know that much about traditional music. Chizuko had gone through a phase of studying *shigin,* Japanese poetry set to music. Most people would think the combination of poetry and music would be relaxing, but *shigin* was anything but. When Chizuko sang, she sounded like she was about to give birth, only this baby would never come out. The shrieking and deep guttural groans continued for months, until Chizuko tired of her classes and, thankfully, joined a needlework group instead.

The *shamisen* tune here was livelier, happy almost. It was definitely singsong, with the melody traveling back and forth over the same notes. Mas watched as the two men guided large, flat picks over the strings and sang of islands and old kingdoms. The woman and the man yapped into the microphone, strong bursts of energy that startled even the most drunk and tired of guests.

Some people were standing and clapping their hands, but Mas sensed great sadness in the song. The man next to him had already gone through two more glasses of iced sake, and Mas himself gulped down one beer and asked for another. After the third one, the music was still going and Mas needed to go to the restroom. The bartender pointed toward the back of the room and Mas slipped off the bar stool to find relief.

As he walked down a narrow corridor, he heard yelling, and not of a musical kind. It was coming from the door marked KANE, men's room. A group of people were starting to gather at the open door, and again

Mas found himself pushed to the front.

G. I. had Randy in a headlock, pressing the top of his head against the hand-drying machine.

"Dammit." Randy shook G. I. off his body like a dog freeing himself of raindrops. "You don't get it, G. I. Never did."

"Listen, wasn't this party for me? You've won half a million dollars, man. Be happy for once."

Randy sneered, and for a moment Mas thought that he was going to do something violent, like throw the trash can against the mirror. But he instead tucked his head down and barreled through the crowd. The room was dead quiet. Everyone felt so self-conscious that no looks or words were exchanged. G. I. walked out, and the rest of the crowd slowly followed. Except for Mas. Filled with three Sapporos, he still had to use the bathroom. As he walked toward the stalls, he noticed a figure cowering in the first stall, the door ajar. It was Jiro, his Hawaiian shirt ripped and the freckles on his face smeared with tears.

Mas had had enough excitement and decided to go straight home without saying good-bye to either G. I. or Randy. The incident in the bathroom had put a damper on the festivities; the feelings of embarrassment seemed to soak throughout the banquet hall. The fake palm fronds began to look wilted up on the wooden beams, and the entertainment had changed to karaoke. An oblivious singer was swinging his hips to the words "I did it my way," convincing Mas more than ever that it was time to leave.

There was plain *haji,* or shame, that people carried with them like heavy stones. And then there was *haji kaita,* when you made a fool of yourself. A good number of the guests had watched G. I. and Randy make fools out of themselves. Old friends, both over fifty years old, they had no business fighting with each other like boys in a schoolyard. After Mas saw Jiro in the bathroom, the freckle-faced man, too, had scurried away in shame. Too bad, too bad, thought Mas. There was no reason for such a celebration to end on this sour note.

Mas took out the screwdriver from his pocket even before leaving the restaurant. Ready for his clean getaway, he shoved open the back door, only to bump squarely into the young hostess, Tiffany, who was coming back into the restaurant. The screwdriver dropped and rolled down the concrete edge of the parking lot. Tiffany bent down to retrieve it. She had a fat bag around her shoulder; she must have been done for the day and realized that she had forgotten something back in the restaurant. She handed the screwdriver to Mas, scrunching her nose in curiosity.

Mas didn't feel like he needed to explain. It was no crime to carry a screwdriver. "Sank you," he said quickly, and headed for his truck. Most of the Toyotas and Infinitis had left, and even though it was early, around five, there was a strange emptiness in the air. The traffic from the nearby boulevard droned like rushing water, but there were no other signs of life — no stray crows or lost seagulls on the telephone wire above. Mas jammed the screwdriver into the lock, swung open the door, and pulled himself into the Ford. It was definitely time to get out of Torrance.

As Mas drove north on the Harbor Freeway, he thought about Jiro hiding in the corner of the bathroom. Had something happened between him and G. I.? Or maybe the argument had started with Randy. These men weren't such close friends; or perhaps they were too close. Sometimes knowing too much about somebody could lead to trouble, Mas knew firsthand. As the traffic started moving, Mas relaxed a little, and stretched out his neck, hearing his bones crack. He didn't have to solve anybody's problems, he reminded himself. His mission today had been to show his face and wish G. I. well, and he not only had done that but had even stayed for a couple of extra hours. His debt to G. I. wasn't paid off, but at least it'd gone down a couple of notches.

Mas took the Pasadena Freeway until it ended and merged into Arroyo Parkway. Within fifteen minutes, he was pulling the Ford into his cracked driveway. He retrieved his mail — all bills and slick advertisements — from his battered, graffiti-tagged mailbox and went inside. He was too full to eat a real meal, so instead he sucked on a Tootsie Roll while opening envelopes and writing checks. By the time he was on his fifth Tootsie Roll, he had finished his bills and returned to his easy chair. Sleep soon followed until he was awakened by the ringing of the phone.

"Hallo?"

"Is this Mr. Arai?"

Mas's ears perked up. A young woman calling him "Mr. Arai" meant only two things — a telephone solicitor or bad news. He sensed it was the latter when the caller identified herself. "It's Juanita. Juanita Gushiken, G. I.'s girlfriend. The police want

41

you back here at the restaurant. Something's happened."

CHAPTER TWO

Juanita had specifically asked Mas to bring over his screwdriver. Mas couldn't imagine why anyone, much less the police, would know or care about the screwdriver he used to lock the door of his Ford pickup. Juanita wouldn't explain what was going on over the phone. "I can't talk anymore," she said. "Just get over here, please."

Mas called Haruo but just got his answering machine. Next he tried Tug and Lil Yamada's house.

"Hello." A male voice, low and distinguished.

"Tug. Itsu Mas."

"Mas, we missed you today. It was quite a spread. Haruo mentioned that you'd be coming, so we were expecting to see you."

"Yah, yah." Mas could only take so much Japanese guilt right now. "Went ova late. Did you hear about some kind of trouble ova there?"

"Trouble? No. After we left? What happened?"

Tug wasn't accepting the boredom of retirement well, and Mas quickly realized that his phone call was throwing more fuel onto Tug's simmering fire.

"Itsu *orai*, Tug. I take care. I see youzu later."

"Monday night, right? Dinner at our house. Give us a full report."

Mas grunted. He hoped the news was the type that could be shared at the Yamada dinner table.

As he drove back to Torrance, Mas's head began to pound. He didn't know if those three Sapporo beers were finally kicking in. More likely, it was *shinpai*, worry that something had gone terribly wrong at G. I.'s party.

Once he arrived at the intersection half a block away from the restaurant, Mas saw that it was much worse than he expected. Parked police cars lined the boulevard, their red lights blinking like bloodshot demon eyes. He passed the restaurant and contemplated driving back home.

But he remembered the urgency of Juanita's voice. He had to follow through, whatever the situation was. He parked in a deserted bank lot three doors down. He cradled his screwdriver in his windbreaker pocket and didn't bother to lock the door. A *dorobo* would be crazy to steal something with the blinking police cars a few feet away. Before Mas reached the Mahalo's door, he noticed a CLOSED sign in the front window.

A young Asian man with a shaven head was walking from the restaurant toward his friends standing on the sidewalk.

"What's happening?" they asked.

"Somebody got killed in there."

"For reals?" "Dang." "What else is open?" They hopped into a car stopped at the curb and took off.

Mas wished his reaction could be so carefree. Who had been killed at Mahalo? Surely not G. I.? Was that why Juanita had called, instead of G. I.? Mas fingered the screwdriver in his pocket and wished this whole business were over. It was one thing for old men to die, but someone in their fifties? G. I. was still in his prime. He could still become a father, albeit an old one. He could still make a bundle of money and maybe help a few more people in the meantime.

Mas tried the front door, and it opened in spite of the CLOSED sign. But instead of some smiling teenagers in fake leis, two grim-faced uniformed police officers

45

greeted him.

"I gotsu go in. My friend, G. I. Hasuike. His girlfriend call me," Mas told them.

One of the officers spoke into the other's ear. Out of the corner of his eye, Mas spied the hostess, Tiffany, pointing toward him. When Mas turned his head to get a better look, she lowered her head. "That's him," Mas heard her say to someone facing her. He was a large man, well over six feet tall. His shirt, blazer, and slacks were all the same tan color; he was as monochrome as a dog biscuit. He looked a little Asian, but not quite. He had dark, wavy hair and big round eyes that seemed to register everything in front of him, like the lens of a camera. Mas thought his roots must be in some Pacific island, a place where they needed their men to be fierce, at least on the outside. He told the hostess something that Mas couldn't hear. She wiped her eyes with a tissue and retreated into the back room while the tan man approached Mas.

"Hello, I'm Detective Alo with the Torrance Police Department." The man's voice was nothing like his body. It was thin and reedy, like the sound of an amateur blowing into a bamboo flute for the first time.

He told Mas to sit down in the next room, which turned out to be another bar for the restaurant guests. In a few minutes, Alo re-appeared with a long, skinny notebook in his hand. He sat across from Mas at a table decorated with a hibiscus centerpiece.

"So you were here for the party?"

Mas nodded.

"How do you know Mr. Hasuike?"

Mas didn't answer immediately. He didn't know how much he had to go into the legal assistance his friends and own daughter had required. He chose, instead, to give a shortcut description. "Friend."

"And Randy Yamashiro?"

"See him for the first time. G. I.'s friend," Mas said, and then wondered if he had said too much.

"You mean Mr. Hasuike."

Mas nodded. "George Iwao, I thinksu." He felt sweat drip down his face. Haven't done anything wrong, he reminded himself.

"I understand that you brought a screwdriver here to the restaurant."

Mas placed the screwdriver on the table.

"My picku-upu key don't work too good. Have to use dis now."

"What kind of pickup do you have?"

"Ninteen fifty-six Ford."

"One of those moldy green ones?"

Mas didn't appreciate his truck being called moldy, but this was no time to be a

47

stickler about car colors. "Yah."

"You a gardener?"

Mas nodded.

"We had a neighbor with one of those. I grew up in the South Bay."

Mas knew that the detective was trying to win him over with small talk, but Mas wasn't a small talk kind of man. "Whatsu happen? G. I. *orai?*" Mas's directness surprised even himself.

"Your friend is fine. But your friend's friend is not. Randy Yamashiro was killed this evening in the parking lot."

Mas's jaw became slack. He couldn't believe it. Randy Yamashiro had been breathing, standing in front of him, that very day.

"Tonight. About six o'clock. Were you still here at the party, Mr. Arai?"

Mas shook his head. "I go home already."

"We heard there was a bit of an altercation in the bathroom after five p.m. A couple guests mentioned a man fitting your description in the crowd."

How many people looked like him? Mas thought. His looks were a dime a dozen.

"You know, altercation. Fighto." Alo was trying his best to make some kind of connection with Mas. But "fighto" was an expression that fans used at Tokyo Giant

48

baseball games, not in reference to a bathroom brawl.

"Izu there, but nutin' much. Those guys just playin' around, not serious."

"Does G. I. often get into physical fights?"

Mas shook his head. G. I. was into battling people in court, not on the street.

Detective Alo must have sensed that Mas was holding back. "Mr. Arai, do you understand that you need to tell us the truth. Everything, you understand? Even the smallest detail can help us. Something that you don't think is important may really mean a lot."

Mas stared at the leaves of the fake hibiscus flower. Someone had worked hard to make it look real. There were even plastic artificial raindrops stuck onto the petals.

"Again, Mr. Arai, can you tell us anything about that argument in the bathroom?"

"Anotha guy," Mas began, feeling like he was ratting someone out. He explained that Jiro had been in the bathroom too.

"Are you saying that he was involved in the altercation?"

Mas shrugged his shoulders. He had walked right into the middle of the scuffle; he had no idea what had really been going on. If the police wanted details, they would have to go straight to the horses' mouths,

G. I. and Jiro.

Before Detective Alo could squeeze Mas for more information, a uniformed officer leaned down and whispered something in Alo's ear.

"Okay, well, I might need to interview you again, Mr. Arai. Here's my card."

Accepting the embossed business card, Mas breathed easy. "I go home now."

"Yeah, that's fine, Mr. Arai." The detective brought out a handkerchief and dropped the screwdriver into a plastic bag.

As Mas pushed the chair back to leave, he found that his legs had become as soft and weak as a cooked *udon* noodle. News of Randy Yamashiro's death had affected him more than he realized. Where was G. I.? Mas could only imagine G. I.'s torment. G. I. and Randy had been close friends. And to have their last interaction be a fight — it was terrible to close the door on a friendship forever that way.

Mas stumbled through the restaurant and back into the waiting area and almost bumped into a man sitting by the hostess station. "Excuse —" Mas said, only to find it was Jiro, now wearing green scrubs, the kind that Mas's doctor customer wore when he went to work. Jiro didn't bother to say hello, and Mas didn't either. Jiro's face, especially around his eyes, was all red and swollen. When some Japanese cried, the skin above their eyes folded up into double or even triple eyelids. Jiro had at least quadruple. His grief was deep — that much was obvious — and it would have been an insult for Mas, a virtual stranger, to say anything. Besides, had Mas in fact betrayed him to Detective Alo? Mas bowed his head and kept it lowered until he pushed open the restaurant door and entered the coolness of the October night.

Mas thought that he had made his escape, but there was Juanita on the sidewalk, talking to the Latino photographer who had taken their photo during the party. He was nodding his head as if he had agreed to something he was already regretting.

"Tonight, okay, Mario?" Juanita was saying.

"Yeah, my editor will be calling you too. First thing Monday morning." Straightening his vest, the photographer then headed toward the line of police cars.

After the session with the Torrance PD, Mas was not in the mood to rehash tonight's events, especially with a PI. He tried to get back to his Ford without being seen, but it wasn't one of those nights.

"Mr. Arai," he heard Juanita call to him.

He stopped in his tracks and cringed before turning around.

"Hallo."

Juanita's eyelids hadn't swollen like Jiro's, but her eyes were shiny and wet. "Thanks so much for coming."

"G. I. ova here?"

"He had to go to his house with the police. Randy's stuff is there. Oh my God, did they tell you? It's so awful." Juanita pressed a hand down on her right temple. "What was that about your screwdriver? You know, never mind. Listen, I know it's late and you're tired. But can you come to G. I.'s for a little bit right now?"

No, Mas said silently.

"G. I. wants to talk with you."

"I gotsu go home."

"Please, please. He's come through for you when you needed help, right?"

Chikusho, Mas cursed in his mind. This Juanita girl must have a big dose of Japanese in her; she understood the power of reciprocity. You scratch my back, I scratch yours. Apparently it was Mas's turn to engage in some back scratching. "Just few minutes," Mas said, knowing that he would end up being there for at least a couple of hours. He hoped his debt to G. I. would finally be paid off in this one trip tonight.

"I'll see you back at the house, then." She waved and went back into the restaurant. Was it her turn to be interviewed by Detective Alo? Mas wondered.

A yellow taxi then pulled up to the curb a few feet away from Mas. It was unusual to see taxis in L.A. People liked to drive themselves places; that's how cars like the Ford became good friends rather than just transportation. People spent more time alone with their cars than with their wives, husbands, or children.

A Sansei man with a sturdy build much like Randy's got out of the backseat. Mas passed the taxi but was close enough to hear the man say to the driver, "Hey, give me a break, eh? My brother just got killed. I'm sure the police will cover the ride."

Mas felt his head spin as he trudged on the sidewalk along the busy boulevard. Too much chaos, too many people. He turned into the bank parking lot. His Ford was the lone vehicle in the lot. He had almost reached the driver's-side door when he heard faint noises coming from down the connecting alley. Mas crept beside the bank building and snuck a look around the corner.

Two police officers aimed bright flashlights into an open rubbish bin. A third person beamed a light on the other side of the alley.

"Hey, I got something over here," one of the two by the rubbish bin said.

"Whadjya find?" the officer next to him, a woman, asked.

The man, who was a good foot taller than Mas, dipped his gloved hand into the bin to retrieve his find. The policewoman followed his actions with her flashlight. In her partner's gloved hand was a long knife as big as a dead trout.

"Jackpot. What's that, blood?" she said.

The third one joined them beside the rubbish bin. "That looks like a bayonet. That's the kind we used in 'Nam."

"Great. I guess we'll get home early tonight." The first officer placed the knife in a plastic bag, and the three of them walked north toward the restaurant parking lot.

G. I. lived in a place called Culver City. Culver City was old, at least for Southern California, and a lot of its streets tangled up in knots like the roots of a tree smashed into a pot that was too small. Luckily, G. I.'s house, a fourplex, was off a large boulevard called Pico, and even if Mas hadn't known where it was, he would have as soon as he spied a black-and-white police car parked on the street.

The unit's light was on, and Mas could see G. I.'s gangly silhouette through the glass door. G. I. lived upstairs, but he had his own downstairs door, which opened onto a set of stairs that in turn led visitors to his small one-bedroom unit. G. I. owned the whole fourplex, and the rent he collected from his tenants apparently came in handy between the infrequent checks from bureaucratic insurance companies and clients on the run.

Even before Mas had parked the Ford, he saw G. I. come outside behind two police officers who were carrying some kind of rectangular box. It turned out to be a black nylon suitcase opened to reveal T-shirts, folded jeans, and tube socks. One of the T-shirts on top had a design of a rainbow-colored snow cone.

Mas waited in the driveway for the officers to pass him by. G. I. brought up the rear. He looked much paler than a few hours earlier. His eyes were bloodshot, like two little red *umeboshi,* pickled plums, on his white, ashen face.

"Mas," he practically whispered. "Thanks for coming all this way. I'll be free in a minute."

The officers placed the suitcase in the

trunk of their car. They were having a few more private words with G. I. when Juanita arrived in a red Toyota pickup truck with a white cab over the bed. After parking the truck, she joined G. I. and the officers for a moment and then approached Mas. "You want to come in?" she asked.

"Izu wait out here for G. I."

"I'll be up there," she replied, and headed up the walkway toward the fourplex.

Mas got out of his truck and made it to the unit's concrete steps and sat down. He ached for a cigarette and massaged the back of his neck. How could he possibly help? Law and order was G. I.'s world, not Mas's.

The police car finally left with the suitcase, and Mas noticed a few of the neighbors peeking out their windows. Many a story would be woven in the neighborhood tonight. But that was the least of G. I.'s worries.

His friend was now approaching, worn-out rubber *zori* on his bare feet. The slippers slapped against the walkway, making a noise slightly irritating and lonely at the same time.

"So sorry." Mas rose, keeping his arms to his sides.

"It's been a nightmare, Mas."

G. I. ushered Mas up the stairs, which

were littered with brown accordion files and other legal-looking papers. G. I. had his share of brains, guts, and heart, but no housekeeping skills. Mas shuddered as he passed by a litter box that obviously had not been cleaned out for a couple of weeks. Since G. I. had a girlfriend now, Mas half-expected his apartment to be neater, but it was actually filled with two times the mess. A top-of-the-line bicycle, resting upside down on its handlebars and rear frame, was in the middle of the hardwood floor. A backpack leaned against the hallway wall, and circles of bright yellow and red rope had been left in corners of the living room. What kind of woman was this Juanita Gushiken? Mas wondered. G. I. didn't seem the outdoor type, although Mas knew that he was coordinated enough to tie himself into knots doing a thing called yoga.

"Sit down," said G. I. "Please sit down, Mas."

Mas opted for a plush purple chair the color of the felt bag for Crown Royal whiskey. It was his favorite resting spot in G. I.'s house; the chair enveloped and soothed all his rusty joints and sore muscles. G. I. squatted on a black leather couch, barely resting his *oshiri*. Juanita, meanwhile, was in a room connected to the living room:

G. I.'s home office, which was filled with more brown accordion files and fat stacks of paper held together by black metal clips. In the middle of the desk, peering out from the mess, were a computer and a monitor. Juanita was typing on the keyboard, her back toward them.

"I saw him, Mas. Just lying there. In a pool of blood." G. I.'s red eyes watered.

"You findsu him?"

G. I. shook his head and stared blankly at his open hands. "One of the waitresses found him collapsed by her car."

Probably the Tiffany girl, thought Mas. This might have happened only minutes after he had left the restaurant.

Juanita turned around in her chair, most likely sensing that she would have to take over in disseminating the news. "He was sliced through his neck. Went right through the carotid artery. Whoever killed him knew what he was doing."

"Didn't know Torrance so *abunai*." In Mas's mind, Torrance was a sleepy suburb with more than its share of straight-A Japanese kids. But wayward teenagers and drug addicts knew no geographic boundaries.

"No, Mr. Arai, this wasn't a random crime."

Mas felt something in the back of his neck go *piri-piri.* He swatted the back of his head just in case it was a spider and not his nerves.

"He still had his wallet, his watch," said Juanita. "The killer had some other motive besides robbery."

Mas frowned.

"Let me show you something, Mr. Arai. C'mon here."

Mas went into the small attached room and stood behind Juanita's swivel chair. "*The Rafu Shimpo* photographer e-mailed these pictures of the crime scene to us," she said.

"I don't know why you had to have him do that, Juanita." G. I.'s voice had a hard edge to it. "I don't want anything to do with those photos."

Juanita ignored G. I. "I made a deal with the photographer," she said. "We'd talk to the *Rafu*'s reporter if they'd send us a copy of their photos."

"You can talk to them. I won't." G. I. lay down on the couch and closed his eyes.

Mas wasn't sure where his allegiances fell, but he was curious to see the photos. The background was familiar — the parking lot filled with Japanese cars. The photos had been taken close to sundown, so most of them had a brownish tint. A group of people gathered in an empty parking space next to a white Honda. Somebody was kneeling over the collapsed body; all Mas could see of Randy was his outstretched arm. His fingers were curled in, revealing that Randy had been a chronic nail biter.

Juanita pointed to the back of the man obstructing the view of Randy's body. "That's G. I.'s doctor friend, Glenn. He's a general practitioner in West L.A. He was trying to revive Randy."

The dark pool of liquid underneath the doctor's shoes looked like an oil leak, but Mas knew it was blood. There were white tufts floating in the liquid.

"Carnation petals," Juanita explained. From the lei, of course. Next to the pool of blood was something that looked like a crushed box.

Juanita pressed down on a few more keys, enlarging the object.

"A-ra," Mas gasped. *"Shamisen."* Indeed, it was the broken face of a *shamisen* like the ones the musicians had been playing at the restaurant, stripped of its neck and its three strings dangling. The *shamisen's* snakeskin covering was peeling off, most likely due to the violence it had just experienced. There was a strange splintered bone next to its

neck, and Mas leaned closer to the illuminated monitor to see what it was.

Juanita nodded. "You can't see it that well here; the picture's too dark. But that's really a bone."

Mas grunted. *Okashii.* Strange.

"See here, though, up by the neck — the other two pegs are bones, you see?" One of them was black, as if it had been painted or dyed.

"So-ka," Mas murmured. The splintered bone must have broken from the *shamisen's* neck.

"I don't think they're human."

Mas was relieved. "Those guys doin' music — police look into them?"

"I saw them being interviewed, but it's not the same *shamisen.* See this picture?" Juanita pointed to a printout of the group photo from earlier, and yes, Mas's teeth were indeed clenched. "The shape of the musicians' *shamisen* on the stage was rounder, and the pegs are made of polished wood — no bones. And the snakeskin on their instruments was new and shiny — see how worn-out the snakeskin here is?" Juanita pointed back to the battered *shamisen* left at the murder scene.

"Ole *shamisen* worth sumptin'?"

Mas remembered watching the public

television show where ordinary people brought in old metal toys and wooden furniture rotting in their garages and attics. What they discovered, more often than not, was this junk could be sold to some fool for thousands of dollars. Maybe the *shamisen* was this kind of valuable junk, so valuable that it was worth killing for.

"Not sure," said Juanita.

"His *shamisen?*" Or the killer's? wondered Mas.

"He didn't have it when we left for the restaurant. We went together," said G. I., now sitting up. "He was staying with me. Actually, he slept on this couch." G. I. patted his hand on the leather cushion underneath him as if it still held the warmth of his friend's body.

"Whatsu dis man's work?" Mas asked.

"He worked in the post office on Oahu," G. I. replied.

Government worker. Not a rich man, but collected a steady paycheck. "Wife?" Mas asked.

"No," said G. I. "He's divorced. No kids. I thought both of his parents were dead — that is, until I got a strange phone call yesterday."

"You didn't tell me about any phone call," said Juanita, swinging the computer chair toward the living room.

"Yeah, I didn't have time to tell you. But I mentioned it to Detective Alo. It was an old man. Kibei, I think. Couldn't speak English too well. He wanted to speak with Randy. He claimed to be Randy's father."

"What did Randy say?"

"You know Randy. Poker-faced Randy. He stayed on the phone with the guy for only a few minutes. Afterward, he said it was an old guy talking smack, but he then left for a couple of hours. I didn't think much of it. I guess I should tell Randy's brother."

"Brian finally came to the restaurant, G. I. After you left. He borrowed forty bucks from me for his cab fare. Can you believe that?"

Mas remembered the chubby Sansei getting out of the taxi. "He from ova here?"

"No, he lives in Oahu, too, but he's been in L.A. on business. He was supposed to show up for the party; I don't know what happened."

"That whole thing is kind of weird, G. I.," Juanita said. "I mean, here he is on the mainland, and he's a no-show. What kind of relationship did they have?"

"Randy never said too much about Brian. Just that he was his kid brother. I guess he thought that their grandparents favored him. You know, typical sibling rivalry."

Juanita turned the chair back to the computer. "Shoot," she said. "I can't open up this one file." Her slender fingers quickly poked the keys on the keyboard. G. I., meanwhile, had risen from the couch and was gesturing for Mas to follow him. Once Mas reached the living room, G. I. pulled him into his bedroom, a plain square with a turntable and stacks of albums in orange crates all against one wall. On the opposite side was a futon on the floor, sheets crumpled below two pillows. Mas narrowed his eyes as he spotted something moving beside the bedsheets. A cat with black and white cow markings that was meticulously licking its paws.

"Listen, I need your help."

Mas waited with dread. Why did he get the feeling that this favor would surpass anything he owed G. I.?

"Juanita is going gung-ho with her 'independent' investigation."

That was obvious, but what could Mas do about that?

"I need you to work with her. Keep her even-keeled. Watch over her."

Mas furrowed his brow. If G. I. couldn't control his own girlfriend, what made him think Mas could?

"I know this is a big imposition. I would ask someone else, Kermit even. But Juanita can't stand him."

Kermit? Mas didn't know any Kermits.

"Jiro, I mean," G. I. corrected himself. "You know, that other guy in our Vietnam group. The short one."

Mas nodded. Jiro he knew.

"Oh yeah, well, we call him Kermit. Like Kermit the frog on that kids' show *Sesame Street*? He looks like a frog, right? We started calling him Kermit at training camp."

Mas gave G. I. a blank look.

"Anyway, she's always talking shit about him. But he's harmless, really. Has a good heart. Got into a little trouble after 'Nam. Drank a little too much, public disturbance violations, a few fights. But he pulled his life together and went through nursing school."

Mas remembered Jiro blubbering in the bathroom. "What happen ova there in the restaurant? Whyzu you *kenka,* fight?"

G. I. pulled the door shut. "This is just between you and me, right, Mas?"

Who else was in the room? The cat?

"Randy was beating the crap out of Kermit. I don't know why. They've always been kind of funny about their relationship."

G. I. swallowed. "I even asked Randy about it recently, when we were in Vegas, but he wouldn't say."

That didn't surprise Mas. Even though he had just met Randy, he could tell that he had been a man who didn't reveal secrets.

"But they were close. Real close. Randy trusted Kermit more than his own brother. You didn't say anything about Jiro to the police, did you?"

"No," Mas lied, feeling shame creep into his gut.

"I'm just glad that he wasn't around to see Randy's body. He had already left to go to work, the six o'clock shift. He's a nurse at Little Company of Mary Hospital, right in Torrance. Juanita thinks he's a jerk. He just doesn't know how to speak with women; he always manages to insult them. He can't help himself. When something gets into Juanita, she can't drop it. She doesn't trust anyone, especially authority figures. I guess that goes with her background —"

Before he could say what her background was, the bedroom door swung open.

"So you guys having some kind of secret meeting in here?" Juanita had one hand on her hip. She was the type who didn't run from confrontation but chased after it.

"No, no," said G. I. "Just talking."

"Yeah, right. I bet." Juanita wasn't convinced.

The doorbell rang, tinny and cheap, followed by banging on the wood frame of the glass door.

"Now, who the hell could that be?" G. I. went back to the living room and drew back his drapes. Looking out his window, he muttered, "Shit."

"Who is it?" Juanita asked, following G. I. down the stairs in the entryway. The cat was next, and Mas, not wanting to be outdone by a cat, went down too.

On the other side of the glass door were Detective Alo and a couple of uniformed police officers.

"What's going on?" G. I. asked.

"We need to do a full search of your residence." Alo's voice had become even softer, barely audible.

"Look, your men were already here to pick up Randy's belongings. What more do you need?"

"We've found some evidence back at the murder scene. We have probable cause."

"Do you have a search warrant?"

"We thought that you'd cooperate, Mr. Hasuike."

"Listen, it's late. I just lost one of my best friends. I'm wiped out, guys. I don't want you ripping up my place. You get a search warrant; better yet, you tell me what you are looking for, and I'll be more than happy to cooperate, really."

Alo and G. I. went back and forth like those tennis pros that Mas occasionally saw on TV while flipping channels. Except what Alo and G. I. shot back and forth were words, legalese that Mas didn't quite understand but still feared. G. I. must have won this match, because Alo was gesturing for the officers to return to their cars.

"We'll be back, Mr. Hasuike." Detective Alo's voice was breathy, but they all could still feel the power of his threat.

The three of them watched the police cars leave the street through the glass door.

"What was that all about?" Juanita asked.

"They found something at the restaurant. Something that implicates me."

"But what?"

Mas then remembered the discovery in the rubbish bin by the bank. *"Katana,"* he blurted out.

"What?"

"Knife. Police found knife in trash. I see it."

"What kind of knife?"

"Big one." Mas held up his hands about a foot apart. "Someone say like in 'Nam."

"Must have been a bayonet," G. I. murmured.

"So that's the murder weapon?" said Juanita. "What the hell? So what were they going to do, try to find a knife in the house?"

"There's two of them here, Juanita. Not to mention my thirty-eight."

"Shit. Well, get rid of them. Where are they?"

"I have nothing to hide. Probably half of the guys at the party own guns and knives. This is L.A., after all."

"G. I., you are their prime suspect. A bunch of people saw you arguing with Randy."

"I was trying to calm him down, I tell you. He just had too much to drink."

"You have to think, G. I. Think about your law practice. It won't look good for a lawyer to be arrested. Doesn't matter if the charges are eventually dropped, or you're declared not guilty at trial. It'll be all over *The Rafu Shimpo.* Your career will be over in a flash. No Nisei grandma will be calling you about her HMO problems. No Sansei's going to be hiring you on his DUI case. And you know the Japanese — they never forget."

G. I. picked up the cat and stroked its fur as Juanita continued. "I spoke to Alo at the restaurant. Told him that he needed to look into the *sanshin.* He said they had a lead on it, that I didn't need to worry about it. He practically patted my head, G. I. They weren't taking me seriously."

"The police could know something that we don't."

"I know, I know. They probably do. But there's something about that *sanshin.* Why was it there? Randy was a postal worker and Vietnam vet. He didn't identify with being Okinawan. I know; I spoke to him about it. There's something behind it. Something more than the police have discovered."

G. I. finally nodded. "All right, you win, Juanita. Stay out of the cops' way, but check out the angles they might overlook. You know, the *shamisen* —"

"*Sanshin,*" Juanita corrected him. "That's what the Okinawans call it."

G. I. chose not to argue with Juanita. "And take Mas with you."

"Why?" Juanita then looked down at Mas, slightly embarrassed. "No offense, but I can do this myself. It's my job, after all."

"But Mas can speak Japanese. He can really help you out with the Japanese people. People always talk to Mas."

G. I. was right. Mas, for his part, was usually dead quiet. It was the other party who would go on and on like a broken faucet.

Many times, these people were just looking for buckets to fill with their stories. But buckets were limited in space, and the overflow usually resulted in a mess that wasn't helpful to anyone.

"My parents can speak some Japanese."

"But Mas can deal with a different crowd." G. I. shoved his hands in his pants pockets. "He'll know the earthy ones."

Mas didn't know what "earthy" meant, but he figured that it had to do with the people who lived close to the bottom rather than the top.

Juanita crossed her arms over her tank top as if she were hugging her tiny breasts. "Okay, he can tag along. But you're going to talk to the *Rafu Shimpo* reporter. Off the record, of course."

"I'll throw her a few bones. But anything you find, report it to Alo, okay?" G. I.'s phone began to chirp. "I better get this," he said. "Thanks for coming all the way, Mas." He flipped open his phone and held it to his ear while walking back upstairs.

"I'll walk you back to your car, Mr. Arai." Juanita grabbed a hold of Mas's elbow and practically led him out the door and down the concrete steps. Once they were outside, Juanita released his arm. "I know what G. I.'s up to. He wants you to watch out for

71

me, right?"

Mas was too tired to deny Juanita's claims. He felt mucus rise up in his throat and spit on the side of the walkway.

"Well, that's fine. As long as we have an understanding. That we go after who did it, no matter who it might be."

Mas hesitated. That wasn't part of the deal. "Yah, yah," he said. Mas thought his daughter was *urusai,* but Juanita was making Mari look like a harmless little lamb.

Mas fumbled for his screwdriver in his pocket and then remembered that he had given it away to Detective Alo. He had parked underneath a streetlight, and the truck's yellow interior glowed like the peel of a ripe banana.

"That's your truck?" Juanita said like she didn't quite believe it.

Mas nodded. He silently dared Juanita to insult his automotive friend, but she was smart enough to back off.

"I'll see you tomorrow evening, Mr. Arai."

Mas grunted. When he got back into the truck, he realized that he hadn't given her his address and phone number. She's the detective, Mas thought to himself, she can figure it out.

The next morning, Mas called Haruo again.

Haruo worked on Mas like a human Alka-Seltzer. He cleaned up any pain in Mas's gut and cleared his head of any early-morning cobwebs.

"Come ova," Mas said after relating the sketchy details of Randy's death and the mysterious snakeskin *shamisen.*

"*Orai,* Mas, we be there." Before Mas could ask about "we," Haruo had clicked off.

Forty minutes later, Haruo was walking up Mas's driveway. And sure enough, right behind him, clinging to his hand and wearing a knit cap, was his girlfriend, Spoon.

"Hello, Mas." For someone with such a narrow face, Spoon didn't have a matching thin *oshiri.* She often wore bulky sweaters, which didn't do her figure any favors. Mas would, of course, never say a thing to Haruo, because, well, there were limits to every friendship, especially comments about a lady friend's behind.

Haruo had brought supermarket donuts adorned with a red sticker: DAY OLD/HALF OFF. Mas didn't mind eating day-olds, and even applauded Haruo's thriftiness. He knew that Haruo was barely surviving on his Social Security and the little he made at the flower market; Mas was always worried

73

that Haruo might someday succumb to his gambling addiction. Hopefully, with Spoon in the picture, the odds of that would be slim to none.

Mas poured some ground coffee into his drip coffeemaker and joined Haruo and Spoon around his kitchen table. He reported what he'd heard at G. I.'s house, that Randy Yamashiro's throat had been sliced open with a bayonet. A bayonet, Mas had once learned on a television show on the Civil War, was a type of *katana,* a knife that sat atop a soldier's rifle. In fact, during World War II, farm wives in Hiroshima had fashioned makeshift bayonets on agricultural equipment to ward off the threat of the barbarians, the Americans, who turned out to be not so barbaric at all. Spoon was apparently surprised that Mas could provide wartime details so nonchalantly, as if he were ordering a cheeseburger with fries.

"Mas and me, weezu seen our share of dead people," Haruo told her as if it were something to be proud of.

Spoon shook her head back and forth. "I can't even imagine," she said. "I would be having nightmares every night."

"Mas does. I hear him whenever weezu go to Vegas. Cries like a baby in his sleep."

"*Orai,* Haruo."

"Unn. Unn." Haruo was apparently trying to re-create one of Mas's night terrors. Haruo closed his good eye while his left one remained half-open. He shook his long white hair from his face, revealing the knotted scar stretching from his left forehead down to his chin. Mas knew that most people would have averted their eyes at this point. But Mas never turned away from Haruo. He figured the scar was part of his friend, like it or not. Why make a big deal out of it?

"Enough," Mas finally said. He knew that Haruo was just showing off in front of his lady friend. Even Spoon gave Haruo a sharp jab in his ribs.

Haruo quit shaking and patted his hair back over his scar. "*Orai,* Mas. Weezu listening."

Mas cleared his throat. "I callsu you ova here to find out whatchu rememba — yesterday's party. Figure youzu there before I come, maybe youzu see sumptin' I don't."

Haruo and Spoon exchanged quick looks. "Well, Spoon and me were talkin' about dis on our way ova here."

"Nani?" Mas waited.

"Dat Randy seem so sad."

"Didn't seem like he just won half a million dollars," Spoon elaborated further. "He didn't look us in the eye. Didn't smile. G. I. seemed happier for him than he was himself," she continued, reinforcing Mas's previous hunch.

Mas asked them if they had met Jiro.

"No, dunno Jiro. So many people at dat party. Maybe Tug and Lil rememba. Youzu gonna see them tomorrow, right?" During the past two years, the Yamadas had had Mas over for dinner every other Monday.

Mas directed the conversation back to the party. "Youzu no see a *shamisen?*"

"Just on stage," Haruo said.

Mas felt the top edge of his dentures with his tongue.

"What's a *shamisen?*" Spoon asked.

"Plays music. Like banjo," Haruo explained.

"You know, I did see someone with that kind of instrument. I think a *hakujin* fella."

"*Hakujin?* Not too many *hakujin* ova there. Maybe somebody's husband?" Haruo asked.

Spoon chewed on the tip of her index finger. "I was buying some peanut butter *mochi* from the cashier to bring back for my granddaughter. And this man came in, bringing in that banjo thing. He left it in the corner, in back of the register, and covered it up with his jacket. I don't think anyone else saw him with it."

"*Toshiyori?* Or young?" Mas asked. His heart began to thump so fast that he began to feel blood pulse up to the tips of his ears.

"You know, I really can't remember. All I know is that it was someone different. Someone who didn't match."

Mas pressed down on his left eyelid with his index finger. Somebody not matching could definitely be a distinguished-looking *hakujin* in a polo shirt. Somebody who was a judge.

Mas knew that he should probably clear his next move with that girl PI. But at times like this, you couldn't waste time asking permission to do something. If he had called home and included Chizuko in his decision to put two hundred dollars on a long-shot horse, Popping Paul, in the third race at Santa Anita, he might have lost the opportunity to win three grand — his all-time high in gambling winnings. And because he had not consulted with Chizuko, he didn't have to tell her about the rolled-up Ben Franklins that he had hidden in different parts of the garage: in the bottom drawer of his toolbox; inside a stack of gray, black, and red duct tape; in an empty box of cigarettes; and finally in the nozzle of an extra garden hose. He could have never imagined that one day Chizuko, fed up with their leaky, worn hose in the backyard, would take it upon herself to replace it with the extra.

Aiming the nozzle at the vegetable garden, she had been shocked to see a projectile of hundred-dollar bills land in her cherry tomato vines. The jig was up, and the money was given over to Chizuko — all except for the stash in the Marlboro box. Every businessman, even a small-time gambler, needed capital to reinvest in his trade.

It only took Mas ten minutes to get to the Parkers' house. It was located just south of Caltech, some kind of technological university frequented by pale *hakujin* and Asian men and a handful of women who all wore the same kind of uniforms — monotone T-shirts and jeans. The tree-lined street was empty as usual, typical for a Sunday. During the weekdays, the only people you'd see were the gardeners working beside their trucks and the maids walking either to or from their bus stops. The landscaping in front of the Parkers' white wood house had changed. The bushes had been removed to make way for agapanthus plants that looked like giant lavender dandelions. Rows of red, peach, and yellow roses were enjoying their final bloom before being clipped for the winter months. Bunches of sky-blue hydrangea, the delicate petals yellowing, seemed on their last legs. Mas was somewhat happy to see the imperfection; he could only imagine what hell the Parkers were giving the new gardener for that.

As he walked up the driveway, he was surprised to see an old gold Mercedes-Benz parked on the other side of their gate. The Parkers had just purchased that car when Mas had worked for them twenty years ago. Mas could tell that it was still in pristine condition; he didn't think of the Parkers as being sentimental types, so he figured that they were rich tightwads. Hiroshima people, in fact, were known as tightwads themselves — whenever other Japanese spoke of their frugality, they balled one hand into a fist to represent how the Hiroshima folks would hold on to their money. Upon seeing the two-decade-old Benz, Mas thought the Parkers deserved a two-fist ranking.

Mas pushed back his Dodgers cap and rang the front doorbell. He felt quite pleased that he was at the front door instead of the back. He was no longer a hired hand; nobody could tell him where to stand.

He saw an eye through the little glass window in the door. "Who is it?" came a muffled female voice from the other side.

"Mas. Mas Arai. Gardener from long time ago."

Locks were turned up and down the door, which finally swung open, revealing the trim figure of Mrs. Parker. Her hair was still dark brown, no doubt due to the help of a beauty parlor. She had a spray of wrinkles around her eyes and mouth, which surprisingly made her more attractive than in her younger years. She seemed more lived in, comfortable with herself, like a well-maintained car seat in a classic automobile.

"Mas, how are you?" she said. "Edwin mentioned that he had seen you recently."

"Good," Mas lied. Good, bad, it really didn't make a whole hell of a difference. "Mista, judge, here today?"

"Oh, no, I'm sorry. He's gone golfing, his Sunday-morning ritual. Is there anything I can help you with?"

Mas blinked. He couldn't come right out and ask, What was Judge Parker doing with a *shamisen* in Torrance? "My friend put on dat party in Hawaiian place," Mas finally said. "Just checkin' if judge didn't leave any-tin' behind."

"Oh, I heard about what happened at the restaurant. Terrible, wasn't it. Edwin has already spoken to the police. Is that what you were concerned about, Mas?"

Mas was struck by how silly he was to have come to the Parkers. Of course the police had already gotten to the judge; he had been the highest-profile guest there. And why would Judge Parker be carrying around a *shamisen,* anyway? Before the party, he had probably never seen one before. *Bakatare, bakatare,* he cursed at himself. He was starting to feel angry that G. I. had put him in this position in the first place.

"Do you live in the same place? Can I have Edwin call you?"

"Ah, no. *Orai, orai.* No big deal." Mas slid away from the door. "Sorry to bother." He almost tripped down the porch stairs on his way out. He realized later, as he rubbed his bum knee, that he wouldn't have almost fallen if he had just gone to the back door as usual.

Mas knew that he had to come clean to the girl PI when she came over that night. Juanita was less than pleased. "Why did you go there, Mr. Arai?" Juanita paced on the linoleum floor in Mas's kitchen. It was close to eight, already pitch-black outside, and a breeze blew through old wind chimes Chizuko had bought in Solvang, causing them to tinkle like shards of broken glass.

"Dis lady saw a *hakujin* wiz a *shamisen*. So I go ova to ask," Mas repeated.

Juanita opened her mouth so wide that Mas could see the filling on her back molar. She then snapped closed her mouth in defeat. "Edwin Parker," she said after taking a deep breath. "The judge on the JABA board, right?"

JABA? Sounded like a children's comic book character.

"You know, the Japanese American Bar Association."

Mas remembered Judge Parker mentioning that group. "Yah, how come he wiz dat group?"

"You know, I asked G. I. the same question a while back. I guess Parker's always felt close to the Japanese. Something about his old-time neighbors being Nisei. And, of course, he's done a lot on behalf of redress." Redress was shorthand for "redress and reparations" for those like Tug and Lil, who had been locked up during World War II without being charged with any crime. Tug spent a year in camp, before shipping out to fight for the same country that had imprisoned him.

"She couldn't say one way or anotha who she saw." Mas didn't know how good

Spoon's eyes were. And she hadn't even known what a *shamisen* was. "Could be some otha *hakujin* man. Maybe singer wiz *shamisen* group."

"Well, I'll check over the guest list. In the meantime, I'll get a photo of Judge Parker — there must be something over the Internet. We can confirm if he's the man your friend saw."

Spoon's not my friend, Mas wanted to say, but that was beside the point.

"Maybe she can at least verify that the *sanshin* she saw was the same one left by Randy's body."

All this detailed work was giving Mas a mean headache. He didn't mind tending to an overgrown bush, but to have to keep returning to people and having them recount their observations was too *mendoku-sai,* too troublesome, for Mas to deal with. Juanita must have sensed his bad attitude, because she said, "Listen, Mr. Arai, if this is too much for you, you can back out at any time."

Mas realized that was Juanita's unspoken desire, but that just made him dig his heels in more. "No, I do it."

"You have to be totally straight with me, even about the little things." Again, just as Detective Alo had said, report on the details.

"Orai."

"Promise?"

"Yah," Mas said. Anything to keep the girl quiet.

Mas walked Juanita to her Toyota truck.

"Dunno too many women with picku-upu," Mas couldn't help but comment.

"Trucks are very handy — as you know, Mr. Arai. You can easily hide dead bodies back there."

It was Mas's turn to open his mouth. Juanita let out a long laugh that seemed to bounce off each metal garage door down the street. "You're too easy," she said, opening the driver's-side door and getting in. She then proceeded to make a U-turn on McNally Street. Mas turned back to his house and then heard a loud boom, like the sound of a shotgun. It had only been the backfiring of an older German car, which was speeding down the street and now practically sitting on the Toyota's tail at the stop sign. It was past twilight. Mas couldn't tell if the car was gold or yellow, but it was definitely a Mercedes-Benz. They both made right turns, one after another, and Mas was worried. "Sonafugun," he muttered. He went inside and found Juanita's cell phone number on her no-nonsense business card.

"Mr. Arai," she answered her phone, surprised. There was a lot of static on the line, and Mas could barely make out her voice. "Something wrong?"

"Where are you?"

"On Fair Oaks. Near Old Town. What's up?" Old Town Pasadena was a tourist area full of lights and pedestrians. Juanita would be safe from there to the freeway.

"Some crazy driver back on McNally. Checkin' youzu *orai*."

"Just some impatient asshole. Lost him a few blocks ago. Why?"

Mas breathed easy. Why would a judge be following Juanita like a no-good spy? Didn't make sense. "Nutin'. I talk to youzu tomorrow."

Mas hung up the phone. Maybe he should have said something, but he felt like a fool. He didn't want to be like a worrywart old woman, jumping at every backfiring car and concerned about whether young people were wearing a jacket on cool autumn nights. But then again, he had told Juanita that he would report everything, even the tiniest of the tiny. He glanced at his Casio watch, held around his wrist with twine. Only ten minutes had passed, and Mas had already broken his promise.

85

CHAPTER THREE

The next day was Monday, the beginning of Mas's workweek, if you could even call it work. He only had ten customers, or two customers a day. His first customer of the week was Mr. Patel, a skinny East Indian man who owned a chain of teriyaki bowl shops in San Gabriel Valley. At one time, after he bought out his partner's share of the company, Mr. Patel had said that he wanted to rename his eateries "Mas's," but Mas told him that was a bad idea. "Think itsu Mexican food," he told Mr. Patel. "People get confuse." Mr. Patel backed down, deciding on the name "Crickets Teriyaki" instead. But he insisted on calling his star menu item — the jalapeño teriyaki bowl — Mas's Special, because it had been Mas's idea to combine the two flavors in the first place.

Mr. Patel had been married twice, and his grown children had left the house. These days, besides his restaurants, his children were his aging Shar-Pei dog (could an animal acquire more wrinkles?) and his collection of curved knives, displayed on the living room wall in his Arcadia home. Mas was staring at one now as Mr. Patel sat down to write him a check. He must have been staring at them too hard, because Mr. Patel commented, "You a fan, Mas?"

"Excuse?"

"Swords. The Japanese are the king of them. You must have some bit of samurai in you."

Mas doubted that he had any drop of samurai blood. Neither did many of his Japanese friends, despite their claims to have a direct lineage to those Japanese warriors. Alas, most of their ancestors had been peasants stuck in the rice fields. But what was wrong with being a plain old farmer? Mas wondered. In some ways, it took more guts and strength to stand out in the humid heat, swatting away mosquitoes as you pulled out green rice stalks, than to wander along dusty roads, carrying around an oversized *katana.*

But with Randy's death, swords were definitely on Mas's mind lately.

"These are *kurki,* the weapons of the Gurka." Mr. Patel pointed to his knife display. Noting Mas's blank stare, he added, "The Gurka were warriors from Nepal who fought for the British in World War Two."

Mr. Patel was an expert on sharp blades, so he might have some insight into the one that had killed Randy. "Knowsu someone killed with knife. Right through here." Mas traced the side of his neck with his right hand, which still stunk of rose fertilizer.

"What kind of knife?"

"Ba-yo-net-o. Dunno who do it."

"Hmm. If the victim was killed with a bayonet, they must have been fighting in close proximity." Mr. Patel tore out his check from his checkbook. "Hand-to-hand combat — the ugliest kind of fighting."

Mas left Mr. Patel's with a dull pain in his stomach. Picturing dead bodies diminished Mas's appetite, and he skipped lunch. By five in the evening, his stomach was jumping with hunger. But Monday was dinner-with-the-Yamadas night, so at least he would be ending his day with a home-cooked meal.

As he entered the Yamadas' dining room, Mas was surprised to see four place settings, rather than the usual three. Stinky Yoshimoto, another Pasadena gardener, was sitting at the table. Mas didn't know why

Stinky had been invited. He didn't travel in the same circles as the Yamadas. Neither did Mas, but their daughters, who had gone to the same preschool, would always tie them together. Those same daughters were now both in New York City: Mas's Mari, a sometime filmmaker, wife of a giant *hakujin* gardener, and mother of three-year-old *warubozu,* little troublemaker; and Tug and Lil's Joy, who didn't seem to be bringing her parents much joy these days. Mas had heard various rumors about Joy from the Pasadena gardener grapevine, but they weren't worth checking out with Mari. None of his business, thought Mas. Young people lived their lives as they saw fit. But he was still well aware of his own character weakness: although he didn't like to spread gossip, at times he didn't mind listening to it.

Stinky, on the other hand, bred and spread rumors like mosquitoes in standing water. Today, however, he seemed to lay low. Must be sick, thought Mas. And then, when Lil inquired when Stinky's wife, Bette, would be returning from her trip to visit their daughters in Seattle, Mas put two and two together. Stinky, a bachelor for the week, was clearly the Yamadas' charity case. Never mind that obviously Mas was too. It was always easier to see the true state of someone other than yourself.

"Sorry it's just curry. Didn't have much time to cook anything fancy today." Lil Yamada brought out plates of sticky short-grain rice covered in a pool of yellow-brown sauce with lumps of vegetables and meat.

The familiar smell — musty like a garage after a rain, mixed in with exotic spices — made Mas's mouth water. Chizuko had made curry, or *kare* rice, as the Japanese liked to call it, once a week from packaged blocks of curry shaped like mini gold bars. You broke each piece off like Hershey's chocolate and tossed it into a saucepan of boiling water with cooked nuggets of chicken, sliced onion and carrots, and cubed potatoes. Occasionally Chizuko would add raisins, but as soon as she could talk, Mari had requested that the raisins be eliminated.

Stinky didn't waste any time after he received his plate. He was raising a heaping tablespoon of curry to his mouth when Tug announced, "Let's pray." The spoon clattered to his plate and Stinky turned to Mas for guidance. It had taken Mas a while to get used to the Yamadas' ritual of saying grace. Mas rubbed his hands on his jeans and then extended his left to Tug. Stinky slowly gave one of his hands to Lil, who smiled encouragingly at Mas to take his other one.

The last thing Mas wanted to do was hold Stinky's hand. Stinky had a habit of going *shikko* without closing the bathroom door. Any other evidence of personal hygiene and decorum, such as the washing of one's hands, was not apparent. But for the blessing of the curry, Mas reluctantly stretched his hand across the table and pinched the cuff of Stinky's flannel shirt. Tug murmured something so softly that Mas couldn't make out everything he said. Mas heard "Lord" and then "friends" and something about Jesus' name. After he finished, Tug would usually squeeze Mas's hand, and a faint electrical shock would go up to his elbow. Mas didn't know if it was a result of a spiritual phenomenon or just static. This time, after "Amen," Mas quickly withdrew both hands. No electrical shocks this time.

Lil passed a small bowl of *rakkyo,* the sweet and tart mini-onions, which she had chopped into slivers. Another bowl held bright-red ginger. Ever since Chizuko had died, Mas kept only a few condiments in the refrigerator — his trusty jalapeño peppers, pickled plums soaking in saltwater, and *takuan,* bright-yellow sliced radishes that stunk like tired feet released from sweaty socks (had to make sure that the lid was tight on that container). To have different types of pickles tonight made Mas happy. He didn't exercise restraint and went ahead and piled two spoonfuls of *rakkyo* and ginger next to his rice.

"So go on, Mas. Tell us about Randy Yamashiro." Tug was looking at Mas intently, and Mas recognized the shine in his friend's eyes. That shine meant that Tug was ready for adventure beyond his three-bedroom, two-bathroom tract house. It also only meant trouble. Hadn't Tug and Lil recently joined some senior citizens' group where they could play bingo and sing birthday songs in honor of still being alive? Tug should concentrate his efforts on that, not living on the dark side.

"Tug, let him eat," Lil said. She had just finished placing four glasses of ice water on the table.

Tug dutifully allowed Mas to take three bites, when he couldn't contain himself any longer. "Do the police have any suspects?"

Mas shook his head, not mentioning either G. I.'s or Jiro's name. The police had questioned both of them, but didn't have enough information to formally charge either man, according to Juanita. Both she and G. I. figured, based on the way Detective Alo was pursuing the investigation, that no prints had been found on the knife.

Mas had already told Tug about the bayonet. Tug had fought in World War II with the all-Nisei 442nd Regimental Combat Unit, leaving a piece of his finger behind on the front line of Europe. He said that it was a small price to pay, considering half of his buddies never made it back. Mas had been shocked that while these young men had been in battle, some of their parents, brothers, sisters, aunts, and uncles had still been held behind barbed wire. If the Japanese Americans had been so disloyal, why had Tug and his fellow Nisei soldiers been handed rifles, grenades, and machine guns and told to fight America's enemy? Didn't make sense.

Being a military man, Tug was familiar with weaponry from different eras. He even got out a heavy book on the military and flipped through illustrated pages. He pointed out photographs of bayonets, which just looked like larger versions of hunting knives to Mas, aside from a ring on the side that was supposed to snap onto the rifle.

"Well, Izu helpin' dis girl. G. I.'s friend. She says sheezu some kind of PI."

"Private investigator?" Lil pursed her lips.

93

Lately she seemed more critical of any woman who pursued a career outside the home. "Does she have children?"

Mas hadn't asked, but he figured she didn't. "Not sure," he said. "Gonna see her tomorrow. Dunno too much about her."

"What are you doing tomorrow?" Tug asked, a white eyebrow arching above his wire-rimmed glasses.

"Lookin' into . . ." Mas said, swallowing a potato, *"shamisen."*

"Sha-MI-sen? You mean that Japanese bamboo flute?"

"Thatsu *shakuhachi,*" Mas corrected him. "*Shamisen* more like guitar. Three strings. A couple of guys doin' *shamisen* at G. I.'s party."

"That's right," said Tug. "I remember seeing the instruments onstage. What does that have to do with Randy's death?"

"Sumbody left a *shamisen* there. Wiz Randy's body."

"Strange," Lil murmured, biting into one of her sliced *rakkyo.*

"So have the police looked into the *shamisen* players?"

Mas didn't know. But he and Juanita were heading out to Gardena the next day to pay the musicians a visit.

"Spoon saw a *hakujin* guy wiz a *shamisen*."

"*Hakujin* man?" Lil frowned. "Somebody at the party?"

At this point, Mas thought that he'd better not mention Judge Parker. No use stirring up the pot now. Juanita had said that they had to verify every detail before spitting out information.

"Is this *shamisen* anything special?" asked Tug. "I mean, is it like those one-of-a-kind fancy violins worth millions of dollars?" Tug's mind seemed to be racing. Mas didn't know whether to make it go faster or try to stop it entirely.

"Covered in snakeskin. From Okinawa," Mas replied.

"There's a lot of Okinawans at Keiro," Lil offered. Every Thursday, Lil volunteered at Keiro, a Japanese nursing home in Los Angeles. *Keiro* meant respect for elders, which made Mas laugh. What person, either young or old, in America had respect for elders? Even Japan's sense of *keiro* had been going downhill. Hadn't Mas, in fact, heard of a story of a Japanese youth who had tied up his grandmother and stolen all of her money? Nonetheless, Mas had to admit that it was good that a place like Keiro existed in L.A. He couldn't depend on his daughter to take care of him, and although he planned to spend his last days in his house on McNally Street, it was reassuring to know that there was a nursing home that served old-time comfort food like *okayu,* soft-rice porridge, and *okazu,* stewed bits of vegetable and meat.

"There's a resident from Okinawa who is a hundred and six years old — they call her Gushi-mama," said Lil.

"That's her nickname, right? What's it short for?" Tug asked.

"Gushiken, I think."

The same as Juanita's name. Mas didn't know how many Gushikens were running around in L.A., but it couldn't be that many.

"By the way, you know who just got checked in?"

Mas shook his head, ready to receive new gossip.

"Wishbone Tanaka."

"Wishbone? Heezu too young to be in there." Wishbone was barely even seventy, wasn't he? Mas could see him in a retirement home, but a nursing home? It had been only four years ago that Wishbone was standing behind a counter at the lawn mower shop, a crooked grin on his pock-marked face.

"Got pneumonia, I guess. And then took

a little spill and twisted his ankle. He was asking about you, Mas. You should visit him sometime."

Throughout this whole discussion, Stinky had been stuffing spoonful after spoonful of curry into his mouth. Usually he would be the one volunteering the latest bad news about his best friend, Wishbone.

"You knowsu about dis, Stinky?"

"Yeah, yeah. Saw him a month ago."

"In Keiro?" Lil frowned. She probably was wondering the same thing Mas was — where had he been since then?

"Yah, right in the beginning," he mumbled, focusing his attention back on his food.

When the last bit of curry had been cleared off each plate, Lil rose. "I'll make some coffee."

Mas stood up to take his dirty dish to the kitchen, but was stopped by Tug.

"You gonna take my job, Mas?" Tug kidded, taking the plate from Mas's grasp. He also followed Lil into the kitchen, and Mas found himself awkwardly alone with Stinky. Although Mas didn't really care how Stinky was, he asked, just to make conversation, "So youzu busy?"

Stinky took a long sip of his water after picking at his teeth with the side of his thumbnail. "Life's shit," he proclaimed. Mas was surprised that he spoke so plainly.

"Whatchu mean?"

"I mean, it don't make sense. A man works hard for his dreams, and what does it get him. Nothing."

Stinky wasn't a philosophical man, so Mas knew that this observation came from something very personal. "Sumptin' happen?"

"A new gardener comes into town. Old friend of a friend. Says he knows of a business deal. Will double, triple my money, he says," Stinky explained. Mas had stopped hanging out at nurseries and lawn mower shops, so he was out of the loop.

"Japan stocks making a comeback, he claims. If a bunch of us pool our money together, we can buy a lot of shares. Foolproof deal."

Mas resisted the impulse to shake his head. There were no foolproof deals, in his experience. Making money meant taking risks, and in both Mas's and Stinky's world, they were the ones who were usually on the losing side of the odds. If Mas had been there to hear the scheme, he would have thrown cold water on it — and fast.

"Some of us were getting returns right away. A guy puts in a thousand, gets five thousand a month later. Pretty soon, all of us want to get in on the action."

Mas waited to hear the damage.

"I lost seven grand. A few other guys got taken for fifteen. None of us can get a hold of the guy now. Phone disconnected. Disappeared in thin air." Stinky closed his eyes and rubbed his droopy eyelids with his arthritic fingers. "I'm goin' to get it bad when Bette comes home."

Even though Mas was no fan of Stinky, he didn't wish him any ill will. He was an *aho* to fall for these schemes, but apparently he wasn't the only one.

Stinky had said that he had seen Wishbone a month ago and had no contact since then. Stinky and Wishbone had been thick as thieves; it was unusual for them to be apart longer than three days. Something was up, and Mas suspected it was money. "Wishbone in on dis deal?"

"How did you —" Stinky closed his mouth and nodded his balding head. He was one of those men who combed the few hairs they had over their bare scalp. For most men, it was vanity. In Stinky's case, he was just too lazy to go to a barber. "He's been giving me money to hold on to so he'll qualify to get into a place like Keiro without paying an arm and a leg. I guess he doesn't trust his own kids. So I thought that I'll surprise him — you know, double his money."

"How much lose?"

Stinky pulled at his comb-over, revealing his pimply scalp. "Twenty grand."

Mas let out a silent whistle.

"Don't have the nerve to tell him — especially with him being sick and all." Stinky lowered his head, and Mas hated to admit that he felt sorry for him.

As the coffeemaker gurgled in the kitchen and cabinets were opened and closed, Stinky snapped his eyes open again. "Don't say a word to them. The last thing I need is Mr. and Mrs. Christian to rat me out to Bette."

Mas nodded.

Lil came out with a tray of coffee cups on saucers. Tug carried out the apple pie that Stinky had purchased from Marie Callender's. "Ready for dessert?" he asked.

Somehow Mas was able to get through the apple pie and decaf and into bed by ten o'clock. He woke up two times, once at four thirty and then at six. He was more anxious than he could readily admit to himself. Juanita had warned Mas that Tuesday would be a long day — she had mentioned something about meeting a musicology professor at UCLA — so he placed some squares of Salonpas over his achy joints, in particular his kneecaps and right shoulder blade. He tried to maneuver another adhesive square onto the middle of his back with a back scratcher he had received from Haruo, but the patch kept rolling up like a cigar. These were the times that Mas thought about the merits of a companion like Haruo's Spoon, but the hassles outweighed the benefits. He would just have to suffer a sore back.

The next morning, Mas maneuvered his truck around the winding Pasadena Freeway, apparently created for Buicks and Fords just a generation away from the Model T. As he neared Elysian Park, the home of Dodger Stadium, Mas was always struck by the silhouette of the palm trees along a hill, giant frilled toothpicks stuck into a meaty mound of L.A. earth.

Juanita lived in Silverlake, named after the concrete reservoir that seemed more for show than for any usefulness. He headed toward Hollywood and got off around Echo Park, passing another fake lake, which bloomed with lotus blossoms, their leaves as large as plates, once a year. More curves, more cracked concrete, more hills that tested the Ford's failing shock absorbers.

The page for Silverlake in Mas's Thomas Guide map had been torn out years ago, indicating how often it had to be used; Silverlake was like Culver City on hills — a web of roads that didn't know the meaning of a straight line.

Luckily, Juanita had been good at giving out directions, and Mas only had to backtrack once. She had said that her house was a little red castle, so Mas spotted it a block away. She had a large wooden trellis that supported healthy vines of bougainvillea, also bright red. His daughter, Mari, had once told him that the bougainvillea was her favorite plant, as it somehow reminded her of the California missions along the coast. Mas thought that it was because it was able to grow wild and flourished in full sun, much like his daughter.

This PI business was lucrative, Mas thought to himself. For how could a single woman afford such a house? He parked the truck in the driveway in back of Juanita's Toyota, since all the street parking was taken. The doorbell seemed to have been rusted for a while, because it emitted no sound. Mas instead took hold of the metal knocker and bore down on the wood door.

A Japanese man in his sixties opened the door. He was tall and thin, with a well-groomed mustache over his thick lips. "Yes?"

"Hallo. Juanita here?" With the same body type as the girl, this must be the father. Mas felt kind of funny asking for a girl young enough to be his daughter.

"She lives out back. Here, I will show you."

The man led Mas through a side gate and down some concrete steps.

"I'm Juanita's father, Antonio," he said when they reached a patio in front of a small back unit. Mas detected a slight clipped accent more reminiscent of his Latino helpers than Japanese Americans.

"Mas. Mas Arai."

"You must be one of Juanita's clients."

"Workin' together," Mas said. He wanted to make clear that his involvement with the daughter was purely professional.

"Juanita." Antonio banged on the door. "Mr. Arai is here for you."

The door opened, revealing Juanita in jeans and a long-sleeved shirt. Her hair was wet, and a towel lay on her shoulders. "Hello, Mr. Arai," she said. "I'm running a little late. I'll be right out." She told him to wait in his car and repark it in the driveway after she moved her Toyota truck.

Antonio obviously thought his job was

done, and excused himself back to the main house. Mas found this father-and-daughter relationship interesting. Living side by side yet somehow able to keep walls between them. The Gushikens were not that Japanese-y, Mas figured.

He returned to his car and watched a couple of squirrels scamper from one side of the road to another. The squirrels here looked different from the ones in Altadena. Instead of being chestnut brown and plump, their tails were shaggy and black. Mas was wondering what that difference meant, when he finally saw Juanita wave to him from the side of her truck. He waited for her to back out of the driveway and then eased the Ford onto the far-right side of their sloping driveway.

"I dunno you live wiz family," Mas said after he had settled into the passenger seat next to Juanita.

"Yeah, it works out pretty nicely. They have their space, and I have mine. My parents have a restaurant business. Peruvian food. A chain of three restaurants. Antonio's."

So-ka, Japanese Peruvian. Mas had had a hunch. He had had dealings with Japanese Peruvians, namely a gambler named Luis Saito, who had fed him a powerful liquor, pisco, in a black bottle in the shape of an Indian warrior. Mas was even familiar with Antonio's; he passed by the Hollywood one whenever he went to a friend's house in the Uptown area above Koreatown.

"That's probably why I can't have a desk job. I'm not used to sitting around. I can't stay in one place." Typical *gasa-gasa* girl, Mas thought. Like Mari, before she had a *gasa-gasa* baby of her own.

Mas mentioned what he heard at the Yamadas'. "Some ole lady named Gushiken ova there at Keiro. Some relation?"

Juanita shook her head. "My relatives are all back in Peru. I just barely knew my grandpa. He came to visit every other year. He died last year."

"Sorry."

"Yeah, it's almost surreal, you know. When someone you don't see often dies. It seems like they are still around in their part of the world."

Mas felt like that about his own parents, who had passed away after he had returned to America. He had not been back to Hiroshima for more than fifty years. He hadn't taken the trek up to his mountain family grave site, looked at the names of his mother and father carved in the long granite obelisk. That would have made their deaths final, and Mas preferred their demise to lack finality.

Juanita explained that she had never gone to Peru. Her relatives ended up there after the quality of life in Okinawa had become so poor. "I mean, Okinawa is so beautiful, even better than Hawaii, but after the Japanese took over, they made everyone work on the sugar plantations, taxed them up the wazoo. No wonder when Peru, Brazil, and the rest of the Latin American countries started recruiting laborers from Okinawa, a bunch of them went over. Turns out that life in Peru wasn't much easier, but it became home, at least for my grandparents. And my dad for a short time."

During World War II, Antonio Gushiken and his parents had been literally kidnaped by the Peruvian government and brought over to a detention camp in Crystal City, Texas. It had been a deal made by the U.S. and Peruvian governments. With a fresh batch of people with Japanese surnames, the U.S. could now trade these hostages for American POWs. It didn't matter that the Crystal City prisoners had little connection with Japan and that their first names were Antonio, Pedro, Juanita, and Maria.

"My dad doesn't talk about it much," said Juanita. "He was a kid, of course. My grandparents eventually decided to go back to Peru, but my father stayed.

"I'd like to visit sometime. Go to Machu Picchu — you know, the lost city of the Incas."

Mas nodded. He had seen video footage of the ruins on a Japanese TV show on UHF and was amazed that such a place could exist. It was a sprawling stone palace amid jagged mountains and swirling mist. Mas knew that he himself could never see Machu Picchu, but sincerely hoped that someone he knew could.

They made more small talk until Juanita revealed the day's plan of action. "We'll meet the UCLA professor and then go over to the *shamisen* player's house. Luckily, the professor lives in the South Bay. She agreed to meet us for breakfast in Gardena, not too far from the *shamisen* player's home. That's where he has his music studio."

"He knowsu weezu comin'?"

Juanita had put on a pair of sunglasses, and it was hard to see any life in her face. "Sometimes it's better to catch them off guard."

Mas didn't like surprises, and he figured that the *shamisen* player was not so different.

"So whatsu youzu gonna say?"

"Well, I may not be saying anything, Mr. Arai. I'm not sure that he can speak English."

Mas stayed quiet. He hoped that Juanita wasn't saying what he thought she was saying. He wanted to just go along for the ride, like a dog in the passenger seat of any other pickup truck. Dogs liked the window open so that the wind could hit their faces. They had no intention, however, of taking control of the entire car.

"Whyzu those people at G. I.'s party in first place?"

"I think that the restaurant contacted the Okinawa group. All of the halaus — you know, the Hawaiian dance troupes — were booked. I'm not sure why they went Okinawan."

Mas tried not to stretch his mind to connect the dots too early. His experience was once you thought you figured something out, you inevitably ended up surprised in the end. He instead looked out the window. To the west of the freeway were clumps of palm trees in between rows of square homes that held precariously to their bits of dirt. Satellite dishes sat aimed at their targets in the sky while clothes dried on the lines. Life as usual in L.A.

They passed the huge monster Hustler

gambling casino. Mas remembered when there had been only a small circle of card clubs in the area. Now that circle had exploded, and giant gambling dens as big as warehouses were clustered by the freeway.

Juanita finally parked the truck in a business district that seemed to be hanging on to the new and the old with each hand. An Italian deli with its crowd of suited men and women standing outside — early business meetings, perhaps? Across the street, customers waited their turn inside a Mexican pan dulce bakery to select pink and brown pastries with pairs of tongs and place them on pastel plastic trays.

Mas and Juanita walked two doors down from the Mexican sweet bread house to a meeting place, another Hawaiian restaurant, called Bruddah's, but this one looked nothing like the place where G. I.'s party had been. Instead of a resurrected chain pancake house, it was in a narrow ramshackle storefront, the kind of place where bleary-eyed fishermen would feel at home. Simple booths on the sides and then a row of tables and chairs in the middle. The photocopied menu was folded next to the *shoyu* (not just any kind of soy sauce, but the Aloha brand, made in Honolulu), ketchup, and Tabasco. There were some old men, probably part-time gardeners like Mas, sitting scattered in a few of the booths. In the corner was a young couple with tattoos all along their arms and legs, and sitting at a middle table, a black woman who looked to be in her sixties.

The black woman rose as Juanita approached. "Ms. Gushiken," she stated more than asked.

"Yes." Juanita stuck out her hand, which the woman gripped firmly. "It's so nice to meet you, Professor. This is my translator, Mas Arai."

The woman took hold of Mas's hand, and Mas was embarrassed that she could probably feel every callus knotted on the palm of it. She was a smart woman; she would realize in an instant that he was no translator, but a plain workingman who had little to do with words. She took out two business cards and presented them in turn to Juanita and Mas with both hands, Japanese style. "Genessee Howard. Please call me Genessee."

Mas nodded, telling himself that he wouldn't be calling the professor any name, especially one he couldn't pronounce, if he could help it. Professor Howard was a small woman with a face round and squat like the shape of a garbanzo bean. She had a short, neat Afro and wore gold-framed eyeglasses and large earrings that shimmered like the inside of an abalone shell. In a strange way, she resembled Chizuko, and Mas was surprised to feel the top of his head go *piri-piri*.

"Thanks again for meeting with us, Pro . . . Genessee." Juanita quickly corrected herself as they joined her at her table.

"Any excuse to eat at Bruddah's." She smiled, revealing a small space in between her front teeth — also just like Chizuko, Mas noted.

Genessee had already ordered, so Juanita and Mas quickly looked over the menu. Something called Loco Moco for Juanita and Hawaiian French toast for Mas.

"I ordered the French toast too," Genessee said. "Theirs is the best, even better than a lot of places in Hawaii." She went on to explain that she had lived in Hawaii as a child. "I was actually born in Okinawa. My father was in the service; my mother's Okinawan."

So-ka, Mas mouthed silently.

"You were probably wondering why this *kokujin* woman has such an interest in Okinawa," Genessee said.

Mas shook his head, and Juanita just looked puzzled.

"You really do need a translator, don't

111

you?" Genessee said to Juanita. "*Kokujin* means black person. African American in my case."

They waited as a waitress in T-shirt and jeans served them all coffee. "So how can I help you?" Genessee, putting some cream in her cup, asked Juanita.

"Well, as I explained to you over the phone, I'm a private investigator. I'm helping a friend with an unusual case. We're trying to get some information about this." Juanita took out a copy of the snakeskin *shamisen* photograph from her back pocket.

"A *sanshin* — what happened to it?" Genessee traced a finger over the *shamisen* image as if it had once breathed air.

"It was found at a scene of a crime." Juanita was obviously not going to get into Randy's death. "Does this instrument have any significance?"

"It's hard to tell from this photo — the resolution isn't that good." Genessee adjusted her bifocals so that she could get a better look at the battered *shamisen*. "It certainly looks like pre–World War Two. Real python skin. Look — the pegs are animal bone. It may even date back to the early eighteen hundreds. The *sanshin* actually originated in China and then was developed in Okinawa, before eventually making it over to mainland Japan. The Okinawans used to use python skin from India, until it became too rare and expensive. After World War Two, when Okinawa was struggling to recover from all the destruction, they made them from tin cans and parachute strings. Now they use python skin again, but from Southeast Asia." Genessee placed the photo back on the table and studied Juanita's face.

"You don't know much about Okinawa, do you?"

Juanita shook her head. "My parents are actually from Peru."

"So many left for Latin America. Couldn't blame them, with all the high taxes and limited economy."

Before Genessee could complete her thoughts, their food arrived. Juanita's was a mess of runny eggs over two hamburger patties and rice, all soaked in brown sticky gravy. The French toast, in contrast, was majestic, thick slices of sweet Hawaiian bread cooked golden brown, cut diagonally and resting so that its powdered-sugar-sprinkled crusts looked like snow-covered peaks.

"I was actually reading something about Okinawa over the Internet." Juanita cut into her eggs and skillfully placed a bite of yolk, rice, and patty on her fork. "Read something about these Japanese warriors taking over Okinawa in the sixteen hundreds. I think they even kidnaped the king and held him hostage in Japan?"

Genessee poured maple syrup on her French toast. "Yes, that's true. They were from the Satsuma clan. Japan at that time was divided into different territories led by these lords, or *daimyo.* The Satsuma leaders saw invading Okinawa, then an independent kingdom, as an opportunity to expand their territory and their wealth without letting the Edo government know what they were really up to. And they hid their relationship with Okinawa from China, who viewed the islands as their tributary. So the Chinese were proceeding with business as usual."

"Yeah, I didn't quite get that. So the Chinese didn't know that Okinawa had been taken over by the Satsuma?"

Genessee nodded her head. "I know that it's a bit confusing. But in order for trade with China to continue, the Satsuma forced Okinawa to pretend that it was still independent. So actually Okinawa had two masters in a sense: Japan and China."

"Weird," Juanita said. Mas had to agree. He hadn't heard about all the duplicity involved in Okinawa's early history.

Juanita wiped the corners of her mouth

with a napkin. "I also read that the king presented some secret *sanshin* music to a shrine in Kagoshima — that's the headquarters of the Satsuma, right?"

"That hasn't been verified. There's a lot of original documents that have never been found. Like the banana-paper *kunkunshi,* for example. The *kunkunshi* are these early music scores that the Okinawan *sanshin* masters created. Famously missing is one created by Master Chinen Sekiko in the early eighteen hundreds. I'm a great fan of Chinen; he really blazed a trail for more modern-day *sanshin* musicians.

"With the Battle of Okinawa in 1945, so much was completely wiped out or stolen. Do you know that some Okinawan treasures, invaluable ancient texts and tablets, were discovered at a military officer's house in Massachusetts in the 1950s? The government never revealed how the items got there, but they were eventually returned. The whereabouts of the royal crown is still unknown. It's a tragedy. As I said, even this *sanshin* in the photo, it could have been constructed way before World War Two. It's a pity that it's been so severely damaged."

Mas remembered seeing a documentary about the battle on a UHF television station. Something like 200,000 killed, half of them civilians. Present-day Okinawans, wearing masks and gloves, were still digging out remains from caves where many families had hidden during the explosives and gunfire.

"So, *shamisen,* maybe worth sumptin'," Mas said out loud.

"Well, maybe to a museum. But *sanshin* aren't really collector's items. It would only be prized by obscure musicians, and academicians like me." Again, Genessee flashed the gap in the teeth. "If you're that interested in the *sanshin,* you should come to the concert at the Okinawan Association next Saturday." She then swallowed the last bit of her coffee and informed Juanita and Mas that she had to leave to make her afternoon seminar. "I'd like to examine the actual instrument, if that's possible."

"It's been entered into evidence at the Torrance Police Department."

"You never told me what the crime was. Robbery?"

Juanita glanced at Mas, who hung his head down as if he had discovered something fascinating in his empty coffee cup.

"Murder," Juanita said. "Someone was killed."

Genessee visibly shuddered as if a cool draft had blown into the restaurant. "Well, good luck on your investigation." She opened up her wallet, but Juanita shook her head and pulled the small plastic tray holding the bill toward her. "It's on me," she said, thanking the professor again.

Back in the truck, Juanita put on her sunglasses and turned to Mas. "Well, what do you think?"

"Nice lady."

"Not her. But the stuff about the *sanshin*. Does any of it help?"

Mas really didn't know how Okinawa's past would have any relevance to the *shamisen* found with Randy's body. "Dunno," Mas said.

"Yeah, I'm not sure either. I hope I didn't freak her out too much."

The mention of murder probably had been too much. Mas didn't think that they would hear from Genessee again. "Nice lady," he murmured again.

Juanita drove less than a mile before she stopped outside a typical Gardena home. It was the color of mint toothpaste, with a square, flat cement porch and a front yard of Bermuda grass and sculpted pine trees.

They got out of the truck and attempted to peer through the large picture window's blinds and drapes. The door was open, but a barred security gate insured the safety of the home's inhabitants. The plucking of multiple *shamisen* sounded from one of the inside rooms.

Juanita tried the bell, but it seemed rusted over. She then dragged her keys along the bars of the security door like she was a prisoner seeking relief. After a few rounds of this, the older basset hound–faced man with bright white hair whom Mas had seen at the restaurant appeared at the door.

"Hai," he said.

"Hello, are you Mr. Kinjo? I'm Juanita Gushiken. I'd like to talk to you about Saturday night. The night of your performance at Mahalo, the restaurant in Torrance."

The man looked from Juanita's face to Mas's. "I'm teaching now," he said in Japanese. His voice came out rough, like the edge of a saw. "This is a very bad time." Yet he didn't move.

Juanita stared at Mas, and he knew that he was on. "I'm very sorry." Mas tried his best in the most polite Japanese he could muster. He had lived in Japan for seventeen years, but he had been in America for more than fifty. The Japanese language was full of rules that were difficult to remember. It was all about who you were and who you were talking to. If you were a boss, you would

118

talk one way to your employee. If you were a servant, you would address someone higher than you in a completely different way. Throw in age and gender, and it would be again another ball of wax. Mas knew that he was tripping over his words. "This girl insisted." Mas gestured toward Juanita. He was selling her out, but she deserved it. "Hired as a police . . ." Mas had forgotten the Japanese word for detective, so he just switched over to English. "Investigate. Lookin' into murder."

"Spoke to police already," Kinjo said, ready to close the door.

"We're looking into the *sanshin,*" Juanita spouted out.

The security gate slowly opened, revealing that the man wore a fleece vest over a flannel shirt, and loose khaki pants that were patched at the knees. Not much of an outfit, especially for a sensei, a teacher.

"Come in," he said in English.

They followed the sensei to his sparsely decorated living room. He gestured for them to sit down on the couch while he tended to his class. In front of the couch was a glass-topped coffee table holding a lacquerware bowl shaped like a squat persimmon and a set of books in Japanese on Okinawan history and the *sanshin.* To the side of the couch was a standard *ningyo,* Japanese doll, in a glass case, and on the wall hung a large framed *kotobuki,* the Japanese character for longevity, assembled out of flattened gold-paper origami cranes. Mas always thought it was strange how Japanese Americans would fold a thousand and one cranes, and then arrange them into shapes of *mon,* family crests, or Japanese characters. Instead of pulling the wings of the folded birds and inflating them, women would lay the poor cranes flat, glue them down, and encase them under glass.

The plucking of strings resumed as Mas sat on the couch. Juanita was leafing through one of the heavy books. "Is this the music that Genessee was talking about?" She pointed to an illustration of symbols handwritten within a grid of squares.

Mas read the caption and section of the story beside the photo. "Um, so . . ." he said. "Datsu *kunkunshi.*" They reminded Mas of the sheets of musical notes that Mari practiced on her piano when she was a child.

Juanita sucked on the earpiece of her sunglasses as she continued to flip through the photographs in the book. Mas, on the other hand, almost nodded off until he heard a jangling and turning of the lock on the front security gate. The door slowly crept open to reveal a Sansei man holding a plastic bag that looked and smelled like takeout from a Japanese fast-food restaurant. He didn't seem that surprised to see two strangers sitting on the couch.

"Hello, I'm Alan Kinjo, sensei's son." It was the other man who had played the *shamisen* at the Hawaiian restaurant.

Up close the man, who was probably around G. I.'s age, wasn't bad-looking. He was tall, with that familiar long face. His cheeks didn't sag as much as his father's, and his eyes were clear and bright, like he was ready to make any negative a positive. He wore a suit and tie and shiny dress shoes.

Juanita rose first. "Juanita Gushiken," she said, brushing her hand on her pants before extending it to Alan. Mas remembered that Juanita hadn't bothered to wipe her hand before she had shaken his when they had first met at the Hawaiian restaurant. Mas merely mumbled his name from his seat.

"I work a few miles from here," he explained. He was apparently one of these Sansei with a Japanese work ethic. To these folk, it was unseemly for a grown man not to be working during broad daylight. "I check in with my dad during my lunch break."

One of these *oyakoko* children, who put

their parents before their own selves. Mas wondered what it would be like to have a son or daughter like that.

"Has he been ill?"

"No, no. But being in his late seventies, well, you know how that is." Mas hadn't made it quite that far, but knew at his age, each additional year was actually worth five regular years.

Alan then studied Juanita's and Mas's faces more carefully. "Are you two waiting to take a class?"

"Us?" Juanita said. "Oh, no. Tone deaf. Never took up an instrument. Chose judo and kendo over piano lessons — do you know what I mean?"

Alan left the plastic bag on a far table away from the living room. "I don't think my kendo dojo even had a girl student. Wait a minute — I think there had been one, but she dropped out after some guy speared her in the chest."

Juanita grimaced. "Ouch. Well, she could have gotten him back easily, if she wanted to."

"She didn't have the killer instinct."

"Oh, well, then. If you don't have that, you're done."

Mas watched Alan and Juanita dance back and forth with their words and felt a little guilty. Didn't Juanita notice Alan Kinjo's gold wedding ring? Was she betraying her loyalty to G. I.? And what was this about Juanita and her killer instinct? Mas could easily picture her in the full kendo garb — wooden face guard and black *gi,* martial arts outfit. It actually wouldn't surprise Mas if Juanita had some of that samurai blood churning inside of her — that is, if Okinawans had samurai.

"We're actually here to talk to you and your dad about Saturday night. The man who hosted the party you two performed at was killed."

Alan's face turned dark for a second, as if a cloud had passed overhead. He recovered quickly, smiling when there was no reason to smile. "We heard about it on Sunday from the police. Were you there too?"

"Yes. The victim was actually a friend of a friend," Juanita said. When did G. I. become just a friend? wondered Mas.

"I'm so sorry. Yeah, we took off right after we performed. We had no idea what had happened until the police called us the next day."

"So you didn't know him, Randy Yamashiro?"

Alan shook his head. "The restaurant booked us at the last minute. We do a lot of gigs there. Maybe with a name like Ya-mashiro, they figured that an Okinawan performance would be appropriate." The music in the next room grew louder, a weaving of treble and bass notes. Alan glanced at his watch. "It sounds like Dad is still with his students. Can you tell him I stopped by? And that lunch is here on the table?"

Juanita nodded.

"Thank you — Juanita, right? Juanita Gushiken."

"You're good," Juanita said, taking a business card from her front pocket. It was bent in the middle from her sitting down. Mas noticed for the first time that she never seemed to carry a purse.

"Thanks." The instructor's son managed a limp wave to Mas and then went out the security gate.

"Nice guy," Juanita said, and Mas wondered if she was joking. Was that all it took to turn her head? A tall Sansei man with good hair and shiny dress shoes? And did she really need to give him her business card? Did her friendliness have to do with the case, or did she have more personal motives? Mas couldn't help but feel protective toward G. I. Normally Mas would stay clear of affairs of the heart, but he didn't want G. I.'s heart to be rolled over, flattened like hot tar over a broken road.

Before Mas could form any more opinions, Kinjo's students walked out from the back room, each carrying something in a black fabric case — most likely a *shamisen.* One was a young man with hair that looked like an old push mower had gone through it; tufts of varied lengths stuck out in different directions. Next came a Japanese woman with graying hair like a skunk's pelt, and finally an older *hakujin* man with a beard. Both looked familiar, and Mas figured out that they had been the singers yelping at the Hawaiian restaurant. Kinjo followed them like a proud parent to three ducklings. "So rememba," Kinjo told them. "Next Tuesday, rehearsal. Then Saturday, meet at OAA. Eleven a.m. sharpu."

At the door, the students all bowed, and Mas noticed the *hakujin* man looked suspiciously over at both him and Juanita.

Kinjo returned to the back room for a few minutes and then emerged with a couple of cups of green tea. He placed each cup on the table in front of his guests and lifted the lid of the lacquerware, revealing *arare* — not just any rice cracker, but Mari's favorite kind, shaped like stars and sprinkled with black specks of dried seaweed. Mas remembered Mari's baby teeth chewing on the points of each star. Later, when she became a teenager, she complained that the crackers gave her "*arare* breath," which Mas learned was not only bad breath, but equivalent to the smell of a dog sick with distemper.

"*Nan desho?*" Kinjo finally asked after Juanita and Mas had taken a couple of sips of tea. Mas poked Juanita with his elbow, a signal that she needed to begin her spiel.

"Well, Mr. Kinjo, as you've probably heard, a man was murdered on Saturday, and there was a *sanshin* found near the body." Juanita slid the photo of the smashed *shamisen* over the glass tabletop until it stopped a few inches from Kinjo's knee. His face paled, and Mas fought the urge to check if Juanita had also noticed the sensei's reaction.

"Have you seen that instrument before?"

Kinjo lowered his chin toward his chest bone. He took deep breaths and then aimed his anger at Mas. "I already told this to the police. Why do you come and bother me like this?" he said in Japanese.

Juanita stared at Mas, waiting for a translation. Kinjo kept going. "This was *my sanshin.* I told the police that I want it back."

"Yours? *Honto?*" Mas wanted Kinjo to be sure. And why would he still want it re-

126

turned in its miserable state?

"Look at the pegs," Kinjo said. "That's real *ho-ne.*"

"What's he saying?" Juanita mouthed in Mas's ear.

"Heezu *shamisen.*"

"He mentioned the bone pegs, huh?" Juanita obviously knew more Japanese than she admitted.

"Nobody else in America have," Kinjo interjected. He also knew more English that he let on. "This peg *kuro.* Black." He pointed to the dark middle peg and repeated it. "Nobody have that."

"When was the last time you saw it?"

"Nineteen fifties."

Before Juanita was even born, thought Mas.

"I'm surprised that you'd even remember it," Juanita said.

Mas could understand. He would always remember the 1950s. That's the decade he acquired the tools of his trade: the Ford and also his Trimmer lawn mower.

"Once you have something like that, you never forget." Kinjo reverted back to Japanese. "I was hit by a *dorobo,* a no-good thief. That *sanshin* is mine; I can prove it." He opened a drawer in the coffee table and proceeded to take out a stack of photographs.

"Here." Kinjo threw down a black-and-white photo of himself with two other Japanese men, all cradling *shamisen* in front of tar-paper barracks. Kinjo's was the only one with snakeskin; the other two were made out of cookie tins and cake pans. "Jerome, Arkansas." He looked at Juanita. "I buy in camp."

"Camp? What? Where could you buy a *sanshin* at camp?"

Tug and Lil had told Mas about internees purchasing clothing and other items from the Sears Roebuck catalogue. Nothing about Japanese traditional instruments.

"An MP. Military police. He had been in Okinawa. Wounded and sent back to the States, to his hometown in Jerome."

"How come youzu lose it?" Mas had to ask.

"I told you, it was stolen. Taken by someone in my very own band. And sold for much money, I imagine."

If what Kinjo said was true, then someone had gotten a raw deal.

Kinjo turned on a lamp in the corner and reexamined the photograph in the light. It was obvious that the *shamisen* was like a child to him. His face had turned gray, like discarded chewing gum. "Ah — *shimmata*," he said, as if the instrument had just experienced a death.

"You knowsu Yamashiro?" Mas asked.

"Why would I know such a person?" Kinjo responded in Japanese. Did Mas imagine that his sagging cheeks were slightly quivering? And Kinjo's eyes: why were they incessantly blinking — *pachi-pachi, pachi-pachi?*

What connection would he have to a fifty-something Sansei from Hawaii? Was it merely a coincidence that Kinjo had been playing the *shamisen* at the same place where his old *shamisen* had been left at a murder scene?

"I have another class coming." Kinjo rose, unlocked the iron security gate, and held it open. "My son is getting a lawyer. I told police that the *sanshin* was stolen and that we need it back."

Mas had little knowledge of police procedure, but he bet that the instructor would not be getting his *shamisen* — if it indeed was his — any time soon. Juanita would have probably agreed if she understood what Kinjo was saying.

They went outside, only to be blocked from a clean exit. The bearded *hakujin* man was still there, sitting on the stairs, running

129

a pocket knife along a dead broken branch. Mas remembered sharpening his pencils back in Hiroshima in the same way. But what was the purpose of doing such a thing to a branch?

"Excuse me," Juanita said, stepping around the man. Mas followed Juanita, not bothering with the excuse. The man squinted up at Mas, the blade firmly held in his left hand. Mas noticed that the man's fingers were long and tapered, the fingernails filed neatly, as if they were cared for by a professional. His face, on the other hand, was cherubic; he was Santa Claus on a diet. *"Konnichiwa,"* he said.

Mas did a double take. The skinny Santa Claus was greeting him in Japanese.

"I heard you asking questions of sensei."

Juanita backtracked and stood beside Mas on the Bermuda grass. "We're just curious about a few things."

Mas wondered why Juanita didn't just identify herself as a PI, but figured that she didn't want to reveal her cards too early.

"Curiosity killed the cat."

"Pardon?" asked Juanita.

"You heard me. It's not the best thing to be sticking your noses into other people's business."

"And what are you doing right now?"

Mas nudged Juanita. No sense in getting into a knock-down, drag-out fight now. They had to save those times for when it really counted. He didn't know if this man was acting as Kinjo's protector or enforcer.

"No trouble." Mas held up his hands as if he were a surrendering cowboy.

"Then we're in agreement." The skinny Santa Claus then left the lawn.

Thankfully, at that moment, Juanita's cell phone rang. She answered, and from the tone of her voice, Mas could tell it was G. I.

"Mas," she said, handing him the phone. "G. I. wants to talk with you."

Mas angled the small phone to his ear. "I'm here with Brian, Randy's brother," G. I. told him. "I need you to help me find a good mortuary. A reasonable one."

G. I., who was lucky enough to still have both parents back in his hometown of San Francisco, apparently figured that Mas would be an expert on death in L.A., and he wasn't that far off. Mas had buried his wife, Chizuko, as well as some assorted gamblers and gardeners with no relatives to speak of nearby. Mas didn't know much about world politics or celebrities, but he did know how you were supposed to handle last rites, at least in the Japanese American world.

He told G. I. not to worry, that he would help him out. They made arrangements to meet the next day. As he finished the phone call, Juanita headed back to her truck. No matter how much ground they managed to cover today, the investigation would have to be interrupted tomorrow. Last rites took precedence over justice, at least for tomorrow morning.

CHAPTER FOUR

Ichiro "Itchy" Iwasaki was an old friend of Mas's from his poker-playing days at Wishbone Tanaka's lawn mower shop. He had little cupped brown ears like those of a monkey, and he often pulled his right earlobe before making a bet. Mas had watched to see if there was some kind of pattern. Did it mean that he had a good hand? Was he bluffing? Sending a message to another player? Or was it just a nervous twitch? In the dead of winter Mas noticed that Itchy had stopped pulling on his ears. In the summer, it started up again. Mas found out later that Itchy was a regular at the public golf course in Monterey Park. Golfer's sunburn, Mas figured. Not any kind of deliberate gambler's signal.

Itchy had been a janitor at L.A. City Hall but, after getting laid off, had taken a temporary detour in the Japanese American funeral business. In L.A., there were at least a couple of mortuaries that specialized in Japanese American death. They knew how to collect *koden,* money from mourners to alleviate the family's financial burden of burying or burning their dead. You slipped a twenty-dollar bill or maybe an extra ten (for someone beyond a passing acquaintance) into a sympathy card. The registrars made sure that you wrote your name and address on the back of the envelope, and within two weeks' time you would receive a printed thank-you card with a book of twenty stamps inside. The Japanese always had to do *okaeshi* — something in return. Mas never knew how the tradition of giving stamps had started in America — probably just the practicality of Japanese immigrants. Like lightbulbs and toilet paper, everyone needed stamps. In Japan, you would give probably five to ten times more in cash, but would receive a ceramic vase or a dish half your gift's value in return. Mas would take stamps over a flower vase any day.

Some people preferred giving and receiving checks instead of cash, because there were occasional incidents of theft during funerals. Chizuko had been appalled to hear of such crimes, but nothing surprised Mas. Where there was money, there were crooks.

If the potential victims were overcome and blinded by emotion, all the better.

To make ends meet after losing his janitorial job at City Hall, Itchy had picked up the dead bodies from people's houses or nursing homes. But after a few months, he couldn't handle touching them anymore. He didn't understand why the bodies got so cold and stiff so fast, he told Mas. What was it about the pumping of blood that kept one's legs and arms so soft and pliable? One time when he was loading an old lady's body into the mortuary's 1975 white Cadillac hearse (they saved the shiny black one for funerals), the stretcher tipped over and the body fell onto the driveway. Wasting no time, Itchy lifted her by her armpits. Rigor mortis had set in, leaving her fingers outstretched like claws. As he dragged her into the hearse, her fluffed-up hair smashed against his face. All he remembered was that she smelled like sour milk and baby powder.

Itchy had gone from funeral work to gardening, but a new mortuary started by an old Latino neighbor of his in East L.A. had called him back to service. This time Itchy would not have to touch the dead bodies but deal only with the living, specifically the Japanese relatives of the deceased. He'd have a nice second-floor office overlooking a plaza in Lincoln Heights.

Lopez, Sing, and Iwasaki Mortuary specialized in cheap funerals, which you'd think would attract a crowd. Itchy's neighbor Mr. Lopez was obviously trying to hit the Latino, Chinese, and Japanese markets. A perfect plan in Lincoln Heights, where Mexican seafood restaurants and Chinese Vietnamese auto repair shops stood side by side. But the idea backfired, because mortuaries were like churches; people seemed to prefer them separated and segregated. It reminded Mas of his favorite Neapolitan ice cream — strawberry, chocolate, and vanilla were packaged together, but the solid lines of flavors never blended into each other.

Normally Mas wouldn't patronize a mixed bag like Lopez, Sing, and Iwasaki, but since G. I. had told him that Brian Yamashiro wanted a deal, Mas knew that Itchy Iwasaki was their man. Mas assumed that the funeral back in Hawaii would be elaborate, so he guessed it made sense to shave a few dollars from the cost to transport the body on the plane.

Itchy was a plain talker who didn't mince words. He wasn't the type to hold anyone's hands or convince them to buy something beyond their reach. He was thorough with his questions: Burial or cremation? Cardboard coffin (covered with a cloth and topped with flower bouquets, of course), sixteen-gauge steel, bronze, or copper? They wouldn't have to suffer through small talk, fake sympathy, or sales pitches.

Itchy was sitting in front of Mas now. He had grown much paler since joining the mortuary business, and his ears seemed like they were drooping.

"Your friends coming soon?" he said. As he moved his swivel chair up to his desk, the springs squeaked.

Mas nodded. G. I. was bringing Randy's brother, Brian, who was staying at a Holiday Inn in Burbank.

"Was this Randy Yamashiro the guy who won the jackpot in Vegas?"

Mas nodded. "Brotha takin' care of every-tin'."

"So what's the brother's story?"

Mas sat on the edge of a metal-framed chair so that his feet could remain on the ground. "Un?" Mas grunted.

"Buddhist, Christian? *Okanemochi?* Has money?"

"Banker," Mas said, not knowing if a person who dealt with money on a daily basis actually had any in their pocket. *"Chotto kechi mittai,"* he added, remembering how Brian had borrowed money from

Juanita for his cab fare. It sounded better in Japanese than in English: *It looks like the guy's cheap.*

Mas could see the numbers being tabulated in Itchy's head. This would be a charity case, done for a future favor from Mas. All this investigating was going to cost Mas — maybe not hard dollars today but a complimentary tree-cutting or sprinkler job tomorrow.

Itchy had to take a call from another customer. "We can make changes if we tell the newspaper by ten," he said. More squeaks from the chair. "If 'girlfriend' is unacceptable, how about 'lifetime partner'?" Squeak, squeak. " 'Friend'? Okay, 'friend,' and mention her last. I got it."

Mas studied the linoleum squares covering the floor of Itchy's office. A huge black scuff mark remained on one square, like a tire skid on the freeway after an accident.

While Itchy continued to negotiate the language of obituaries, Mas heard footsteps on the rubber-covered stairs and then voices in the front office. G. I. appeared with Randy's brother, who was wearing a pink polo shirt and jeans and had a cell phone case clipped to his belt. Mas noticed that he was thick around the middle like Randy — only his brother had been more solid, while

Brian's belly seemed squishy, as if he were resting a pillow inside the front of his shirt. G. I. made the introductions, and Mas was surprised to see Brian smile widely. Mas could see his teeth lined up prettily, like a string of pearls. "Thanks, eh, for all you doin' for us," he said to Mas. Brian had a lilt to his voice, and as he spoke, a dimple appeared on his left cheek.

He certainly didn't look like a grief-stricken brother. His shirt looked freshly pressed, and so did his jeans. Who had time to iron when you were on the road, not to mention planning the transportation of your brother's dead body?

Itchy ended his phone conversation, and finally the four of them got to business.

"We'll pick up the body from the coroner's office after they are done with their report," explained Itchy. "In cases like this, we can also provide shipping services. I can put the body in a recycled box and shave off about twenty dollars."

"How about cremation?" Brian put the tips of his fingers together. He wore a gold bracelet, the kind with two magnetic balls that rested inside one's wrist where a nurse might take your pulse.

"Cremations are cheapest way to go," replied Itchy.

"Cremation is good enough, I think."

G. I.'s thinning eyebrows were pinched together. "But don't your relatives want to see the body?"

"What relatives? Got no family over in Oahu. Mom, grandparents died years ago. And my father — who knows where that guy's at? Have some distant uncles, aunts, but they're over in the Big Island. Wouldn't come to a funeral in Oahu."

This still didn't seem to sit right with G. I. "Did you clear this all with police?"

"They know what I'm doing. The coroner already completed his investigation."

"Once you cremate him, there's no going back," G. I. continued. "Maybe you need to think about it for a couple of days."

"I don't need to think about it," said Brian. "Cremation."

G. I. clutched his knees in his seat, and Mas noticed that a blue vein on his forearm was distended. "I don't know if I mentioned this. But an old man called a few days ago. Said that he was your father."

"That's a good one. He left us when we lived here in L.A. Mom, with two of us kids, had nowhere to go. So she went back to her folks' house. I doubt our old man is alive. And if he still is, he's dead to me. Probably just called about the money."

Yes, the money, thought Mas. It had been on Mas's mind, and most likely on G. I.'s. And now they knew that it had been on the brother's mind as well.

"I saw Randy was in the newspaper," said Brian. "Crazies come out of the woodwork, eh, when you talking about half a million dollars."

Itchy nodded, squeak, squeak. Mas snuck a look at G. I. He didn't look happy. But G. I. had no real say — this was a family matter, a decision that only blood relatives could make. If they were in Hawaii, the door would have been closed to both G. I. and Mas. They were allowed in here only because they were locals, and Randy had died thousands of miles away from home.

Brian signed some papers and then shook Itchy's hand. "Well, I guess we're ready to go," he said to G. I. "If we get back to the hotel by eleven, I'll be able to make my lunch appointment."

Itchy's telephone rang and he excused himself to answer it. Brian, on the other hand, went down the hall to the restroom.

After Brian had disappeared from view, Mas felt G. I.'s breath against his ear. "I can't believe this SOB," he hissed. Water was seeping from the sides of his eyes, and Mas could see bits of *hanakuso* stuck in the hairs of his nostrils. G. I. was still suffering; there was no doubt about that. "There is something fishy about this brother."

Mas waited to hear more.

"The whole time on the drive over here, he's on the cell phone. Talking business with his colleagues. Nothing about Randy."

Before he could go on, Brian was walking down the hall toward them. "Come to the house later on," G. I. said to Mas. "We need to talk more." He then brushed away his tears and straightened his back. It was clear that G. I. did not want to reveal any weakness to Brian.

Itchy returned to the group, a little bit of tension in his sad eyes. "There's a bit of a problem."

"What kind of problem?" Brian pulled at his golden bracelet.

As usual, Itchy didn't sugarcoat his message. "The police are refusing to allow you to take the body for cremation. Says that you're a prime suspect in their murder investigation."

"Whatthe— ?"

"Did the police actually say that?"

"Well, it's my friend in the coroner's department, Hajime Kaku."

That was a name that Mas had not heard for decades. Hajime Kaku had worked for the Los Angeles County Coroner's office since the fifties. "Hajime still alive?"

"Still kicking. Kind of putters around the office. But my best source of information," Itchy explained. "I was trying to figure out what the hang-up was in getting the body released. I guess they don't want the evidence getting burned up."

"This is messed up. I did everything for my brother. Saved his ass I don't know how many times. And now the police think I killed him?" Brian's brow was furrowed and a large crease connected one eye to another. "What's this guy's name again — Kaku?"

"He has nothing to do with it," Itchy said, seeking to protect his messenger. "Call the police. They'll let you know."

"You bet I'll call them." Brian opened his nylon case on his belt for his cell phone and charged down the stairs without saying thanks or good-bye.

"Well, Mas, I'll catch you later," G. I. said, his voice now a couple of octaves lower.

When they were finally alone, Mas turned to Itchy. "Boy's *okashii*. Heezu brotha's dead and he trying to make some bizness deal. Maybe he did have sumptin' to do with the murder."

"You never know, Mas. He may not show it right now, but when he's alone, it'll hit him. It'll hit him hard." Mas had to give some credit to Itchy's judgment. He dealt with grief-stricken faces on an hourly basis — he could probably smell a faker a mile away.

Mas then remembered his conversation with Lil. "Oh, yah, I hear Wishbone's at Keiro."

"Yeah, big surprise. He was so *genki,* huh, but then all of a sudden got struck down with a cold that turned into pneumonia and then fell down. Luckily he just hurt his ankle. But after he lost the lawn mower shop, he hasn't been himself."

With all the big-box home improvement centers, how could a shack like Tanaka's Lawnmower Shop survive? Mas knew that the loss was most keenly felt among old gamblers rather than any working gardeners. And now, because of Stinky, Wishbone would have to brace himself for another loss.

"He's been asking about you, Mas. You should stop by and say hello sometime."

CHAPTER FIVE

When Mas had first met Wishbone Tanaka, in the fifties, Wishbone had a ducktail that looked like wild beach grasses gone awry in the wind. He'd parted his pitiful matted hair down the back of his head and then greased it plenty with dabs of Brylcreem. The ends were folded onto the top of his head, resembling a bowing Buddha. Most Nisei and Kibei sported a crew cut or flattop. Itchy, with his straight-as-pins hair, had been a flattop man and still was (no wonder his earlobes kept getting sunburnt). Mas hadn't been foolish enough to go with a ducktail back in those days, but when he'd had a full head of hair, he did carry a bit of a pompadour, which he held in place with his standard hair cream, Three Flowers oil.

Wishbone was as unmanageable as his hairstyle. While everything had been well stocked and arranged in his lawn mower shop, you couldn't tell him what to do regarding anything else in his life. He had a short fuse, and Mas did his share of lighting it. The other guys were a bit wary and afraid of Wishbone, but Mas didn't hold back when necessary.

Mas had had a falling-out with Wishbone years ago. He swore that he would never step foot in Tanaka's Lawnmower Shop again, and he didn't. But when it was closed and resurrected as a hair salon, Mas had to admit that he'd felt a pang of regret. Hair salons were a dime a dozen; a lawn mower shop, full of decades of memories, card games, and the juiciest gossip in town, was irreplaceable.

And now Wishbone, like his dead enterprise, was being cast aside. Mas could have laughed and announced, You got your big *bachi,* payback, for all the meanness you sowed. But what was the use? They both were cut from the same cloth, and Mas knew that what had visited Wishbone would visit him someday.

After checking in with a nurse at Keiro, Mas made his way down a corridor, its clean floor covered in linoleum. A few residents, trapped in wheelchairs, were out in the hallway like lonely space satellites, not connected to anyone. Mas found Wishbone's room and poked his head through the doorway. There were two beds, both with mint green curtains to one side. The roommate was obviously somewhere else, but Wishbone, slumped in a wheelchair, was looking out the window toward the flatlands of Lincoln Heights.

"Wishbone."

Wishbone jerked up, startled. He slowly turned toward Mas.

"Who's dead?" he asked.

"Huh?"

"Well, someone must be dead or close to it for you to be here. Who you come to see?"

"You."

"Who told you? Lil?"

Mas wasn't going to mention Stinky's name; he didn't want to get in the middle of that fallen deal.

"That Yamada lady has a big mouth. Volunteers are supposed to keep their traps shut about who's in here."

"Well, Itchy tole me too."

"Itchy? Well, I was right, somebody must have died. You over at the mortuary today?"

Mas gave in. "Actually G. I.'s *tomodachi*. From Hawaii."

"The guy who won the Spam jackpot. Got knifed in Torrance."

Mas was surprised. Even within the confines of a nursing home, Wishbone was at the height of his gossip game.

"Saw it in today's *Rafu Shimpo*," Wishbone said. "Ugly goddamn photos." In the old days, *The Rafu Shimpo* used to be delivered by paperboys on bicycles and in cars, but with the Japanese sprinkled all throughout the Southland, now the U.S. post office was the better way to go. Obviously Keiro's mail service was a lot faster than Mas's.

"Yah, kinda helpin' G. I. find out what happened," Mas said, immediately regretting that he was revealing his activities to Wishbone, of all people.

"Well, the *Rafu* had the photo of the *shamisen* right on the front page. It was the talk of lunch today. This old Okinawan lady was going on and on that she knows who owned that *shamisen.*"

Mas pressed down on a small, painful bump on his hairline. Did Wishbone say Okinawan? "Gushiken?" Mas asked.

Now it was Wishbone's turn to be impressed. "You know the old lady?"

"Hear about her. You knowsu?"

"Sure, sure, she's down the hall. Follow me." Wishbone wheeled himself toward the open doorway. At first Mas thought about helping to push Wishbone forward, but he realized the last thing Wishbone would want was help.

"Hey, Gushi-*san,* somebody wants to meet you," Wishbone called out down the hall. He was fast with his wheelchair, and Mas noticed that Wishbone's shoulders were still pretty toned. His hands, as worn as a workingman's gloves, advanced the wheelchair into another residential room.

A slight, pigeon-faced woman was resting on one of the beds. "Where's Gushi-mama?" Wishbone asked.

Mas hated to be *meiwaku,* a bother to anyone, especially anyone who was trying to get some shut-eye on a quiet afternoon. Wishbone, on the other hand, was known to blow so much hot air into something that it would burst at the seams.

"Terebi," the woman said, pointing to the next room.

The room next door had a couch and chairs facing a large television playing an NHK soap opera straight from Japan. Mas preferred samurai series to this type, which starred teary-eyed women and salarymen in blue suits.

Two women were watching the soap opera, and Wishbone wheeled right in front of the one knitting a rainbow-colored blanket.

"Gushi-mama, this guy here wants to talk to you. About that *shamisen* in *The Rafu Shimpo.*"

Gushi-mama raised her head from her knitting. Her face looked progressively sunken, like a muffin that had failed to rise. Either she had forgotten to wear her dentures or at the age of 106 it was a grooming detail reserved for only special occasions. Her black and white hair shot out from her head like dried-up desert brush.

"Who you?" she asked.

"Mas. Masao Arai."

"I dunno you."

"Izu a friend of Lil Yamada. You know, she come here all the time."

"Yamada-*san.* Nice, nice lady."

No one could dispute that fact. The Yamadas, with their stellar reputations, often served as Mas's calling card. A friend of Tug and Lil Yamada's was seen to be a person who could be a friend to just about anyone.

"Tell him," Wishbone interrupted, inching the wheelchair so close to Gushi-mama that the blanket was almost underneath one of its wheels. "Tell him what you were saying about the *shamisen.*"

"Youzu see dat *shamisen?*"

Gushi-mama nodded. "Kinjo-*san's san-shin.* He played with Sanjo Brothers." Kinjo sensei had mentioned that somebody in his band had stolen his *shamisen.*

"Kinjo, whatchu knows about him?" Mas asked.

Gushi-mama shook her head. "No good. No good. But thinks he good." The old lady balled up her freckled hands into fists and placed them one alongside the other on the end of her nose. *"Hana ga takai,"* she said, and Mas understood instantly. Kinjo's nose, or *hana,* was tall, stuck up in the air — too much pride.

"Always say he has connection to kings. Oh, yah? I say, 'Show me.' But nothing."

"Howzu about Sanjo?"

"The *niisan* Sanjo, big brother, best *sanshin* player around. *Ichiban, yo.*" She lifted a bent finger in the air to simulate the number one and peered into Wishbone's face for emphasis. Wishbone retreated a few inches back. "Everywhere he go, everybody like him. Good-lookin', too. Big brother's name was Isokichi. He got into trouble before war. *Aka.*"

"Aka," Mas repeated.

"Red?" Wishbone translated out loud. So something from Wishbone's Japanese school experience had stuck in his brain.

"You know, *aka,*" Gushi-mama said to Mas.

Mas nodded. A Red. A communist. He

151

didn't know how to say it in English, so merely murmured, "Trouble."

Gushi-mama nodded back.

"What happen to Isokichi?" Mas asked.

Gushi-mama returned to her knitting.

"Gushi-*san*, what happened to Isokichi?" Wishbone repeated loudly in Gushi-mama's ear.

But Gushi-mama continued her knitting as if they weren't in the room.

A nurse in a smock dotted with flying elephants appeared in the doorway. "Mrs. Gushiken, you ready for your sponge bath?"

"Yah, yah," she said, rolling up the remnants of her knitted blanket.

"Waitaminute," Mas said, trying to stall. "Sanjo name. Whatsu *kanji?*"

Wishbone crinkled his nose. "Why do you need to see the Japanese character for it?"

"Please, dis one thing, then I no bother no more," Mas insisted.

Gushi-mama looked up, attempting to judge whether Mas would keep his end of the deal. *"Orai."* She finally gave in.

Mas handed her a felt-tipped pen and a piece of scratch paper from a craft table in the corner. Gushi-mama bent her head, revealing a bald spot in the center of her grizzled hair. Using her half-finished blanket as a surface, she carefully maneuvered the pen on the paper and created two complete Japanese characters — one for *san* and the other for *jo.* After completing the final stroke, she presented the writing to Mas. She then waited like a queen as the nurse took hold of the handles of her chair and wheeled her out of the television room.

Mas examined the paper. Gushi-mama's scrawl was difficult to read, but sure enough, there was the first character, mountain. The second one, castle.

"You got a lead on something?" Wishbone asked. Wishbone was like any other self-respecting Nisei — he didn't know how to read and write Japanese. Mas himself hadn't been much of a student in Japan, but he had caught on enough to know the basics. One was that the reading of a Japanese name was unique to its holder. The same two characters could be read a dozen different ways. And the most common reading of the two characters in front of Mas was not Sanjo, but Yamashiro.

"Izu don't think Yamashiro their real names." Mas was back in G. I.'s Crown Royal purple chair, a beer at his side. He watched as G. I. paced back and forth on his hardwood floor. His cat, Mu, squeezed himself in between G. I.'s legs. At first Mas thought Mu was named Moo, as in the sound of a cow, but found out later that G. I. was using the Japanese word *mu* — nothingness, a philosophical notion that *hakujin* hippies and Sansei baby boomers like G. I. subscribed to. In some ways, Mas preferred Tug's straightforward religion better. They had concrete symbols — the cross, the silver fish on the back of people's cars, and sometimes the statue of the lady with the outstretched hands. G. I.'s beliefs, on the other hand, didn't seem to take much shape or form, just the smell of incense and silly cat names.

"That doesn't make sense. I mean, why would Randy and Brian's family change their name? And what does this have to do with Randy's murder?"

The doorbell rang before Mas could respond. "Who could that be?" G. I. said.

"Juanita?" Mas offered.

"She has a key." G. I. checked his watch and went down the stairs to the door.

Mas heard two pairs of footsteps climbing up the stairs and then saw Jiro's freckled face in the doorway. "I was in the neighborhood, so I thought I'd stop by," he was telling G. I. He was taken aback to see Mas in the living room. "Oh, hello. You doing some landscaping around here?"

"Mas is helping me out," explained G. I. "We were at the mortuary today."

"Oh." Jiro pursed his lips together.

"Randy's brother wants to cremate him. Before he takes him back home to Hawaii."

"Makes sense, I guess. It's cleaner. Easier to deal with."

"But no one will see him. No ex-girlfriends. No coworkers. No friends."

"Maybe they don't want to see him like that," Jiro said.

"Well, anyway, the coroner's not going to release the body to him right now. So it's a moot point, I guess."

"G. I., it doesn't matter what you think. Brian is his family. Not us."

"But Brian isn't focused on Randy. He's not thinking clearly. He doesn't know what we know, Kermit."

"What the hell do you mean about that?"

"We were in 'Nam, man, that's all. And Mas here, he knows. He was in Hiroshima when the Bomb was dropped."

"So what does that have to do with anything?"

Mas wasn't that clear either.

"Only that sometimes you need to see death. To make it real."

"You're talking crazy, G. I. Just let it alone." Jiro circled G. I.'s hardwood floor.

155

"That's what would get you off the hook, huh?"

"What?"

"That night. The night that Randy was killed."

Jiro sucked his lips into his mouth.

"What were you two arguing about, anyway?"

"Stupid shit. You know Randy. Little things would set him off."

"Don't lie to me, Kermit. Randy was really pissed off about something."

Jiro crossed his short but powerful arms. He was certainly built like a fireplug, Mas noted. "Listen, I don't need to be accused of anything. You don't know Randy. Not like I knew him."

"Okay, then tell me. If you were so damn close to him, tell me about the real Randy Yamashiro."

"Go to hell, G. I." Jiro then headed down the stairs, with G. I. right behind him. They exchanged more words by G. I.'s front door as Mas and the cat stared at each other in the living room. Mas edged toward the foyer, but their voices, bouncing against the bare walls and high ceilings, were hardly distinguishable. Mas returned to his beer, moving to the couch with Mu. Mas had to admit that the cat was decent enough, as

156

far as animals went. "Moo-moo," Mas teased, raising the half-empty can above Mu's head. In response, Mu squarely swatted the can's bottom with his paw, sending the beer and its contents onto the leather couch.

"Sonafugun," Mas spat out. He leapt up and grabbed the beer can, but the damage was already done. A bubbling stream of Budweiser was making its way in between the cushions. Mas scanned the room for a napkin, a dishrag, anything. Leaning in one corner was a *shamisen* — what was that doing there? Mas frowned. He finally used one of G. I's discarded T-shirts to mop up the mess. Mas began to toss the cushions from the couch to make sure that the beer hadn't soaked through to the springs. On top of the couch's frame, he found old peanuts and pretzels, a few pennies and a dime, and an envelope whose middle had gotten wet. Although the envelope was blank, there was something inside, Mas could see, because the ink was starting to bleed through.

"Chikusho," Mas cursed again. He felt bad opening the envelope, but there was no time. And there, on an extra-long check, was the name GEORGE IWAO HASUIKE, and then the sum: FIVE HUNDRED THOUSAND DOLLARS.

CHAPTER SIX

Mas wanted to blame everything on the cat, but he figured that wouldn't go very far with G. I. Mu was now on a *tansu,* a Japanese chest of drawers, raising his paw as innocently as one of those *maneki neko* statues of cats welcoming good luck into businesses and homes.

From the living room window, Mas had seen Jiro leave in his dark Toyota Cressida. It was dusk, and the whole street was enveloped in a brown haze.

G. I. finally emerged, the top of his head sopping wet with sweat. All this business was taking a psychological toll on the fifty-something lawyer.

"Gomen, ne," Mas apologized as G. I. surveyed the cushions dumped on the floor. "Beer all ova your couch."

"No biggie, Mas," G. I. said. "It's survived worse."

"No, your check. Check all damage." Mas

pointed to the limp check.

G. I. frowned and took a look. "What the — Where was this, Mas? Exactly where?"

Mas pointed to the center of the naked couch.

"I don't know where this came from," he said. "This is a cashier's check. Look, it was issued five days ago. The day before Randy was killed."

"Jackpot check?"

"No, he deposited the money into a new account at a bank in L.A. I told him to wire the money to Hawaii, but he didn't want to for some reason. I don't understand this, Mas. This cashier's check is from his bank. Why would he do this?"

Mas stayed quiet. It did look bad. Doubts about G. I. even hit Mas for a second, but then he brushed them aside, making his mind work like heavy-duty windshield wipers. If G. I. had known about the check, why would he have hidden it underneath a sofa cushion like a Depression-era old lady? G. I. wasn't that *baka.*

"Maybe Kermit was right." G. I. wiped his oily forehead with the edge of his sleeve. "He said that I didn't really know Randy. What do you think, Mas? What the hell should I do with this check?"

Mas shrugged his shoulders. He didn't

know what to advise. G. I. could turn the check over to the police, but eyebrows would be raised about G. I.'s connection to Randy's murder. He certainly couldn't cash it — that would be plain wrong. What had Randy Yamashiro, or Sanjo, or whatever his name was, been thinking?

Mas made up some excuse about needing to go home to meet a friend, completely forgetting to ask G. I. about the *shamisen* leaning against his bookcase in the corner. As it happened, his fake excuse came true. Somebody was sitting on Mas's porch as he turned onto McNally Street. Mas checked his Casio watch. Nine o'clock. Too late for salesmen or evangelists. Mas didn't recognize the boxy Honda parked outside his house, but after easing his truck into the driveway and approaching the front door, Mas could see a familiar sloped back and balding head. Stinky Yoshimoto.

"You couldn't wait to tell him." Stinky dispensed with a plain hello, which was fine with Mas.

"Who?"

"Wishbone. He left me a message — called me every four-letter word in the book. In English, Japanese, and Spanish. Didn't know he knew that many languages."

160

"I had nutin' to do with it." Mas was tired after driving all the way from Culver City. Beginning with the mortuary session at Lopez, Sing, and Iwasaki, it had been a long day.

"Bette came home first to hear the message. Now she's asking me a bunch of questions. I told her that Wishbone had lost his mind in the nursing home. But that's not going to hold water for long."

"Youzu ask him."

"I went to Keiro this evening. He's AWOL. Gone."

Mas licked his lips.

"His roommate said that he had a visitor today. An old Japanese guy. And they were arguing."

Mas tried to go back in time. He hadn't even run into the roommate. And his conversation with Wishbone had been low-key; no angry words.

"The roommate said the guy was probably a Kibei."

Mas braced himself for what was to come next.

"On the visitors' sign-up sheet, there was only one visitor for Wishbone. You."

"I see him, but I no *kenka*. Nutin' about your money deal."

"Then what? You were there for one

straight hour. A long time to say nothing."

"Just hallo. And then sumptin' came up. Sumptin' that I lookin' into for G. I. We talk to Gushi-mama."

"About that guy who won the jackpot? What the hell would Wishbone have to do with that? He's been sick this whole time. He can't offer you much about something that happened over in Torrance."

That's where Stinky underestimated Wishbone. Wishbone wasn't a hundred percent, but when it came to gossip, thirty percent of him could rival any investigator — maybe even Juanita — in tip-top shape.

"So you're telling me that between the time you saw him and the time he called me, he spoke to some *other* Kibei who spilled the beans?"

Mas shrugged his shoulders. "Youzu believe what you believe. I tellsu Wishbone nutin'. None of my bizness."

Stinky stepped into the light set off by the motion detector attached to the next-door neighbor's house. He studied Mas's face as if he were looking at a map directing him to lies and truths. But Mas wasn't the type to blab bad news, so Stinky finally let out a long sigh. "Okay, Mas, I'll have to take your word for it. But in the meantime, I'm going to find that guy."

"Who, Wishbone?"

"No, the guy who swindled us. His last phone number was in the 213 area code. Downtown. I'm going to check every fleabag Skid Row hotel. Once I get my hands on him, he's going to wish he was dead."

"Yah, yah," Mas said, not believing Stinky's threat. Do what you need to do, he thought, just leave me out of it.

Sometimes when Mas repressed his feelings, his feelings broke loose at night while he was sleeping. Often they took the form of Chizuko, her piercing eyes shining light on every weakness in his character. Other times, it was a person who Mas wouldn't think twice about — like Frank, the black man who operated the local liquor store. In a recent dream, Frank had floated above him, legless, saying that he had a job for him to do. Normally Mas would need a lot more details, specifically how big the job was and, more important, how much money he would get, but here he unquestioningly followed Frank. Frank brought Mas to a dead sparrow lying in the street, maggots wiggling out of its stomach. *Bring it to life,* Frank shouted. *Bring it to life.* Just like how Mas had felt stumbling in between corpses in Hiroshima.

Early this morning, Mas was visited not by Frank, but by Gushi-mama. For some reason, she was much, much younger — her skin smooth and spotless and even real teeth in her mouth. She had her hands outstretched in front of her — palms facedown. On the back of her hands were tattoos of a boat, its sail full mast. *"Herupu-herupu,"* she called out for help.

She then turned her palms up. Blood ran down her arms and pooled into the cups of her hands. What could Mas do? He was afraid to touch her, but he couldn't run away either. He stood frozen and waited, feeling drops of blood soak his bare feet.

It had been a bad night and an early morning, so Mas wasn't happy to be answering the phone at ten thirty. "Guess what?" The voice was breathless and female. Juanita Gushiken.

Mas waited.

"Mr. Arai, are you there?"

"Yah." He wasn't in the mood for guessing games.

"You were right. It looks like the Yamashiros may have been Sanjos." G. I. had apparently told Juanita of Mas's hunch. She went straight to the computer and found a handful of information, mostly death records, on

164

Sanjos in Los Angeles. One with the same first name Gushi-mama had given: Isokichi. Date of death: June 4, 1953. After talking with Brian Yamashiro, Juanita had figured out that was the same year that Brian and Randy had moved to Hawaii with their mother. She also discovered Randy's middle name: Isokichi. Too much of a coincidence. All these years, the two brothers had assumed their father to be a deadbeat dad, but not really dead. Juanita's findings indicated otherwise.

"Randy's brotha believe you?"

"I don't think he cares, one way or the other. But G. I. thinks it's worth checking out. Do you know Hajime Kaku?"

Mas grunted. Kaku's name again, in less than forty-eight hours. Ever since he'd been hired by the coroner's office in the fifties, Kaku had had some kind of low-level job, processing stiffs as they arrived. But when another man straight from Japan became the top dog in the sixties, the head coroner of Los Angeles, Hajime became his countryman's biggest champion. Hajime was often the one to visit each of the twenty-some-odd gardeners' associations, telling them that Japanese Americans needed to band together to rally against any criticism leveled against the coroner, who was dealing with the autopsies of Hollywood's biggest stars. Marilyn Monroe, Natalie Wood, Robert F. Kennedy — no man could withstand the pressure and limelight, especially one with yellow skin, Hajime told them. With four to maybe even eight thousand Japanese American gardeners throughout the Southland at the time, many politicians, even the mayor of Los Angeles, had eventually made their way to these meetings to convince gardeners to think their way on the latest bill or election.

"I say we pay him a visit," Juanita declared.

Mas's first inclination was to refuse, but then he stopped himself. It wouldn't be bad to see Hajime Kaku after all these years. Old acquaintances were hard to come by these days, with the Nisei and Kibei dropping like flies. When the opportunity came to see a familiar face, sometimes you needed to take it.

Hajime Kaku told Juanita to meet him outside the building where he worked. Hajime was a company man, but he was a community man too. If he were to spill any secrets, it would be to friends or friends of friends, and only outside the walls of the coroner's office. And since Kaku and Itchy had been close all these years, Juanita and Mas apparently qualified as friends of a friend of a friend.

Hajime was sitting at a plastic picnic table, a manila envelope in his hands. It was half past three, and the only other people were a man and woman wearing identification tags around their necks, sitting on one of the benches. The building was right next to the L.A. city emergency center and across the street from Lopez, Sing, and Iwasaki — offering full services for fallen bodies within one square block.

As Juanita and Mas approached Hajime, he stood up. He wore thick plastic-rimmed glasses that had seen their heyday about thirty years ago.

"Hello, I know you?" Hajime was Issei; he had moved to America as a child, Mas remembered, and his English came out smooth as motor oil. Mas figured that his family must have been high-toned, the learned kind that actually read books and didn't work with their hands like Mas's lineage.

"Member of Crown City gardeners. Youzu came to talk to us."

"That's right, that's right. Way back in the sixties. Sheesh. A lifetime ago."

Mas nodded.

Hajime turned his attention next to Juanita. "So Itchy told me that you're an investigator. Looking into a case from the fifties."

"Yes — 1953. His name was Isokichi Sanjo."

"Yes, yes, Itchy filled me in on all the details. Why are you investigating this, may I ask?"

"You know that I can't say."

"Well, I'm not supposed to be giving out information either." Hajime straightened his back as if he were facing a noon showdown. It didn't take long for Juanita to back down.

"Our friend was killed. Over in Torrance."

"The jackpot winner?" It seemed like everyone they talked to knew about the case.

Juanita nodded. "Something was left at the crime scene. Something that can be traced to a man named Kinjo who was friends with the Sanjo Brothers. And now we're thinking that our friend's family might have once been named Sanjo. The father hasn't been heard from since 1953. He may have had the same name as a man who died in L.A. in 1953."

Hajime pushed up his glasses. He had a typical Japanese nose with a low bridge. "I remember that dead man," he said.

"Honto?" Mas couldn't help to express

doubt. "Ova fifty years ago."

Hajime tightened the grip on his envelope. "I started working in the office that year. The first Japanese to be a clerk in the coroner's office. One of my teachers at L.A. City College got me the job. I was assigned to the graveyard shift. I was so nervous; I wanted to make sure I did everything right.

"Then, one evening, I was outside having a smoke. I shouldn't have, because my supervisor was still out on his break — but he was twenty minutes late and nothing was going on in the morgue. I heard some noises in the parking lot, and there's a *hakujin* man dragging something from the backseat of his car. He sees me and says that he has a dead homeless man. Needs my help to get him out.

"It was a black Ford — that much I remember. And then, when I get closer, I see an Asian man just a little older than me. He was fully dressed, with a knit vest, hat, slacks, and shoes that were unscuffed. It was the same kind of shoes that I had purchased myself in Little Tokyo. Only his shoes had no shoelaces."

Strange, Mas thought.

"I tell the *hakujin* man that he needs to call the police. The police need to get involved for sure. He then shows me a

169

badge. He's a G-man. A government man."

"What, FBI?" Juanita asked.

"Something like that. Law enforcement for sure, and if I just listen to what he says, there will be no trouble. He seems official. An important man.

"I don't know what to do. I tell him that I'm going to call my supervisor, and he says that's a bad idea. He asks me what my name is and writes it down in a small notebook. He can make it so that they send me back to where I came from.

"I was scared. He tells me to report that I found the body lying outside the coroner's office. A John Doe. No identification. And then he drives away.

"I put the man on a gurney and bring him inside. I'm filling out the paperwork, and I'm not sure what I should write down. My supervisor will be returning from his break any minute. But I need more time to think things over. This was the year after the McCarran-Walter Act passes. I'd filed papers to become a citizen — the first year someone born in Japan could do so."

Juanita scrunched up her nose, and Mas knew that this piece of information was a surprise to her. Young people had no idea what the Issei had had to go through, toiling away on farmland and in people's yards with no promises that America could be their home. And then everything was taken away from them during World War II. It was a wonder that the whole lot of them didn't commit mass suicide together in camp. But they were too tough for that. The West Coast sun had hardened them; calluses had developed not only on their hands but also around their hearts. Inside, however, all was gentleness and gooeyness, like the soft center of a See's chocolate. Most of them never lost hope in their new country; so when they were able to go completely American, in 1952, many of them jumped.

"I couldn't let anything ruin my chances to be naturalized. But I couldn't abandon this man either. I searched his clothing, his felt hat, his shoes. He had a piece of Japanese rice candy in his pocket. You know, the kind with rice wrapper that melts in your mouth?"

Both Mas and Juanita nodded.

"So how could I report that he was homeless, a regular John Doe? Him being Japanese, I could have gotten away with it. I mean, who would have really cared?

"But I decide to store him away in the cooler for just one night. Until I can figure out my next step.

"I can't sleep that day; I can't mention

this to anyone I know. I go back to work, and a Japanese gardener comes to see me. I know he's a gardener because he comes in his gardening truck. He tells me that he's looking for someone. He's hoping that his friend — that's how he referred to him — is not dead, but he has to check, just to make sure. He's heard of me, so he thinks that I can be trusted.

"I know instantly that he's looking for the man who was brought in the night before. A part of me hesitates. I remember the G-man's threat, that he's going to send me back to Japan. But I look into the gardener's face, and I know that I can't keep this from him.

"So I take the gardener back into the morgue. The dead man's face and hands are bluish now. The supervisor's out again, but he'll be returning any minute. 'Is this him?' I ask. The gardener's crying. *'Niisan,'* he says."

"Niisan," Mas repeated.

"Yes," Hajime nodded. " 'Big brother.' "

"I go get the paperwork for him to fill out. When I get back to the front desk, the man's disappeared. I don't have his name; all I know is that he spoke to me in Japanese.

"My supervisor comes back and starts yelling at me about this new body in the

172

cooler. I tell him that someone left the body outside. He's suspicious and makes me fill out a full report. I do, but I mention nothing about the G-man.

"A few days later, I come to work and two police officers are waiting for me. They want to know more about the discovery of the Japanese man's body. They question me for three hours, and I finally break down. I tell them everything. Then they show me a photograph of a *hakujin* man. 'Was it this man?' they ask me. It's the G-man who delivered the body to the morgue. His name is Henry Metcalf. I say, 'Yes, what's he done?' But they tell me nothing. I think that they are going to arrest me, but they just tell me to keep what I know under wraps. My supervisor reprimands me, but I still have my job.

"The supervisor tells me the dead man's name is Isokichi Sanjo. The body is never claimed. It's like the whole Sanjo clan has flown the coop. No one in the community seems to care. So we handle it like we handle all the other abandoned bodies."

"How's that?"

"Cremation. And then burial in the Los Angeles County Cemetery."

"Near Evergreen," Mas couldn't help but spout out. Chizuko's resting place.

Hajime nodded.

"Did you ever find out more about the G-man who brought Sanjo in?" Juanita asked.

"No. They didn't tell me, and I didn't ask. For months and years, I had nightmares of him taking me away, but I never saw him again. When I finally got my citizenship papers, I began to rest a little easier. But I knew that citizenship alone wouldn't be able to protect me." Hajime took a deep breath, and Mas realized that this event had been weighing on him for decades. It was a relief for him to tell the story, to let it go so he could float back to the surface, leaving dark waters behind.

Hajime handed the manila envelope to Juanita. "Here's a copy of the death certificate, if you don't have one already."

"Thanks."

"I hope that me being quiet all these years didn't cause this man's family any problems."

Mas lied and shook his head no.

CHAPTER SEVEN

Mas and Juanita walked back to the Toyota in silence. The weight of their thoughts was overwhelming. Who was this Isokichi Sanjo? Had Metcalf killed him? And how much did this have to do with Randy's demise?

Mas began to fear what they were dredging up from the past. Randy was already dead. Why blacken his family's history by traveling in dark places like plumbers pulling out smelly decay and bringing it up to the surface for all to see?

When they were back in the truck, Juanita opened the envelope and spent some time examining the death certificate. "It says here, under cause of death, blunt force trauma. How did the police justify not fully investigating this case?"

Mas shrugged his shoulders. The fifties were a different era. Some of his old customers called it America's Golden Years, but it looked mighty different in the eyes of anyone who wasn't a clean-cut *hakujin* man. Besides, no one had been fighting for Sanjo, which made it all the easier to forget that he had ever been alive.

"Maybe we betta give Detective Alo dis information."

Juanita frowned.

"Alo, you knowsu, the one with Torrance Police."

"I know who you're talking about. Mas, we have nothing."

What about Kinjo being in the same band as Randy's father? And Randy's father's subsequent murder?

Juanita must have read Mas's mind. "I mean nothing concrete," she said. "If we start talking about a murder that occurred fifty years ago, the police are just going to say, 'Wow, that's nice. Give us your documents and we'll call you — don't call us.' We have to keep digging until we find something that definitely links Randy's murder to this Sanjo's. Then we can start talking."

Mas squeezed the fingers of his left hand together. Juanita was starting to get on his nerves.

Juanita then handed Mas an envelope, a smaller, white one.

"Whatsu dis?" he asked.

176

"I keep forgetting — this is Judge Parker's photo from the Internet. I want you to check it out with that woman — your friend Haruo's girlfriend."

Mas removed a plain piece of white paper folded in thirds and opened it. Sure enough, it was Judge Parker's portrait, shot from the shoulders up so you could see that he was dressed in a dark robe.

At that point, they were more ahead than behind, so Juanita should have called it a day and headed home. But she was *ganko,* just like most of the women Mas encountered in his life. Mas was hardheaded himself, but whether it was at the track or the poker table, he knew when to quit. Juanita, on the other hand, didn't.

They sailed along the Harbor Freeway toward Kinjo sensei's mint green house. What they were going to say, Mas didn't know. Accuse him of lying? Of concealing his connection to Randy Yamashiro?

Juanita rattled the security door again, this time with the edge of her ring. The wood door was closed, and no plucking of *shamisen* strings was heard.

"Not home," Mas said, relieved.

"Isn't the Okinawan Club around here somewhere?"

They got back in the truck and drove to

the corner of Western and 166th Street, where a modern glass building stood next to two older brick ones painted light yellow. Mas was impressed. These Okinawans had money, he thought, for not only one building but three.

The gate to the parking lot was closed, so Juanita found a space along a curb below a large, shady elm tree. Mas was ready to jump out, but noticed Juanita scanning her rearview mirror. "The same SOB," she murmured.

"Huh?"

"Back there. That Asian guy in the suit. I saw him in Kinjo's neighborhood."

Mas looked back and saw a tall man with a neat hairstyle sitting in the driver's side of a black Mercury. "Youzu sure?"

"Sure," Juanita said, pulling out a Chap-Stick from her purse. Why did she want to waste time putting makeup on at a time like this? "Okay, Mas, that is what we're going to do. Walk south down Western, and then you make a run for it and I'll stay back. If he chases you, I'll know that he's up to no good."

Mas frowned. This didn't sound like much of a plan. He didn't know the last time he had actually moved his legs at any quick speed. Besides, wouldn't running as if he

178

had something to hide invite something undesirable, like a big hit on the head? "Youzu just ask him. Datsu easier."

"He's not going to tell me what he's up to. I need to catch him off guard." She placed her hands on his shoulders. "Don't worry. I won't let anything happen to you. I just want to test this guy out."

Mas grimaced. He usually had good sense; he was no *bakatare.* But being in Juanita's strong presence made you do things you couldn't imagine. He shuddered to think what she made G. I. do behind closed doors.

They both got out of the truck slowly, walked over to the corner, and, as Juanita had instructed, turned south. Once they crossed the street at a light, Juanita nudged Mas. "Now," she whispered.

Mas bit down on his dentures and churned his legs as fast as they could go. He felt his joints go *piri-piri* and then heard hard soles hit the pavement behind him. And then the sound of a dull thud and a few grunts.

Mas turned back to see the Asian man and Juanita lying in the middle of the street, grappling with each other like two-bit wrestlers. The man was attempting to get away from Juanita, pulling at her hands to free himself. A Toyota Camry was coming toward them, so Mas stepped in front of the car, waving down the driver to switch to the far-right lane. *"Kuruma.* Car, *yo,"* Mas shouted. When Juanita lifted her head, the man was able to wrest free from her hold and ran down the street into a Korean barbecue restaurant.

"Don't let him get away, Mas." Juanita was still on the ground. She breathed hard, her small, compact breasts heaving against the pavement.

Mas followed the man into the restaurant. No windows and dim light. Only orange flames and smoke from a handful of gas grills embedded in the middle of tables. About a dozen customers sitting in booths. But then, in the back near the emergency exit, Mas saw him. *"Ko-ra,* you!" Mas yelled out, and then immediately regretted it. What the hell was he doing? If he ended up apprehending the man, what was he going to do? Hang on to his ankles like a child?

Before Mas had to make any hard decisions, he felt someone push him aside, and then he saw the back of Juanita's jeans as she leapt toward the man. Mas was afraid that they would end up on a burner — he could imagine the man's helmet hair going up in flames — but Juanita had effectively tackled the man in the middle of an aisle.

"Get his ID, Mas, in his back pocket." Juanita was sitting on top of the man, her elbow digging into his shoulder blades.

Mas was not happy about sticking his hand in a stranger's pants pocket. Didn't that constitute robbery, anyhow?

Some of the customers were standing now, and Mas heard a waiter yell, "Call the police!"

"Mas, hurry."

Mas gave in and drew out the man's wallet, which was thin enough to hold only a couple of credit cards.

"Police coming," someone reported. The patrons had left their seats and their barbecue meat to gawk.

Mas tossed the wallet to Juanita, who quickly registered its contents. Her face grew pale, and she slipped off the man's back. "Why have you been following us?"

The man pushed himself up, brushing dirt from his hands and his expensive slacks. He then faced Juanita, his chiseled features stern and menacing. "What did that coroner's clerk tell you?"

"What does that have to do with you? Or who you work for?"

"Just watch your back. People are watching."

Juanita returned the wallet to him, and he pressed a business card in her palm. "Call me. We can help each other." Police sirens wailing in the distance. "You better get out of here," the man said.

The man continued to brush dirt from his fancy suit. Mas noticed that in spite of his spill, not a hair was out of place. "Go now," he said more forcefully.

Juanita and Mas left from the front door — the sirens were only about a block away. Mas felt his heart working overtime; even his fingertips were pulsing. He was shocked that his legs were moving so fast as he and Juanita went down a side street to get back to the car. He couldn't feel his feet, his worn-out joints and knees. If he hadn't heard his own loafers slapping against the pavement, he wouldn't have believed that it was really him running.

Once they were back inside the cab of the Toyota, Mas asked, "Whozu he?"

Juanita handed Mas the man's business card. It read:

BUCHANAN LEE
SPECIAL AGENT
HOMELAND SECURITY

The ride back to Juanita's house, where

182

Mas had left the Ford, was dead quiet. What had Randy been involved in? How was his death related to Homeland Security? And why had this special agent been following them?

Mas knew that after the World Trade Center towers went down, America had changed — but for how long, who knew? He himself had felt his gut fall down to his knees as he watched on television the towers crumble, disintegrate, leaving survivors covered in gray ash. He, too, had anxiously called to see if his daughter, grandson, and son-in-law were all right; he knew that Brooklyn was across the water from Manhattan, but compared to the distances in L.A., it was right next door. But Mari and her family were safe in their underground apartment, and Mas even whispered a prayer of relief before he realized what he was doing.

He felt the worst for those actual eyewitnesses. Mas knew the curse of surviving, of looking normal and unblemished years later but feeling the Bomb still burn in his chest at the strangest and most unpredictable times. Now Homeland Security was supposed to protect them all, but Mas knew they were only words. What was home, and what could be secure? Was it only an excuse to push out the poor and unwanted? And what about that statue in New York Harbor, the one that Mas had seen when he had visited his daughter? Wasn't she holding a torch for newcomers? Or was it now a warning that immigrants should keep their distance?

Like the G-man who had brought Sanjo's body to Hajime, was this agent sending a message to Mas and Juanita?

Mas left Juanita's house without saying good-bye or making plans to meet again. He figured that she needed to talk things over with G. I. Mas also needed a sounding board, so he stopped by Haruo's that evening.

It was cool, with a dampness that seemed to soak into the top layer of their clothing, but they sat outside in lawn chairs anyway. Tomato and cucumber season had passed, but now Haruo was facing a bumper crop of persimmons, or *kaki,* so much so that he had lined up plastic grocery bags full of the fruit against the side of his rented duplex like mini sand bags. There were two kinds of persimmons in Mas and Haruo's world: the pointed, mushy kind, called Hachiya — overproduced by Haruo's small tree — and then the Fuyu, which was as hard as a squished baseball. Mas preferred the Fuyu;

in the days before getting false teeth, he had crunched them like apples. Hachiyas were better for drying, and Haruo had hung them up by their stems with strings on his laundry line. The full moon was out, reflecting an eerie blue light on the hanging persimmons above them.

"So whatsu it again?" Haruo said.

"Homu-lan-do Security," Mas repeated.

"What, like FBI?"

"*Chotto* different. FBI still around; Homeland swallow up INS, I thinksu."

"Whatsu dat gotta do wiz Randy-*san*'s murder?" Haruo muttered, and Mas didn't know what to tell him. He then remembered the folded paper in his pocket.

"You gonna see Spoon at work tonight?" In three hours, Haruo would be on his way to his graveyard shift at the Southern California Flower Market, which was where he had first met Spoon. She had inherited her route business, basically a wholesale floral delivery business, from her dead husband in the fifties. Now Spoon's daughters had taken over the business, renaming it Spoon Sisters Route Services.

"Yah, she comin'."

Mas handed him Judge Parker's photo. "Datsu Judge Parker. Maybe Spoon rememba if he da one with the *shamisen*."

185

"Youzu gotta ask her directly. None of my bizness." Haruo left the photo on his chair and went into the house.

Mas cursed. When didn't Haruo want to stick his nose in someone else's business? And "directly"? When did Haruo ever use words like that? This must be some kind of hocus-pocus from Haruo's counselor, Mas said to himself. Mas thought that Haruo had abandoned his Little Tokyo counselor after dating Spoon, but apparently he was still going in for mental tune-ups.

Haruo returned to the backyard with a cordless phone and the ripped edge of a newspaper with a phone number. "Call her youzuself and ask."

Mas shot Haruo a killer look. *Chikusho.* Damn him. But he still accepted the phone. After a couple of tries, he heard a woman's voice on the other line. Mas cleared his throat. "Spoon-*san?*"

"Pardon."

"Su-poon," Mas repeated, louder and slower.

"Yes, is this Mas?"

"Yah, itsu Mas."

"My caller ID displayed Haruo's number, but you're obviously not Haruo."

Mas didn't know how to take her comment, so he decided to ignore it. "Yah, can you take a look at a pic-cha?"

"What picture?"

"Photo. Of a *hakujin* man. See if itsu same guy you saw wiz *shamisen*."

"Oh, I don't know, Mas. My eyes aren't that good, remember? But have Haruo bring it to work with him, and I'll get back to you."

Mas handed the phone back to Haruo to receive his instructions. Mas understood how it worked now. Haruo had a new boss now, and it wasn't Taxie, the guy who operated the flower stall where he worked at. "Yah, yah, yah," Haruo was saying into the receiver.

Mas left soon after with a bag of Hachi-yas. He was sitting at the kitchen table, in fact, biting into the soft tip of a *kaki,* when the telephone rang. Haruo. They seemed to have a bad connection, because Mas heard clicking noises after every three sentences.

"The photo . . ."

Mas waited.

"Youzu right," Haruo said. "Spoon say dat man, Judge Parker, was the one with the *shamisen*."

187

CHAPTER EIGHT

In Japanese Noh puppet plays, a stagehand called a *kurogo* runs all the behind-the-scenes activities right on stage. Dressed in all black like a killer ninja, the *kurogo* moves furniture or changes the actors' clothing as surreptitiously and unnoticeably as possible. Mas knew that to properly handle Judge and Mrs. Parker, he had to do the same. But Mas wasn't much into subtlety or deception. So he dutifully dug out Juanita's phone numbers. He dialed both her home office and cell phone, but came up empty and didn't bother to leave a message. Strange, Mas thought. Juanita always seemed to answer her cell phone whether she was in the toilet or speeding on the freeway. She must be involved in some heavy-duty business to ignore its ringing.

After watching a television rerun of a detective who lived in a trailer in Malibu, he called Juanita's cell phone again, but got her voice mail. *Shikataganai.* What could he do? He went ahead and left a message: "Itsu Mas. Give me a call. Important."

About an hour later, the phone did ring. "Hallo, Juanita?"

"Juanita, who's Juanita? Your new girlfriend?" It was Mari in New York City.

"*Baka yo,* have nutin' to do wiz girlfriend."

"Okay, okay," Mari said, almost sounding relieved. Mas, for a minute, thought about Professor Genessee and then berated himself. Don't be *kuru-kuru-pa.* A sensei like that would have nothing to do with a no-good gardener.

"Howzu baby?" Mas asked.

"Takeo's not a baby, Dad. He's almost three. We're talking about visiting you in California someday. Now, wouldn't that be something?"

Mas couldn't picture the presence of his active grandson bringing life to his dust-filled rooms. He hadn't seen Takeo for two years, but traced his development through regular telephone calls and letters from Mari.

Then there it was again. A clicking noise.

"What's with your phone, Dad?"

Okashii. "Dunno," Mas said. "Keep happenin'."

"You should get the phone company to

189

check it out."

Mas grunted.

"You're not going to do it, are you? You're going to wait until the phone goes dead and you're in trouble."

Urusai, thought Mas. Sometimes Mari was as much of a nag as her mother. The line crackled again.

"Has it been raining over there? Didn't your line go dead during El Niño?"

"No, no rain."

"Weird. Well, get it checked out." She then began asking if there was anything new in his life.

"You knowsu, same, same."

Mas didn't mention to Mari anything about his volunteer investigative work for G. I. She would tell him to drop it, take it easy instead, and find friends to play his favorite game, go. But most of his peers were buried or close to it. And since Haruo had his lady friend, Mas was pretty much on his own. He spoke to Mari a few minutes more and then got into bed. The chase, news of the dead Japanese man, Spoon's identification of Judge Parker, it was too much for Mas to take right now. That night, another nightmare visited him. Gushi-mama again, this time wearing a bright-red wig like a kabuki lion dancer's. She was stomping in circles, her feet wrapped in *tabi,* the traditional white socks with a split for the big toe. She was gesturing for Mas to come, but then she would hide behind a giant tree or a concrete post. Mas felt himself getting angrier and angrier. "Ole lady, what do you want?" Mas called out. Either show yourself or disappear. And then, as if adhering to Mas's demands, she vanished, and Mas found himself in complete darkness in a huge wet tomb, water dripping from the sides of the walls, slippery algae accumulating on the floor.

Mas woke up cocooned in a cotton sheet and worn blanket. He shook his shoulders free and wiped the sweat dripping from his ears. Gushi-mama kept visiting him in his dreams, and Mas was beginning to see that it was no coincidence. Gushi-mama had revealed that she had known Isokichi Sanjo, but said nothing about his death. When it became light, Mas called up Haruo to accompany him back to Keiro. Haruo could be his anchor at times, a solid weight that prevented Mas from drifting into unsafe waters. But Haruo, again, was otherwise occupied. He was going over to Palm Springs to help Spoon and her daughters with their floral decoration job at a hotel.

"Gonna see Wishbone at Keiro?" Haruo

191

asked. He obviously wasn't informed of the latest news. Mas told him about Stinky's Japanese stock scheme and how it had imploded, spreading debris all over its victims.

"*So-ka,*" Haruo murmured. A perpetual loser and gambling addict, Haruo had deep empathy for anyone who found their pockets empty. "You knowsu, Mas, I've been thinkin' about this killing. Don't have a good feeling about dis, Mas. Betta if you forget about it."

But it was too late to forget. As much as Mas hated to admit it, Sanjo's story had gotten under his skin.

Gushi-mama was knitting in her room. Her roommate, the pigeon-faced woman, was again tucked in her bed. Must be depressed, thought Mas, who in the past had also opted to shut himself from sun and people. When Gushi-mama looked up and saw Mas, her chin quivered a little. Mas knew that she was afraid.

"*Kaerinasai,*" she ordered, rather than said. And if Japanese wasn't sufficient, she added the English translation, "Go home."

Mas shuffled his feet, but he didn't leave. "You tell me lies," Mas said in broken Japanese. "Neva mention Sanjo *oniisan* dead," he continued in English.

Gushi-mama dropped her knitting and attempted to move her wheelchair. Her roommate remained listlessly on the bed. "Sachi," Gushi-mama called out, trying to stir her roommate. "Sachi." But depression had firmly taken its hold on the roommate.

Mas felt a twinge of guilt about hassling a woman who had made it into her hundreds. But being that age didn't come by accident. It took not only a strong body, but a spirit that was not easily crushed. Gushi-mama was toothless, but her mind was like a steel trap.

Mas stepped forward to Gushi-mama. She threw a spare knitting needle at his chest, a pitiful arrow that just grazed his T-shirt.

"Izu not making trouble. Sanjo's *musuko* dead. Just trying to findsu out who did it." Mas made it a point to say *musuko,* instead of "son" in English. *Musuko* evoked the sounds of a mother with her child, laughing and playing in a freshly mowed park.

"You know Uchinanchu?" Gushi-mama finally asked.

Mas cocked his head. The term was somewhat familiar. Wasn't it what Okinawans called their own kind?

"Uchinanchu not only in Okinawa. In United States. South America. Australia."

Mas had known about the Uchinanchu in Hawaii and Latin America. But way down south in Australia? Okinawans were like the Chinese; they knew no borders.

"We all Uchinanchu — feel it inside — even though we everywhere. Do you know why?"

Mas had a clue. He knew that Okinawa had been a kingdom at one time. The Ryuku Islands.

"Kuro. We know *kuro."*

Suffering, yes, Mas could appreciate that. Like the Indians in America, Okinawans were the native people. Indians had been pushed out to make room for the *hakujin,* and now people of every country and race were pushing on each other to get into the best houses, schools, and companies.

"Yamashiro, Tamashiro, Kaneshiro, all these names have *shiro* at end. Castle. For king."

Mas nodded.

"Japanese names all about trees, farming. Nothing about kings."

Mas's last name could have different meanings, depending on how you wrote it. Arai could be "New Well," but in Mas's case it meant "Rough Home." The only one who would truly know the correct characters would be the owner of the name himself.

Nonetheless, Gushi-mama's contention was correct. The meaning of the Arai name had little to do with royalty.

"Uchinanchu *kokoro,* heart, strong. Food best. Music best."

Aside from the Okinawa *dango,* a fried donut that Chizuko used to make in an electric skillet, Mas didn't know much about Uchinanchu food. But Gushi-mama was speaking so adamantly that Mas had to take her word for it.

"Your home is where?" Gushi-mama asked in Japanese.

Mas was going to say Altadena or his birthplace, Watsonville, California, but he knew she meant Japan. "Hiroshima," he said, for his parents' hometown.

Gushi-mama's mouth fell open. "So," she said. "You know *kuro* too."

A little suffering, more than a little happiness, always seemed to draw people together. It certainly seemed to work on Gushi-mama. "What Sanjo-*san* to you?" she asked finally.

"His son, friend of friend."

Gushi-mama's heavy-lidded eyes rested on Mas's face as if she were taking in every line and blemish. "Last time I hear about Sanjo-*san*" — Mas practically held his breath in anticipation of what would come next — "fifty years ago. INS call him in. Sanjo never come back."

"Nobody do nutin'?" I thought you Uchinanchu all stick together, he said to himself.

"Whole family leave for somewhere. Nobody want to get involve."

"You knowsu sons' names?"

"Just *oniisan*'s. His name Randy."

Mas caught his breath. More proof that Isokichi was indeed Randy's father. "So you knowsu about Isokichi dying?"

Gushi-mama bunched up her knitting. "I just choose good things to remember. Throw away the bad. My husband the same way, and he go to *The Rafu Shimpo* to ask them not to write anything about Sanjo-*san*. It was *haji* for the family and the Okinawa people too."

This shame was deep; it could not be erased by merely censoring journalists. Mas could imagine how the *haji* burned red-hot inside. It was no wonder that the wife escaped to Hawaii with her children.

"You in L.A. in 1950?" Gushi-mama asked.

Mas nodded.

"Then you know. You hear about government taking Issei."

Mas did faintly remember some stories

about questionable Japanese being arrested and threats of them being sent back to Japan. But it hadn't been in the papers, not even *The Rafu Shimpo.*

"I become citizen in 1952," Gushi-mama said proudly. She pointed to a plastic American flag that was hanging from the panel light above her headboard. "My boys fight in 442nd." That was Tug Yamada's outfit, the all-Nisei combat unit that battled and died all throughout France and Italy.

Mas got where Gushi-mama was coming from. She chose to embrace the American way, while others were still smarting from their families being barred from buying land and then being sent into camps during World War II. If Mas hadn't been born in America himself, he didn't know how enthusiastic he would have been about switching allegiances from Japan to the United States.

"I no think about Sanjo for fifty years. Then, all of sudden, you come. And this morning the other one."

Another person had been asking about Sanjo? Mas could barely find his voice. "Who?"

"Tall, good-looking, all dressed up in a suit. Nice hair. Chinee, I think. Didn't say his name, only that I shouldn't say anything about Sanjo to anybody but him."

"When?"

"Hour before you come."

Mas jammed his hands down his jeans pockets so hard that he could feel the lint gathered in the corners of the lining. The description fit Agent Lee, no doubt. "Heezu say anytin' else?"

"Not much. You know, your *hyoban* pretty bad here right now."

Hyoban, one's reputation, was everything to a working-class man. A reputation is what you built slowly and deliberately over a lifetime. Anyone could have a success at the track, and some were born with good looks; but the windfall could be easily taken during one bad session at the poker table, and an accident with a Weedwacker could put an end to a handsome face. Mas couldn't afford to have a bad reputation, but it wasn't anything that he could take hold of and remedy. You couldn't beat your own shadow in a boxing match. Mas figured Stinky must have done his share of damaging Mas's reputation in his futile search for Wishbone.

"Wishbone not back?" Mas asked.

Gushi-mama shook her head. "You want to see Tanaka-*san's* roomu?"

Mas nodded. Gushi-mama gestured for Mas to take hold of the handles of her wheelchair. The queen had returned in full form.

Mas wheeled Gushi-mama down the hall to Wishbone's residence. This time a thin, bony man was sitting by the window. He had large bags under his eyes as if they were holding decades of sorrows. He listened to Gushi-mama's question about Wishbone's visitor and then pointed to Mas. "Look a little like you. Dark skin. Short. They were talkin' *okane.* Money," the man said for emphasis.

"That's all?" Gushi-mama asked in Japanese.

The man pointed to his right ear. "This *mimi* no good. Can't hear too well. But Wishbone was mad. Even began to hit the man with his crutches. I had to call a nurse to get him to stop. Then, a few hours later, he gone."

This was all *kusai,* as smelly as fish skin left in a trash can on a summer day. Strange things were going on in this nursing home. It wasn't Wishbone's style to go MIA. He wasn't a man who did well solo. His disappearance was an act of desperation. Whether it was Wishbone's desperation or another's, he was in trouble.

When Mas went home, he disconnected the

telephone. Since he had just spoken to Mari, it would be another two weeks before she'd call again.

It wasn't worth it to continue with this investigation, Mas decided. This situation wasn't black-and-white — it was full of grays. He couldn't tell who was bad or good, guilty or innocent. He was standing squarely on one side, Isokichi Sanjo's side, but what if it was the wrong side?

He felt bad for Randy Yamashiro, but realistically, what could he do? Mas was just a good-for-nothing gardener who didn't even have a full lineup of customers. G. I. and Juanita had the degrees and licenses. They didn't really need him. The next time they asked, Mas would politely beg off any more visits to *shamisen* instructors or Uchinanchu community leaders, he vowed, and then he went to sleep.

The next morning was peaceful. Mas didn't bother to get up at the crack of dawn, and instead lingered in bed. He listened for the sparrows outside in the boxwood bush and could smell the edges of the sycamore tree's leaves turning brown. He wondered what the next season, winter, would bring. Another El Niño, with the deluge of water that could melt a boulder and hillsides? Or would it be a sporadic sprinkling that would leave the ground hardened and lawns withered?

After twelve hours of being disconnected from the outside world, Mas finally felt strong enough to deal with outsiders again and plugged in his phone. If Juanita or G. I. called, he would just tell them he was too busy, too old, to take up his time going *gasa-gasa* over the murder of a man he barely knew. He didn't have much time to practice his *kotowari,* his regrets, because the phone soon began to ring.

"I've been calling and calling you, Mas." It was G. I.

Mas took a big breath, but before he could spit out his second thoughts, G. I. shocked him with this: "Homeland Security arrested Juanita's father. A glitch in his permanent residency status. Doesn't make sense."

Antonio Gushiken, the mustachioed man who stood rail straight and somehow knew how to respect his grown daughter's space. Mas knew that Juanita had been born in the U.S.; Mr. Gushiken must have been in this country for at least forty years.

"Now they're saying that he illegally entered this country," continued G. I. "But he was part of the prisoner-of-war exchange during World War Two. That's how he and his parents came over. Later, the government made provisions for these Japanese Peruvians to stay, so I don't understand why it's a problem now."

Mas had a clue. Something to do with Juanita's run-in with Agent Lee. The line crackled, inciting a response from G. I.

"That damn noise — I bet they've been wiretapping your phone; they bugged Juanita's. Better if you use a pay phone from now on."

The telephone receiver grew slippery in Mas's sweaty palm. Wiretapping, electronic bugs — these weren't a part of his life.

"Juanita's helping her mom with the restaurants. They don't even know where her dad is being held. I got the best hotshot immigration lawyer working on the case. This is beyond me, Mas. We need the big guns."

After getting off the phone, Mas just sat at the kitchen table, listening to the ticking of the wall clock. He was not a superstitious man. He believed that crop circles (and, yes, they even showed up in Japanese rice paddies) were created by teenagers with too much time on their hands, not by space aliens. He didn't give much credence to secret societies, although he did once see a former customer leave his house in a silly red hat with a long yellow tassel to meet three other men in the same outrageous getup. But it all made sense now how Agent Lee had been one step ahead of him, at least in this last visit to Keiro. He had been listening to Mas's conversations all along.

Juanita must be worried sick about her father. She was the type to take charge and put out fires before they got out of control. But this fire was much bigger than any one person could extinguish. The only way to stop it was to light another one, but then you faced the risk of the flames joining forces and swallowing you whole.

Mas felt his chest grow tighter as the clock continued its ticking. Years ago, he had had to throw away their old, defective clock and replaced it with a plastic one he'd gotten free at Santa Anita Racetrack. The face featured a jockey holding on to a racehorse, the image blurred as if they were going top speed. There were no numbers, so sometimes Mas was an hour off the real time.

It was either four or five when Mas drove to Frank's Liquor Store on Fair Oaks Avenue to use the beat-up pay phone outside on the sidewalk. He took out a couple of business cards from his wallet and propped them up in the graffiti-covered pay phone enclosure.

"Your phone not workin', Mas?" Frank walked outside to rearrange his stacks of the *Los Angeles Times,* the L.A. *Sentinel,* and *La Opiñion* by his open door.

"Broke," Mas said.

"Here, here, on me." Frank stuffed a couple of coins into the slot and went back in his store to give Mas some privacy. Mas knew who he would be calling first.

"Alo here." The detective's voice was surprisingly loud over the phone.

"Hallo, Mas Arai."

"Mr. Arai, how can I help you?"

"Findsu out the man with *shamisen —* Judge Edwin Parker."

"Yes."

What? Alo knew already?

"We got that information on the day of the murder. Anything else, Mr. Arai?"

Mas felt like a fool. What had taken him and Juanita days to uncover had already been in the hands of Detective Alo, a real professional. He thought about mentioning his having been followed by Agent Lee, but he wasn't sure what the relationship was between the Torrance Police Department and Homeland Security. It would be better to wait on that revelation.

"Well, call if you happen to get a hold of any other information."

Mas ended the call and considered going back home. But instead he stuck more coins in the pay phone.

At the third ring, she finally answered. "Hello."

"Professor Genessee." Mas was surprised how her name rolled off his tongue, as easily as ordering *hamachi* from his favorite sushi bar in Little Tokyo. "Itsu Mas Arai."

"Mas, so nice to hear from you again. How can I help you?"

"Sumptin' happen." Mas could only manage to whisper.

Mas told Genessee a condensed version of events — from the Spam jackpot to the Hawaiian restaurant to the *shamisen* sensei, the Homeland Security agent, and the funny sound on his phone. And, of course, the arrest of Antonio Gushiken.

"I think your Mr. Gushiken may be in serious trouble." The professor didn't mince words. "After 9/11, everyone's on high alert about immigrants."

"Just a boy when he come ova," Mas explained the little he knew. "The U.S. government the one who bring the family here in the first place."

Genessee knew all about it: Japanese Peruvians who were taken to a camp in Crystal City, Texas, to be part of a prisoner-

205

of-war exchange. Only the exchange was never totally completed, and even if it had happened, what purpose would it have served? Japan wasn't home for these Peruvians, as much as it wasn't home for Americans like Tug and Spoon. So then the leftover Peruvian folks were truly homeless. Peru didn't want them, and neither did Japan or the United States. It was only after work by some lawyers that the Japanese Peruvians were allowed to stay in the States, Genessee explained.

"I hope your man has a good lawyer," she added.

Mas nodded. Big guns, wasn't that what G. I. had said? "Don't wanna be too involve," he inadvertently murmured.

"Mr. Arai, I think you're already involved. You need to help Juanita. And her family. Isn't that why you called me?"

Mas felt his face grow hot. He glanced at his image in the metal faceplate of the pay telephone. On the scuffed surface was a distorted tan swirl with two dark holes, his eyes, staring back at him. Why was he calling this woman, whom he barely knew? What about her seemed safe and strong, somebody who could point him in the right direction?

"Listen, Mr. Arai, I think I know of a place

that can help you out." She mentioned something about a library and then an address in South Central L.A.

South Central? What kind of help was the professor offering?

"It's a private library — I've heard that records belonging to immigration attorneys in the fifties are stored there. I can even meet you there on Tuesday. Maybe we can find out information about this Isokichi Sanjo."

When Mas hesitated, Genessee added, "What do you have to lose?"

My life, Mas thought, recollecting the daily reports of shootings in the area on the television news. But if the professor was not afraid, Mas wasn't either.

On Tuesday morning, Mas went down the Harbor Freeway, but this time not as far as Gardena. He got off at the Florence exit, recalling the intersection where the 1992 riots had started. Hadn't there been a Japanese man pulled out of a melee by a black man who turned out to be a TV actor?

He parked on the street, fed money into a parking meter, and approached a building with a long mural featuring a bunch of women — a bespectacled black woman in a suit and hat, a woman bent over a sewing machine, a woman wearing a hard hat with her arm raised. What kind of library was this? Mas wondered. Looked like a place for troublemakers, not researchers. But there, in front, wearing a dress that looked like it was made of Japanese batik cloth, was Genessee Howard.

"Had any problems finding the place?"

Mas shook his head. Genessee was wearing new earrings this time, simple pearls that made her earlobes look like open oysters. Instead of a purse or briefcase, she carried a large straw handbag.

The metal folding security gate had been pushed aside to make way for visitors. The tint on the locked glass door was too dark for Mas to see inside. Genessee went straight for the black doorbell on the frame of the door. It was obvious that she had been there before.

A large woman wearing a Mexican-style embroidered shirt opened the door and gestured for them to come in. Her salt-and-pepper hair was all mussed up — definitely a look of an *asanebo,* a late riser who had just rolled out of bed to come to work.

The cavernous room felt a bit dreary, as if it had been drizzling inside. A few colorful posters punctuated the stark walls, but what took center stage were rows of bookcases filled with books of every size — yellowed tomes as solid as bricks, flimsy booklets as thin as mud flaps on a truck, and new paperbacks that glistened with hope and expectation. The whole place smelled like old paper, and Mas felt his body growing itchy, as if silverfish had gotten underneath his clothes.

Mas's eyes attempted to adjust to the dimness. How could anybody read in here? The professor, meanwhile, had been talking to the bedhead-haired librarian, who nodded and disappeared in some stacks. The professor set her straw bag on a fake wood table and pulled out a laptop computer and a yellow legal pad. She handed the pad and a pencil to Mas. "We're not supposed to use ink," she said to Mas, who let the pencil slip through his fingers. Now what was the professor expecting him to do? Mas preferred reseeding someone's lawn to anything dealing with books and writing. But he needed to be strong and keep all his petty *monku* locked up inside, he told himself. Juanita and her father were in trouble, in need of any kind of break. So when the librarian emerged with a box full of files, Mas did not say one word of complaint.

"These files have been popular lately," the

librarian said. The front of the box was marked AMERICANS TO PROTECT IM-MIGRANTS COMMITTEE FILES, 1952–1960.

"What do you mean?" Genessee asked.

"Well, no one's asked for them in years, and all of sudden, we've received three — well, four — requests, counting yours, over the past couple of weeks."

"Who's asked for them?"

The librarian denied the professor's request. "You know, Genessee, that that information is confidential. You wouldn't want me to be telling other people what you've been up to, right?"

They went through file by file, paper by paper. There were newspaper articles from the fifties, legal documents, and finally correspondence. Letters from people Mas had never heard of, written to people he had never heard of. The pages of Mas's legal pad remained empty, and his eyes began to slide shut. Before his forehead hit the table, Mas heard the professor's voice: "I think I've found something."

Mas wiped the drool off the sides of his mouth and pushed his reading glasses back over his eyes. *"Nani?"*

"Isokichi Sanjo, wasn't that his name?" The professor traced a section of a letter with her smooth index finger. She sounded out the name: "I-so-ki-chi San-jo."

"Yah, datsu him," Mas said, looking over Genessee's arm. It was some kind of mimeographed letter. Dated 1953.

"I guess he was among immigrants arrested for their affiliations with the Communist Party in the thirties."

Communists — *aka,* that's what Gushi-mama had told them. But it didn't make sense. If the letter was dated 1953, what did that have to do with something from the thirties?

"It was the height of the Red scare. The McCarran-Walter Act enabled the government to deport 'undesirable' aliens, which was open to interpretation, let me tell you. Some of the deported had even fought for the Allied Forces during World War Two. But on the flip side, the act was the same legislation that allowed Issei to finally get naturalized. So most Japanese Americans view it as being beneficial."

Mas nodded. He did recall photographs in *The Rafu Shimpo* of Japanese men in suits and felt hats and their wives in dresses and sturdy black shoes raising their right hands to take oaths to be Americans. Just like Gushi-mama, these folks couldn't wait to pledge allegiance to the country where they had spent most or all of their adult lives. Didn't matter that three years of it might have been behind barbed wire. Didn't matter that the government had forced them to leave their strawberry and lettuce fields ready to be harvested. Their love for America was deep; it went far beyond material possessions. It was wrapped up in their children, grandchildren, great-grandchildren. They didn't care about severing ties to the past, because they wanted to hold on to the future.

"Let's see." Genessee rubbed the backs of her ears as if that move would help her think. "This letter mentions his defense attorney, Isaac Delman. A very well-respected civil rights lawyer. Helped a lot of people placed on blacklists during the McCarthy era."

Mas had never heard of him.

"He died about a decade ago. His daughter Olivia is still alive. She's on a few boards at UCLA. I've met her a couple of times."

Genessee flipped through different pages of the correspondence. "Wait a minute," she said. "I guess Delman backed out and another lawyer filled in. Edwin Parker."

"Paa-kaa?" Mas's voice came out high, like the cawing of a crow.

"Edwin Parker," Genessee repeated.

"Sounds familiar. Isn't there an Edwin Parker who's a county judge?"

Mas gave the professor a fake excuse to cut their meeting short. Genessee made some copies of the letter before they left. She lingered by the sign-out sheet at the front counter and finally joined Mas outside.

"Well, I figured out who at least two of the three other people looking at the Americans to Protect Immigrants Committee files were. That agent you mentioned, Buchanan Lee? And a reporter for the *Times* — Manuel Spicer."

Mas didn't know which one surprised him more — the government agent who had been tailing him and Juanita, or this new name, Spicer. But reporters were always sniffing around in dark corners. Who knew what other stories were buried in those files?

Mas knew what he had to do. There was no reason to involve the professor further. She had done enough. She was a woman with a lot to lose: a good job, a title, a *hyoban*. According to Gushi-mama, Mas's *hyoban* was dirt anyway. To hell with being a *kurogo;* Mas had to play it his way: straight.

Mas knew where Judge Parker worked. Years ago, he had been called to jury duty and in spite of Chizuko clearly having written DOES NOT SPEAK ENGLISH on his jury response form, he had received instructions that he needed to call a number during a certain week in the summer. Chizuko indeed called for him, and, of course, his assigned number was selected. He would have to go in. "Tell them that you cannot speak *Eigo*," Chizuko said, handing him a note on which she had typed: TO WHOM IT MAY CONCERN: MASAO ARAI DOES NOT SPEAK ENGLISH.

On the day he was scheduled to appear for jury duty, he parked in a three-story parking lot across the street from the Music Center, walked four long blocks, and, after passing through a metal detector, waited with another group of people to go on the elevator. As he'd walked down one of the long corridors, he'd seen a familiar name on a plaque outside a courtroom: JUDGE EDWIN PARKER. His first instinct had been to hide; he didn't know exactly why, because the doors were closed. But he did move across to the other side of the hall, protected by lines of taller people.

Mas's name was not called the whole day as he waited in a large room with year-old magazines and a television whose sound was muted. He had thrown away Chizuko's note, anyhow. Despite what she thought, he wasn't a child. He could speak and understand enough English, probably better than most, he thought. People usually just listened for words, while Mas knew that you needed to listen to the spaces in between the words.

Mas headed to the courthouse now, locking his door with another screwdriver that he had fished out of his toolbox. He had only one hour to make his point or else face a sixty-dollar fine. He would keep it short. As soon as he stood before Judge Parker, he would know. Parker wouldn't have to even say a word; Mas was sure he could read his face.

But Mas didn't count on being foiled at the door. He walked through the metal detector, only to have it buzz, causing the uniformed officers to straighten up after an apparently uneventful morning. One of them took him aside, waved a wand around his body, and then stopped at his jeans pocket. Sonafugun. The screwdriver. The officer with the wand made Mas lift his arms higher and patted the sides of his body. The man wasted no time in extracting the screwdriver; the next move was by the officer sitting on a stool by the metal detector. He removed a walkie-talkie from his belt and cupped it to his mouth. Mas couldn't hear exactly what he was saying — all he knew was that it wasn't good.

A mustachioed man in a suit and tie and plastic-laminated badge crossed the lobby and spoke to the officer with the wand. He kept his eyes on Mas at all times. What did he think? That Mas at age seventy-two would make a run for it?

The man in the suit finally approached Mas. "You can't bring something like this into the courtroom," he said, holding up the screwdriver.

A new officer had joined him. A burly-looking one the size of a giant refrigerator.

"Itsu my key. Open car door," Mas tried to explain. His voice was high-pitched, and in the cavernous lobby, it sounded tinny and cheap.

The officers exchanged glances.

"What's the nature of your business here?" the man in the suit asked. Mas tried to make out the name on his badge. The photo was old — in it, he had the same mustache, but was wearing a fat tie and glasses with thick plastic frames.

"Judge Edwin Parker."

"Judge Parker? What business do you have with him?"

Mas didn't know what to say now. So he

said a half-truth, half-lie. "Gardener. Izu Parker's gardener." So what if he was off by a couple of decades.

The faces of the men instantly softened, relaxed. It was an identity that they could believe. And only a gardener could be *baka* enough to try to bring a screwdriver into a criminal courts building.

"Parker behind on his gardening bill?" the officer with the wand asked. He smiled widely, as if he wasn't really expecting an answer. The man in the suit whispered something in the seated officer's ear, who began talking into his walkie-talkie again. Mas had to stand on the side for ten minutes until a familiar person appeared. Judge Parker, in a suit, without his robe.

"Hello, Mas," he said. The judge then addressed the officers. "It's all right. I've recessed early anyway. He can come on up."

"You can get your key on the way out." The officer smiled again, waving Mas's old screwdriver.

Mas awkwardly followed the judge to a set of closed elevators, joining a crowd of men in ties and women in nylon stockings and dresses, carrying either briefcases or carryout food. Mas said nothing. There was no sense in either of them attempting small talk.

They rode an elevator to the fourth floor. It was the same courtroom that Mas had passed before, only this time they went through a small door next to the double doors, down a narrow hallway, and finally into Judge Parker's private chambers. Papers and accordion files were neatly arranged on his desk. A black robe hung from a wooden hanger on the edge of a bookcase. Freshly dusted photos of the judge, Mrs. Parker, their children (who had grown up so much that Mas barely recognized them) were on display on his desk. Mas was surprised to also see on his wall a framed illustration of the ten camps that had once held Issei and Nisei. He had never pegged Parker as having been a lover of Japanese America, but if he really thought about it, some kind of connection was there. After all, Judge Parker had represented Sanjo and was on the board of the Japanese American Bar Association.

The judge sat in a black padded leather chair. "What are you doing here, Mas?" he asked.

"Needsu to talk to you. About Isokichi Sanjo."

"Sit down." Judge Parker gestured toward a wooden chair on the other side of his desk. Mas did as he was told. His feet could barely touch the floor, and he couldn't help but wonder if that was Judge Parker's way of making him feel like a child.

"I was his attorney. Yes," Parker said.

"You knowsu Randy Yamashiro, his son?"

"Yes, well, at least that's what Randy told me."

"He say?"

"He called me on the Friday before the party. He wanted to talk to me."

"How —"

"I'm not sure how he found out that I had been his father's attorney. He wouldn't say. I think that all of this was new to him, that he needed to absorb everything as soon as he could. It was unbelievable — he hadn't even known that his father had a different last name. I told him all that I could. That his father had been a target of political propaganda. He was no more a threat to American security than I was. He hadn't even been an official member of the Communist Party; he had just gone to one meeting. And most of those people were there because they were antifascist, more than anything else."

Mas couldn't follow all that the judge was saying, but got the impression that Sanjo was innocent, at least of being a threat to national security.

"So whysu he end up dead?"

Parker shook his head. "Yes, that was tragic. But there was nothing I could have done. I was out of the picture by then. Mr. Sanjo had terminated my services."

"Fire? Makes no sense."

"His brother Anmen was behind it, I believe. A week later, the coroner's office contacted me to identify the body. The whole family, including the brother, had moved without telling anyone their whereabouts. I did think Isokichi's death was suspicious. The INS agent who had arrested him previously, Henry Metcalf, was missing. Quite a coincidence, I thought."

And yet you did nothing. Mas's eyes must have betrayed his thoughts, because the judge sighed and stroked his lined forehead. "I had other cases, Mas. I didn't have time to run around playing Hardy Boys."

Mas didn't quite understand Parker's reference to the Hardy Boys, but felt the *hiniku,* sarcastic jab. Mas obviously did have time to waste, because here he was, playing around and asking questions. All this didn't explain how the *shamisen* had gotten into Randy's possession. "Youzu bring the *shamisen* to party."

Parker nodded. "I had hung on to it all these years. The police released Sanjo's possessions to me after he was cremated. I was hoping that I could return it to his family someday, and Randy asked for it."

"He knowsu about *shamisen?*"

"Yes, again, I'm not sure how. But I assured him that I would get it to him as soon as possible. And then he proposed that I bring it to G. I.'s party. I didn't mention all this to you, Mas, because I thought that it was none of your business."

Fair enough. Mas could accept that. "Somebody else's *shamisen.*"

"Well, I don't know anything about that. It had been in Isokichi's possession when he was arrested."

"Yamashiro found dead with *shamisen.*"

Judge Parker's body stiffened as if he were posing for an official photograph in the *Los Angeles Times.* "I hope you're not suggesting that I had anything to do with Mr. Yamashiro's death. I barely knew him. But I must say that I was surprised to see Mr. Kinjo performing at G. I.'s party."

"You knowsu?"

"Well, not personally. But I remember him well. He was the one who informed on Mr. Sanjo fifty years ago."

CHAPTER NINE

Mas kept thinking about what Judge Parker had said: Kinjo sensei had been the informant who had led to Isokichi Sanjo's arrest. Kinjo, who had denied that he knew Randy Yamashiro. Kinjo, who had been at the Hawaiian restaurant the day Randy had been killed.

Mas was so jumpy that he almost ran over a Chinese woman at the crosswalk on Hill Street in Chinatown. She had been pulling a metal handcart full of green vegetables from the local farmers market. Mas was late to brake, causing the woman to run, her cart overturning and releasing about half a dozen bok choy onto the street, a tumble of edible bowling pins.

The handcart of food reminded Mas of dim sum. Dim sum, with its steaming-hot round tins transported in carts pushed by uniformed women, was high-pressure dining. In dim sum, you had to make a snap decision right then and there. Yes, pork shu-mai. Yes, taro cake. Yes, egg custard tart. If you didn't respond fast enough, the cart would pass you over, leaving a wash of regret in your stomach. In honor of snap decisions, Mas made one in the Ford. For his own peace of mind, he needed to find out the truth. And he didn't want to burden Juanita with the latest information until he had turned over all the bowls in the shell game. So, instead of north, he found himself going south: back to the house of the *shamisen* sensei.

Kinjo sensei's street was full of cars; Mas had to drive two blocks away to find a parking space. He noticed a familiar car, a dusty old Cressida — a dime a dozen, Mas thought to himself. Something was going on in the neighborhood, and Mas quickly discovered that it was happening at Kinjo's house. The security gate and door were closed, but Mas heard music coming from the back. He walked around the back of the house, where windows revealed a bunch of black and white heads. Once Mas stood on his tiptoes, he saw what the crowd was there for: six *shamisen* players, including Kinjo and his son. Mas had seen this before — Mari's tiresome piano recitals, where one

223

child after another banged on the keys, producing a sound that could be called anything but music.

He couldn't just charge in there and confront Kinjo. He had no choice but to wait. He leaned against the corner of the outside wall and wished that he had a cigarette to pass the time. He didn't want to smoke it, just finger it, hold it, smell it. Even the dead man, Randy, had understood Mas's compulsion. Hadn't he had an unlit cigarette hanging out of his mouth during the party?

Standing out there alone in the driveway, Mas couldn't help but listen to the music. Before, he had been definitely a *shakuhachi* man more than anything else. The sound of the bamboo flute was a searing wind that blew in and out the cracks of his heart. It was as if his own breath were going into the *shakuhachi,* leaving behind a hollow husk, his pitiful body. The *shamisen* was different. The twang of the instrument first bit into the back of his jaw like ice on a filling. But then the notes quickly wove a pattern that moved from his head to the pit of his stomach. The *shamisen* music made his insides dance. Even listening to Kinjo and company's music now, in spite of the anger he felt toward the *shamisen* instructor, Mas felt like his soul was elevating and almost leaving his body.

After a couple of songs, the music stopped and Mas heard clapping. The black and white heads were moving; people were getting up from their folding chairs. There must have been some food, because people were gravitating to a corner like summer flies to a picnic table.

Mas contemplated his next move. He still might have to wait some more for the crowd to thin out. He raised his heels again, and he was surprised at what he saw: Jiro, in green scrubs again, talking to Kinjo. What did those two have to say to each other? They didn't travel in the same circles, with the exception of that tragic day at Mahalo. Mas was looking around the corner to the back stairs when the door opened, revealing a Nisei couple accompanied by the skinny Santa Claus man Mas had seen here last time, when Kinjo had been giving lessons. Now the man wore black pants and a turtleneck.

The three must have just wanted fresh air or quiet, because they didn't come down the stairs; they stayed on the top step, balancing paper plates on the wooden handrail. The couple spent a good five minutes oohing and aahing over how im-

pressed they were by Santa Claus's performance. Mas grimaced. It was like those
Japanese straight from Japan who were
impressed by a *hakujin* saying *konnichiwa*
instead of hello. It wasn't rocket science or
brain surgery.

The couple addressed the man as Mr.
Halbertson. Mas closed his eyes and tried
to concentrate on their conversation as hard
as he could.

Mr. Halbertson was telling them that he
had fought in Okinawa during World War
II. The three of them were eating some kind
of cake, and the man paused to swallow. "It
was a nasty time, but I just fell in love with
the Islands. And the *sanshin,* of course."

The couple again oohed and aahed in af-
firmation. They were doing the classic *aizuchi* — literally "hammering togetherness"
— which in Japanese was *hai,* "yes," or
sodesuka, "is that so?" These Nisei, on the
other hand, did their *aizuchi* in the form of
saying "really" and "that's right." It didn't
mean that the listener was agreeing, only
that he or she was actively hearing. So Mas
hoped Mr. Halbertson wasn't under the
delusion that he had a real fan club in the
couple.

"How long have you been playing?" the
Nisei woman asked.

"Not that long, in fact. About three years."

"But you do it so well. Will you be performing this Saturday at the Okinawan Association?"

Mas couldn't hear Mr. Halbertson's response. It must have been yes, because the wife said, "Oh, I'm so looking forward to it. We could listen to the *sanshin* every day. It's medicine for us. I think that's the secret to the Uchinanchu living so long. Has nothing to do with eating pork and vegetables."

"How did you meet Kinjo sensei?" the husband interjected. Mas could have pounded the man's back right then and there — that was the exact question he wanted answered.

Mr. Halbertson hesitated — maybe just a couple of beats, but enough so that Mas knew that he was considering feeding them a lie. "Arkansas," he finally said. "I worked a stint in the Jerome camp after I came home early from the war. I was recovering from a minor injury — I'm the type that needs to keep busy."

"Oh," the couple said in unison, probably mulling over how they felt. Jerome brought back memories of incarceration. Mr. Halbertson didn't seem like a teacher or social worker type. Mas could easily picture him as a scrawny, beardless Santa Claus hefting a rifle in a guard tower.

There was a lull in their conversation. Mas then heard some voices out front, the jangle of keys, and the opening and closing of car doors. Before Mas could duck behind a car or garbage can, he was staring at the pure-white crown of Kinjo sensei, who apparently had come out to move his car. "*A-ra* — you again. What are you doing here? This is a private event," Kinjo said in Japanese. Instead of the worn fleece vest and patched pants, Kinjo sensei was wearing a turquoise kimono.

"Izu come to talk. About the dead man."

"I told you everything I know. Nothing. Just that the *sanshin* is mine. My son is hiring a lawyer to get it back from the police."

"Maybe Judge Parker will helpsu."

Kinjo's face suddenly lost all expression. His eyes darted back and forth as if he could find the answer in the bushes or his pine tree. His savior came in the form of his son, dressed in a black kimono-style top and *hakama,* the same clothing he'd had on at the Hawaiian restaurant. He squeezed in between two cars to get closer to Mas.

"This is private property. You need to leave now, or I'll call the police," said Alan. Long gone was his ingratiating smile, perhaps reserved for women like Juanita.

"Judge Parker, rememba him?" Mas repeated to Kinjo.

Kinjo's eyes took on a strange color, like that of a diseased animal.

"Who's Judge Parker?" Alan asked.

"Parker knowsu Kinjo real good. And Kinjo *tomodachi* of Randy Yamashiro's father."

Randy's name sparked interest in the faces of both Kinjo and Alan. Mas didn't keep them waiting. "Isokichi Sanjo."

"Sanjo no friend of mine."

"Dad — you don't need to say anything." The ever-faithful son again.

"Youzu in same band."

"He's a *dorobo*," Kinjo spouted. "A thief."

Mr. Halbertson emerged from the back of the house. "Don't tell him a thing, Kinjo." His tone of voice surprised Mas. It was authoritative and demanding. No way to talk to one's sensei.

He then called out to no one in particular — the Nisei couple, perhaps — "Call the police."

Mas felt a sense of calm wash over him. Maybe it had been the music that made him feel stronger. He wasn't going to leave unless Kinjo explained what exactly he had done to Sanjo in the fifties.

Mas decided, as Tug would say, to go for

229

broke. He thought of the worst thing a man could call another man — a dog, an informant, a back stabber. "You *inu*," Mas stated.

"Who are you calling *inu?*"

"You tellsu INS dat Sanjo *aka*. I knowsu. Judge Parker tell me."

"Sanjo was *aka*. I saw him myself at that meeting."

"Then youzu *aka* too. Whysu you at the meeting in the first place?"

Kinjo's face looked frozen again, as if he were stuck in the past and couldn't move forward.

"You make deal with government, *desho?* You finger Sanjo, and then you free." Mas kept going. "But Sanjo neva come back after they get him. He found dead at coroner's. And now his son dead too."

The backyard had gotten stone quiet; even the birds seemed to know that they shouldn't hang around anymore. The Nisei remained silent on the steps, still holding on to their empty paper plates. Mas didn't know if they had heeded Mr. Halbertson's demand to call the police. The couple had been joined by at least half a dozen other guests who were all the type to slow for auto accidents — not to help but just to survey the damage.

The son, meanwhile, had also gotten as still as a statue. Mas could see a couple of veins were distended on his forehead, and his hands were shaking. Pure rage, Mas first thought, but then quickly realized that Alan was actually scared out of his mind.

Mas figured that if the police had been called, they were going to take their time. A crazy old Japanese man crashing a *shamisen* concert obviously wasn't a big priority. Still, Mas knew that he shouldn't push his luck, and he left, walking two blocks down and finding refuge back in his Ford.

He hadn't even started the engine when a car pulled up next to him. It was the Cressida, the passenger window wide open. Jiro was in the driver's seat, a mean scowl on the frog face of his. "What the hell are you trying to do, old man?"

Mas could ask Jiro the same question. "Youzu big fan of *shamisen?*" he said sarcastically.

"This isn't a joke. It's no game. Randy's dead, and you have to honor that. Honor his memory."

"G. I. tryin' to findsu his killer." That in itself seemed pretty honoring.

"He needs to be at peace now. He can't be, with all of you running around."

Mas would usually be the first to agree

with that philosophy. But something still didn't sit right with him. Why was Jiro talking to Kinjo? "Why, then, youzu runnin' to Kinjo?"

"Just go back to your plants, Mas. You don't know what's going on." Jiro revved his engine and sped forward down the residential street. Then what was going on, and how was Jiro involved?

As Mas turned the truck's ignition, he was surprised to see that his hands were trembling. What had possessed him to stand up to the *shamisen* instructor, and do it in front of an audience, anyway? Perhaps, ironically, it had been the effect of Kinjo's music, music that he had inhaled, absorbed into his blood and bones. He thought more about Jiro's accusations. Was he in a sense dishonoring Randy's memory by looking into his family's past? Mas cringed to think about strangers investigating his own legacy after he died.

Confused, Mas needed an emotional release. No tobacco — that his vow after his grandson had recovered from a serious case of jaundice. So instead, it would have to be alcohol. He didn't know if Peruvian beer would be any good, but he was willing to give it a try.

It wasn't that hard to trace Antonio's. The

main hub of Juanita's family restaurant chain was on the second-busiest street running east and west in Hollywood, north from Sunset Boulevard. It was in a mini-mall, next to a Spanish-speaking podiatrist's office, rental mailboxes, and a Laundromat. The parking lot was full, but on Mas's third circle, he was finally able to find a spot next to a beat-up Nissan sedan and an abandoned laundry cart.

Like Juanita, the restaurant was nothing fancy, but up-front and full of color. There were posters of Peru — yes, even Machu Picchu — on the walls, weavings of dancing men in costume, a mirrored wall to make the space look double its size, and a large menu above a register. A sign by the door stated SEAT YOURSELF, so Mas chose a small two-seater in the corner.

A glass of water came immediately, and then a laminated menu folded into thirds. Mas looked for any sign of Juanita, but the help were mostly young Latino men in white shirts and black Dockers. Before Mas could take a good look at the menu, a pile of octopus tentacles, cooked shrimp, whitefish, and scallops was placed on his table. He was ready to protest, but it was Juanita, her hair pulled back in a rainbow-colored headband and wearing a full-length red apron.

"I saw you come in," she said, slipping into the chair across from him. "Peruvian ceviche — you'll like it."

Mas felt so glad to see Juanita that he almost forgot about his day's adventures.

"I guess you've heard about everything," she said.

Mas wanted to ask about her father, but didn't want to open that door if there wasn't good news. Juanita was at her family's business anyway; no place for such conversations. Surely she would bring up any new developments on her own.

Mas had his own news to tell. "Buncha things happen." He revealed that Sanjo, too, had faced possible deportation. "He gotsu lawyer, but had to get new one. Parker."

"What do you mean?"

"Judge Parker was Sanjo's lawyer. Same Parker wiz *shamisen.*"

"So that's how they're connected."

Mas also added that Kinjo had been the informant in the Sanjo deportation case.

"That SOB," Juanita murmured. "I wonder if he knew that Randy was Sanjo's son."

Well, if he didn't before, he knows now, thought Mas, wondering if he should have even gone to the recital in the first place. "Jiro at Kinjo's," Mas said as an afterthought. "Tell me to mind my own bizness."

Juanita frowned. "Kermit's been busy. He was over here too. Asked me to drop the case completely, for Randy's sake. It doesn't make sense. Randy's dead. How can anything help him now? Why is Kermit on this personal mission for us to stop investigating?"

"Hidin' sumptin'?"

"Most definitely."

Mas tried to dislodge a piece of chewed octopus stuck on the back of his dentures with his tongue.

"Have you run into our other friend?"

Mas frowned.

"You know, Agent Buchanan Lee."

"Heezu at Keiro. Right before I go ova."

"Doesn't surprise me. Do you know that I found a tracking device on the Toyota? Lee was monitoring everywhere I went. I found the tracer in my wheel well — it was a cheap sucker. Very old-school. Looks like it could have been twenty years old. We're in big trouble if that's the best Homeland Security can come up with."

Mas couldn't understand why the U.S. government would want to invest good money in monitoring Juanita and even himself. A girl PI whose family owned some Japanese Peruvian restaurants? An old gardener? Mas knew that the most devious could be packaged in ordinary clothing, but this was a bit much.

"Agent Lee even left a message on my cell phone, saying that he wanted to talk to me. I haven't called him back yet. I know I have to — I guess I'm scared."

Mas peeled off some dead skin from the side of his thumb. It was a lot for Juanita to admit that she was afraid.

Juanita then quickly changed the subject. "So what would you like to order? You want fish? Chicken? Beef?"

"Beef."

"Okay, I have the dish for you." Juanita wrote something on her receipt pad. "And beer too, right?" She had read Mas's mind.

The beer came first, in the form of an ice-cold bottle of Cusqueña. Mas had never had it before and sipped it tentatively. It was light, like Sapporo, with a kiss of sweetness. Mas took another swig. The restaurant was getting crowded. Even through the tinted windows, Mas could see a line forming outside. He ate a forkful of the ceviche and enjoyed the crunch of firm baby octopus tentacles, tang of vinegar, and *piri-piri* of hot sauce. *Oishii,* thought Mas. So delicious and fresh. If Mas had known that Japanese Peruvian food was this good, he would have started to eat it much earlier.

The main course was a stir-fry of beef strips, red peppers, and French fries. Mas had never eaten his fries mixed up in a main course, but he had an open mind when it came to food. In ten minutes, the plate was empty.

"So I guess you like Peruvian food." Juanita was back with another Cusqueña and picked up the plate.

"Good bizness," Mas said. He was impressed. One after another, the customers came in, ate, and left. The turnover was high — Antonio's wasn't a place where you took your time and relaxed in candlelight. This wasn't for illicit lovers or big-business types. The restaurant was for no-nonsense eaters, longtime married folk who understood that a full and happy belly beat foreplay any day.

Juanita made her rounds to a couple of other tables and returned to Mas's.

"Chotto taigi, ne."

"What?"

"Tired. Youzu look tired."

"Yeah, with my father in custody, I've been at the restaurant twenty-four/seven. My mother really needs my help." She looked behind her, toward a sixtysomething Japanese woman clearing off a neighboring table.

237

"Mom —" she called out, getting the woman's attention. The mother obviously liked to keep her hands busy, because she managed to stack four dirty plates and three half-empty plastic glasses in the brief moment she took to turn around.

"Mas, this is my mother, Maria."

The mother had bright eyes like her daughter. *"Konnichiwa,"* she said, doing a little bow over her dishes.

"Her English is awful," Juanita whispered into Mas's ear. "You'd think after forty years in America that she'd catch on."

Juanita shot out a string of Spanish, and her mother responded with a string of her own. Maria placed the dirty dishes on a counter and returned to their booth. She looked straight into Mas's face and clutched his shoulder. *"Osewaninatta,"* she said in Japanese. "We could not get through this without good friends."

Her black eyes then welled up with tears, reminding Mas of the deep sea at night. Mas felt his heart being pricked with something sharp. Here he was, so concerned about paying off his debt to G. I. that he had not felt the full pain of the people who got hurt along the way. Maria pressed down on her eyelids, releasing a trickle of tears. Then, as quickly as the few tears came, she excused herself and turned her attention to an errant busboy, letting loose another string of Spanish.

Juanita's eyes, twins of her mother's, were also wet with tears. "I was afraid that they would have shipped him to another state, maybe even another country. But he's still in Southern California. Terminal Island."

"Terminal Island?" Mas knew that the speck of land by San Pedro had once been home to about two thousand Japanese American fisherman and cannery workers and their families before the government kicked them all out a few weeks after Pearl Harbor. From then on, the island had never been home to anyone else except the military.

"The government has a holding center for immigrants there. Some say that it's the last place in the U.S. for deportees before they are shipped out."

What was Juanita saying? That her father was next on the list? "Youzu daddy —" Mas couldn't help but say.

"It's all bullshit, Mas. Luckily, G. I. has mobilized JABA members and a bunch of community groups to write support letters on behalf of my father. There's going to be a huge article in the *Rafu* and maybe even the L.A. *Times*."

Mas wanted to reach out and pat Juanita's hand, say that it would be okay. But Mas didn't do such things, and he didn't know if everything would indeed turn out all right. Instead of verbal encouragement, Mas pulled out his wallet.

"No, no." Juanita shook her head. "It's on the house."

"No, no." Mas pulled out a couple of twenty-dollar bills and pushed them toward Juanita, who just pushed them back.

They played this game, four rounds each, until Mas finally relented. "*Orai,* I do sumptin' for you."

"Mas, you already have." Juanita got up and began cleaning Mas's table. If that wasn't enough, she brought him a small plate of flan, his favorite, for dessert.

"So how's Professor Howard, by the way?"

"Huh." Mas enjoyed how the egg custard dissolved in the middle of his tongue.

"You said she helped you out."

"She *orai.*" Mas felt awkward talking about Genessee. Juanita probably sensed his schoolboy crush, and if he verified it in any way, it would be out to G. I. and then the rest of the circuit. "She seems to knowsu lots about Sanjo's first lawyer."

"He's alive?"

Mas shook his head. "But daughter is.

Looks like Genessee knowsu her."

"Do you think the daughter will be able to shed light on Sanjo's case?"

Mas shrugged his shoulders.

"Do you think that you could find out? I know I'm imposing a lot —" Juanita's bushy eyebrows made her eyes look even more dramatic.

"Maybe," Mas said. That's the most he could promise.

When he finally left the restaurant, the sun had already sunk, and the lights in the parking lot gave the tops of the cars a yellow-green sheen. Dinnertime launderers, perhaps desiring clean underwear above food, had started to claim laundry carts and washing machines. Amid the scent of stale powder detergent, Mas fished out his screwdriver and opened the door of the Ford. He wasn't going to worry about his nonmonetary debts and IOUs anymore. To hell with the personal checks and balances of favors that all self-respecting Japanese kept in the backs of their minds. This didn't have to do with any sense of obligation; Mas needed to make things right just so he wouldn't have to see any more women cry.

CHAPTER TEN

He began the next morning with a drive to Frank's Liquor Store to use the pay phone.

"Phone not working again?" Frank asked, sticking his head around a stack of newspapers.

Mas grunted. He needed to get his phone untapped, but he didn't want to burden Juanita further. In the short run, Frank's was a good enough option. Mas went inside the store to buy a pack of Juicy Fruit gum and get change; he couldn't have Frank keep subsidizing his phone calls. Genessee must have been a morning person, because she answered the phone at its first ring.

They spoke for a few minutes, and then Mas hung up the phone and waited. He watched two stray dogs cross the street. They seemed oblivious of the cars traveling toward them, other than the pads of their paws working the concrete as fast as they could. The oncoming cars slowed. Another day of life for the mutts.

The phone rang, and Frank stuck his head out again, curious.

"Hallo," Mas answered, and listened. Olivia Feinstein, the daughter of Sanjo's first lawyer, had agreed to meet with him Saturday morning.

Mas went to his only customer that day — Mr. Patel in Arcadia. Mr. Patel had one of those newfangled mansions that was built on a lot that had once held a ranch house. But somehow the builder had preserved the old landscape, with a bottlebrush bush on the side and clumps of birds-of-paradise in the front. Per Mr. Patel's request, Mas had also constructed a rock garden next to the birds-of-paradise, creating a Japan-meets-South Africa kind of look. As Southern California had become overdeveloped, rocks had become expensive and hard to come by. For Japanese community gardens, the gardeners had gone to various dry washes and old mines in pickup trucks, hauling boulders into truck beds with rope. But the authorities were cracking down on rock grabbing, so now you had to pay a pretty penny for jagged pieces of granite. Mas had purchased the rocks for Mr. Patel's garden at a local quarry that also sold headstones and Chinese statues.

"What's going on with your friend's case? You know, the one whose throat was slit?" asked Mr. Patel. He was taking his prune-faced Shar-Pei out for a walk, and the dog was sniffing the leg of Mas's jeans.

"Police dunno yet. They don't take nobody in." Mas put on his gloves and pulled out some wilted stalks of the birds-of-paradise, their once-proud headdress of orange and purple now shriveled and brown.

"Well, I hope they catch the guy. Soon."

Mas nodded.

After Mr. Patel's, Mas went home, took a shower, and drank a Budweiser. He knew that it was early to be drinking, but somehow the Cusqueñas yesterday at Antonio's had gotten his taste buds craving beer. He thought one would be enough, but he went ahead and had another. My lunch, he thought, and laughed. His face grew hot and he opened the front door, hoping to catch some kind of breeze. But the air was warm and still, even oppressive. Earthquake weather, Mas thought. The worst *jishin* that he had ever been in was the San Fernando quake in 1971. The Northridge earthquake some twenty years later was bad, but he, Chizuko, and Mari had felt the 1971 more. Dishes came crashing out of cabinets, and

Mas bounced back and forth from the hallway walls as he went to collect Mari from her bedroom. Her bedside lamp had been knocked down, and she was sitting up in bed, her eyes wide-open with fright. "Daddy," she cried, and held on to his shoulders when he scooped her up from her tangled sheets. That might have been the last time they embraced like that. It took Mas going to New York City to mend their broken relationship. Now Mari was trying to let bygones be bygones and forge a new way of interacting.

He then thought about Juanita, her father, and her mother. The parents' home government had sought to spit them out, while their new country had tried to trample them. But the Gushikens had gamely fought back. Hanging on to their heritage, they had created a market for octopus ceviche and beef-and-French-fry stir-fry in Hollywood. Now the government was trying again, but they wouldn't succeed if Mas had anything to do with it.

Mas signed in at the front desk of Keiro as he had done two times before: *M. ARAI.* Under "Person Visiting," Mas wrote *Tanaka,* for old times' sake. Luckily for Mas, there must have been a couple of Tanakas, because the receptionist waved him through.

Mas crept into Gushi-mama's room, but he quickly discovered that he didn't have to this time. The roommate was sitting up, knitting in bed. The mattress beside her, Gushi-mama's, was stripped, without any sheets, blankets, or pillows.

Mas licked his lips. Surely the stripped-down mattress was not what he feared. But then, Gushi-mama was 106. Each additional day of living was a miracle when you were that age.

"Arai-*san, desho?*" The roommate's voice was barely a whisper, like wind between two rocks. If you weren't listening, you'd think the sound might be a figment of your imagination.

"Are you here for Gushiken-*san?*" she asked in Japanese. The roommate's face was still pinched like a pigeon's, and her small, beady eyes were magnified by her reading glasses, but today, instead of having a grayish tint, her skin looked healthier — even her cheeks were pink.

Mas nodded, waiting for the worst.

"She's in White Memorial. She stopped eating, so they had to hospitalize her. Feed her from tubes," she continued in Japanese.

"Sheezu sick? *Byoki?*"

"Probably *sutoresu.*"

246

"Sutoresu," Mas repeated. Stress. From what? Mas's visits? Had Agent Lee returned?

"She's been having a lot of visitors. You, the Chinese man, and then Tanaka-*san's* friends."

Wishbone? "He don't have no *tomodachi,*" Mas murmured to himself.

"One was a Kibei. I didn't catch his name. But the other was Yoshimoto-*san.* I think you may know him."

Mas almost laughed at Stinky being referred to with the honorific of *"san."* Stinky was no *san,* or even a *chan,* usually used for children, or *kun,* for boys. He was a chump who deserved no sign of respect or affection.

"Arai-*san,* may I say something to you?" The roommate's voice was less tentative this time.

Mas braced himself. He deserved anything the roommate wanted to throw at him.

"Everything seemed so quiet and calm before you arrived. Breakfast, lunch, dinner — everything predetermined and set. Dependable. And then you came to visit Gushiken-*san,* and from then on, people not acting themselves. Fighting. Asking questions. Soon we don't know what tomorrow will bring."

Mas hung his head.

"I just wanted to say something to you —"

Mas hardened his gut for the hit.

"*Domo arigato.* Thank you so much."

Mas was glad that he was a tiny bit drunk, that his face was already flushed red with alcohol. Otherwise, receiving her thanks would have been too unbearable. He understood what the pigeon lady was saying. Having nothing to do all day, being comatose mentally and emotionally, wore on the body. Involvement with the outside world meant inconvenience, irritation, and frustration but, like a spur digging into a horse's side, made everything move forward.

So while Gushi-mama had been down, the roommate had come to life. Mas knew that the pigeon lady didn't hold any ill will toward Gushi-mama; it was just that the monotony of life had conquered her, beaten her into a robotic pulp. But now the pigeon lady was breaking free. Perhaps Gushi-mama had sucked all the life out of the room, not leaving any for her roommate. With Gushi-mama gone temporarily, the roommate was growing her wings. When Gushi-mama returned — and Mas was pretty sure that she would — she would have a fight on her hands. But fighting would be good for both of them and would most likely restore Gushi-mama's appetite.

When Mas was waiting to sign out at the reception desk, someone grabbed his elbow. He turned to see the bespectacled face of Lil Yamada. She was wearing a gray smock and a huge name tag that had her name in both Japanese and English above a smiley face. "Hey, I saw that you were here."

"Who tellsu you?" Mas couldn't help being a little paranoid.

"You had signed the book," she said. "But Wishbone's not here. Hasn't been for days."

Mas felt his face grow hot. It *would* have to be Lil who uncovered his duplicity.

"Listen, Mas, can I speak to you for a moment?" Lil motioned to a small room across the way.

That tone of voice was familiar. Usually what followed was *Mas, we're going to have to let you go* or *Mas, we like you, but we're just cutting back on our unnecessary expenses.*

As Mas followed Lil into the room, which turned out to be a supply closet, she said, "I'm worried about you, Mas. So is Tug."

"I'm *orai.*" Mas banged his chest a couple of times. As healthy or *genki* as a person could be, standing next to boxes of tongue

249

depressors and adult diapers.

"No, it's this Yamashiro case. I think there are some very unseemly people involved."

"Whatchu mean?"

"A government agent's been coming by to talk to Mrs. Gushiken. I think he's bothered her so much that he made her sick. And he's been asking questions of a lot of the other Okinawan residents here. He even came here today, you know."

Mas nodded.

"The administrator had to ask him to leave." Lil adjusted her eyeglass frames. "Your name has come up, too, Mas."

"Oh, yah?"

"Yes, as a person to watch out for. I told them that I knew you, that you were a close family friend. I told them that I'd talk to you."

Who were "them"? Mas wondered.

"There's been another man, named Saito, who's been causing a lot of trouble too. You know, Wishbone's friend."

So this other so-called friend was named Saito.

"Anyway, they've been calling it a *yogore* epidemic. You know, *yogore* —"

Dirty scum.

"I mean, I didn't mean you, Mas." Lil blushed, desperately trying to rewind her comment.

But it was too late. And besides that, it was true. If there was a king *yogore,* Mas would have a decent chance at winning the title.

"*Orai,* I gotcha, Lil."

"Mas, I really didn't mean —"

Mas left the supply closet for the door, but was stopped by the receptionist. He was young, probably a fourth-generation Japanese American, a Yonsei. "Sir, we need you to sign out."

Mas found his name and signed. As the receptionist took care of a phone call, Mas quickly glanced at the names on previous sheets. He traced his dirty fingernail down the column that stated "Person Visiting." Gushiken, Gushiken — there was Buchanan Lee, and then S. Yoshimoto. And after that, having signed in two days ago, was another name, the Saito Lil had mentioned, written above a scratched-out name. Who'd cross out their own name? Even Mas wouldn't have any problems writing "Arai." He looked closely at the scratch marks. He could at least make out the second-to-last letter. It was definitely a J.

Stinky lived on a street in Altadena called Calaveras, which apparently meant the

251

skulls and skeletons that danced around during a Mexican holiday, according to one of the day laborers whom Mas had once picked up on Pine Street. It was appropriate, because when Stinky and his wife, Bette, had first bought their house, in the sixties, it was a skeleton of a home. The house was obtained during a fire sale; a big chunk had burnt down when a piece of bread got stuck in a defective toaster. But due to Bette's enterprising spirit, the home began to get more meat on its bones year after year, until by the eighties, it was downright pretty. Bette had also tried to work her magic on Stinky; he had proved to be a harder challenge. Most recently, she had been able to get him elected to the presidency of the Crown City Gardeners' Association for two terms. (He ran unopposed the first time; his opponent died before the election the following year.) Crown City was the old name for Pasadena; Mas wasn't quite sure why it had been called that, but being the home of the Rose Parade and its beauty queens, it wasn't much of a stretch to connect Pasadena with royalty.

Mas parked the truck on Calaveras, right across from the Yoshimoto house. They had redone the sloped driveway, and it looked like the shutters were being repainted. Mas climbed up the driveway, impressed that all the cracks had been covered over. The Yoshimotos had a huge jacaranda tree with invasive roots that seemed to push up the ground within a ten-foot radius.

Bette must have been waiting for a delivery, because she opened the door before Mas had a chance to ring the bell.

"Mas, how are you doing?" she asked. Bette was a small, compact woman shaped like a missile ready to be launched. She had no waist to speak of, and no *oshiri*, or rear either. It was surprising that her pants could stay on her body — perhaps that's why she always wore a black leather belt that looked like a man's.

"Orai," Mas said, adjusting his Dodger cap. "No *monku.*"

"That's what I like about you, Mas. You don't complain. My husband, on the other hand — *monku, monku, monku.* Do you know now that he refuses to eat leftovers? And no fast food for him. I have to cook up a fresh batch of food every day for two old people. Isn't that ridiculous? You'd think that now he's working part-time, he'd lend a hand around the house."

Mas didn't know how to answer. If he agreed with Bette, Stinky would be in hot water. Normally, Mas wouldn't care, but since he needed information from Stinky, he adopted another strategy.

He shifted his weight from one foot to another, cleared his throat, and sniffled hard, as if a huge *hanakuso* had blocked his ability to smell or hear. "Stinky ova here, by the way? Needsu to talk to him."

"Well, you'll have to go to his office to see him."

Office? When did Stinky have enough money for an office?

Bette smiled. "Eaton's Nursery. His so-called office is right there — outside on a picnic table. He even keeps his Crown City Gardeners files over there."

Mas should have known. Ever since Tanaka's Lawnmower Shop had closed down, Wishbone's gang had had to find another hangout. Like a flock of cawing crows, they needed to exist in numbers or risk never being heard. And for Wishbone and his like, not being heard would be worse than death. They had finally landed at Eaton's Nursery on Altadena Drive, right below the county wash, a flood control drainage area.

Thanking Bette, Mas headed down the driveway back to the Ford. Eaton's was actually owned by a *hakujin* fellow, an old-timer who spent his nights gambling with the Japanese. His number-two employee was a Nisei, Bill Kamiyama, who everyone called Kammy.

Eaton's was pretty far north, so the purple-peaked San Gabriel Mountains loomed close. One time, Mas's second cousin came down to visit him from San Francisco and was shocked to see the mountain range just above Altadena. "Didn't know L.A. had mountains," he said. Outsiders rarely knew of L.A.'s true charm. And the ones attracted to the region's superficial glitz and glamour weren't the type to ever see it.

Mas parked in the gravel lot and this time didn't bother to use the screwdriver to lock the car. This crowd wasn't the thieving kind, at least not beyond a poker table.

Mas walked underneath a lattice roof where potted plants hung, and then past gallon containers of bougainvillea and ficus trees. On the side, in front of the bathrooms and around a plastic table and umbrella, sat the *renchu,* the gang of five. For the customers, having Japanese gardeners on display might have made Eaton's Nursery feel more authentic. But if you bothered to spend any time with them, you would learn the truth: that the gardening trade hardly came up in their conversations. Even now, they were busy eating sunflower seeds, taking turns flipping the shells into the center of the table.

"Mas, haven't seen you around for a long time. How are you doing?" one of the gardeners exclaimed. He had a plastic cooler at his feet, and Mas knew that although the top would be filled with Coke and Hawaiian Punch cans, the bottom would be all Budweisers, reserved for after-hours. Stinky must have been in a good mood, because even he was smiling up at Mas.

"*Orai.* Getting ole, datsu all." That was about all the small talk that Mas could manage. He then turned his attention to Stinky, sweat dripping underneath his comb-over. "Stinky," Mas said, pulling him aside, "I gotsu to talk to you."

"Sure, sure, around the back."

They went past the bathrooms down a walkway to another gravel lot, which faced an alley. A rubbish bin was so overwhelmed with chopped-up greens that its lid didn't properly close.

"Whaddya want, Mas?"

"Go to Keiro today. Youzu went ova to talk to Gushi-mama dis week?"

"The old lady? Yeah. I know that she was tight with Wishbone, so I thought she might know where Wishbone was."

I thought you were running from Wish-bone, Mas thought to himself. And now you're running toward him.

Mas's thoughts must have been worn on his face, because Stinky asked him, "Didn't you hear about Wishbone?"

Mas shook his head.

"Turns out he was in on the deal with that gardener from the very beginning. He knew that it was a scam. That's why he got so mad at me for investing in his own scam. I guess the guy pulled a fast one on him and disappeared with all the money, his and everyone else's."

"How youzu find dis out?"

"Well, I went over to Skid Row, you know. Every low-income hotel down there. Finally, at the Chesterton, these guys say that they've seen my man. Saito."

Mas's eyes widened. The same Saito who visited Keiro.

"I know, Saito. What a joke, huh? That name is a dime a dozen. Should have known it was fake. Anyhows, I give them the two-one-three phone number, and it's confirmed. It's the phone number for their pay phone. So this Saito, or whatever he is, had moved out a couple of days ago. I bribe the receptionist to let me in his room so I can look around. And guess who's there, doing the same thing?"

Mas knew before Stinky said it.

"Wishbone. He's walking with crutches. He tells me the truth — that he was working with Saito all along. Only now he's been double-crossed. Just deserts, I guess. He said that he would have warned me not to get involved, if he knew what I was doing. Everything's all right with us now."

No wonder Stinky's disposition had gotten sweeter. But there was still the monetary loss, which must have smarted bad.

"Where's Wishbone now?"

"Home, if he's not following Saito's trail. I guess this Saito's still hanging around L.A. Not sure exactly why. You'd think he'd hightail out of here, you know. With everyone talking about him."

Mas pulled down on the back of his cap. Stinky was right. The longer Saito stayed in L.A., the more likely that he'd be spotted by someone on the lookout for him. Unless he avoided Nihonjins completely and stayed and ate in Japanese-free areas. Mas felt he had exhausted all the information he was going to get from Stinky. "Sank you, *ne*. I gotta be somewhere."

The only real place Mas needed to go was

home. And more specifically, right into his bathtub. It had been a killer day, and Mas was rubbing Irish Spring soap onto his arms and shoulders when he heard a knock at his door. *A-ra.* He wasn't expecting anyone. Mas waited, afraid to make any splashing noise to confirm that he was in. But the knocks became more insistent. Finally, Mas gave in and got out of the bath, suds and all. Drying himself with a towel, Mas found his pajama bottoms and quickly stepped into them. He looked through a side window and nearly passed out right then and there. Agent Buchanan Lee was the one banging on his door.

"I know you're in there, Mr. Arai. I just need a few minutes with you."

Mas first thought about calling the police, and then wondered if that would do any good. Men and women with badges, wouldn't they stick together? Mas kept the chain on his door as he opened it. He imagined the crime article in *The Rafu Shimpo:* Altadena gardener killed in his pajama bottoms.

"Listen, I'm not here to hurt you. I'd like to talk. Explain myself."

"Waitaminute." Mas went into his bedroom and got a clean T-shirt from a dresser drawer. After pulling it on, he undid the

259

chain lock and slowly opened the door. "Come in," he said. The house, as usual, was a mess. But Agent Lee wasn't concerned with good housekeeping anyway.

"Sorry to barge in. Really."

They spoke standing in the hall. That way Lee wouldn't overstay his welcome, Mas figured.

"I've been trying to talk to your partner, Juanita."

"Sheezu not my partner."

"Well, whoever she is to you, she's extremely stubborn. She won't hear me out. My agency has been investigating a man named Metcalf. He worked with the INS in the fifties."

"Why youzu interested now?"

"They found his skeleton buried underneath a city building that is being renovated for residential lofts. It just so happens that one of the future loft owners is an investigative journalist, Manuel Spicer. Now he thinks that he's on one of those TV crime shows; he's made it his mission to find out how Metcalf was killed."

Spicer. That had been the name that Genessee had mentioned back at the library.

"You go to South Central Library."

"Yep. Been there a couple of times."

"Ole history."

"Yes, but my agency is very PR sensitive right now. We don't need a story about how the INS contributed to the Red scare. So myself and a partner were assigned to dig up the truth and see what we are dealing with. And it's not pretty. We think that he might have killed somebody on the job. The man you're looking into. Randy Yamashiro's father. Isokichi Sanjo."

Mas nodded. He felt a little proud that he and Juanita had been able to piece together that much on their own.

"But the more we uncovered, the deeper it got. And then my agency told us to stop. Drop the investigation. My partner was more than willing — like you said, this is old history to him. I, on the other hand, can't let it loose. I mean, what's everyone so worried about?"

Mas studied the agent's face. He was young, probably only in his late twenties. His face held hope and innocence. He was a true believer. "So youzu doin' dis on your own?"

The agent nodded. "I wanted to work for the government to make a difference. And that's what I'm planning to do."

Agent Lee was going to learn the hard way that there was a great cost to making a difference. But that was his life, his decision.

What use was it to give the boy warnings?

"Can you tell Juanita what my intentions are?"

"You gonna help her daddy?"

A flicker of either pain or sadness passed over Agent Lee's face. "I'm trying the best I can on that. I'm low level."

So much for making a difference, Mas thought.

As Mas steered Agent Lee back to the door, he made a request. "Get rid of dat phone bug, *orai?*"

Lee didn't openly admit that he had participated in any electronic surveillance, but he did dip his head, ever so slightly.

"And no more bugs in cars."

"Tracking devices?" Lee seemed genuinely surprised. "I didn't place tracking devices in any vehicles."

Mas didn't know whether to believe the agent or not. But his gut told him that someone else was on their tail, someone perhaps not as congenial as this Buchanan Lee.

CHAPTER ELEVEN

The next morning, Mas was in the garage, sharpening the blades of his hedge clipper, when someone walked up his long, cracked driveway. Mas tried to focus through the haze on a man with a large frame. It was Tug, carrying a sweet-smelling baked good.

Mas knew what this was before Tug spoke. Lil's apology, wrapped up in a brown sugar coffee cake. So Mas accepted it, placing the warm pan on his workbench next to a can of WD-40 and jars of nails and screws organized by size.

"Whatever she might have said, she didn't mean it. She's been under a lot of stress lately."

Mas could tell that he and Tug were going to be having one of their talks. So he wiped his hands and pulled out his dust-topped Coleman cooler. A few brushes from a rag, and Tug's seat was ready. Mas then went into the house and poured what was left in his coffeemaker into a mug for Tug. Mas had been around him enough to know he liked his coffee super sweet, so he also threw in a couple teaspoons of sugar before he brought it outside.

"Thanks, ole man." Tug gratefully took the half-full mug of coffee and declined an offer of coffee cake.

"Mari's probably already told you about Joy," he said.

Actually Mari had said nothing. She was a little like Mas — well, truth be told, she was a lot like Mas, in all respects. She kept dark stories locked inside, even from family members.

"Joy's living with a girl now. They are coming together here for Thanksgiving."

Girl roommates? What's the big deal? Mas almost spouted out, when he fully realized what Tug was getting at. So the whisperings in corners of local nurseries were true.

"I've been praying about this, Mas. Two years straight. Hoping to get answers. Were we bad parents? I told Lil that she was too strong, and she tells me that I was too soft. Tell me the truth, ole man. Did we do something wrong?"

In her diplomatic way, Lil did call the shots at home. Tug, meanwhile, had fought various obstacles in the *hakujin* world as he worked as a county health inspector. When he got home, he deflated, pushing out all the pressures of work to readily receive the pleasures of being a father. They were a typical Nisei couple; as a family, better than most.

"It's really my fault to have put so much expectation on her. I told her that she could do anything. Be president, even." Tug pulled at his white beard. "Maybe the pressure was too much for her."

Mas slowly chewed his coffee cake.

"We've kept quiet about her situation, and now, with the whole extended family coming over to our place on Thanksgiving, everyone's going to know. I was telling Lil that maybe it's better that way. It'll all be out in the open. It won't be like Lil will be carrying this huge secret burden on her back. It's Joy's life, after all. It doesn't have to be a reflection of ours."

The *hakujin*s preached openness, but Mas didn't know how well that worked in the Japanese American world.

"So, that's enough about me. What's going on with you and your investigation?"

Mas didn't know if it was a carryover from his health inspector days, but Tug loved studying evidence. Mas could imagine him getting on his hands and knees to check underneath stoves for any signs of rodents and cockroaches. Measuring the temperature of meat in the refrigerator. Especially in light of his friend's down mood, Mas gave Tug what he wanted. A blow-by-blow description of what they had uncovered about not only Randy's death, but his father's.

"Getting mixed up with Homeland Security? This is serious, Mas." Tug's eyes were shiny with excitement.

A car then pulled up into the driveway. G. I. stuck his head out of the driver's-side window. "That asshole just served me with papers saying he's suing me for the five hundred thousand dollars."

"Huh?" Mas licked some of the sugar from his fingers.

"Brian Yamashiro. I'm so pissed, I could kill that guy. I'm going over to that Burbank hotel to tell him off. I need someone with me so I don't do anything crazy."

Mas stood staring at G. I. His face was bright red, making his pockmarks more noticeable.

"I think he means you, Mas," Tug said, rising from the Coleman cooler. "I'll lock up your garage for you."

Mas thanked Tug and told G. I. to wait. He went into the house to get a khaki work shirt. Securing all his doors, he got into

G. I.'s car and waved good-bye to Tug, who looked wistful, as if he wanted to change places.

Brian was sitting by the hotel pool, wearing sunglasses and typing into a rectangular object that looked like a calculator. Next to him on a table was a glass of tomato juice garnished with a leafy stalk of celery. The recent stifling heat had subsided, and now the sky was gray. The only person in the rectangular light-blue pool was a woman in a white bathing cap and goggles.

"What the hell is this?" G. I. threw some papers in Brian's lap.

"I thought you were a lawyer. I think it's pretty self-explanatory."

"Your brother's body is still warm and you pull something like this? You are something else." G. I. adjusted his tie. He was wearing a suit for a court appearance later in the day.

Brian set his mini-computer on a table and calmly sipped from his drink. "What I think is even more interesting is that you would have received a half-million-dollar check from my brother and not even mentioned it to the police. But don't worry — they know now. I'm sure they'll be giving you a call."

G. I.'s face looked grim, his mouth drawn in a straight line.

"There are more PIs in L.A. than your Juanita Gushiken. It wasn't that difficult to trace my brother's bank accounts, especially since he didn't have that many."

"I didn't know anything about the check until after he died. He hid it. Underneath my sofa cushions."

Brian then began to laugh and took another sip of the tomato juice, only this time the leafy celery almost went up his nostril. "That's a good one. I like that story."

"No story," Mas piped up. "Izu da one who found it."

"Yeah, right," Brian said. "That's going to hold up in court." He then readjusted himself in his lawn chair. "Listen, we can put an end to this. I won't even ask you for all of it. You can keep ten percent. That's still fifty grand."

G. I. crossed his arms. "No, let's go ahead. Let's solve this in the courts. Greedy little brothers don't do well on the witness stand."

Brian spit out a couple of obscenities and slammed his glass against the table so hard that Mas feared it would shatter. The tomato juice ran down the sides of the glass. "Greedy? That's why you think I'm doing this? Who do you think has been helping him financially all these years? Who has to pay off all his debts?"

"He had a job. Why would he need help?"

"He got laid off six months ago. I guess he didn't bother to tell you that."

G. I. was quiet. It was obvious that he had not been informed about this latest downturn in his friend's life.

Brian, perhaps influenced by his liquored tomato juice, was getting relaxed with his language, slurring words and dipping them up and down the musical scale. "You didn't know the real Randy. I know that he idolized you. The one guy from 'Nam who made it. Randy had problems, okay? I was the one who was always behind him, helping him. Did you know that he was hospitalized once? Nervous breakdown. Had some drug addiction problems too. You can ask anyone back home. Why do you think his wife left him? Jiro knew all of this. I don't know why he didn't tell you. Jiro was actually the one who called me, convinced me to come to L.A. Told me that Randy was in trouble. That I needed to talk sense to him."

"What kind of trouble?"

"Dunno. Jiro was going to tell me at that party. I never made it, because my rental car got broken into. Stole my laptop and everything. I was dealing with the theft when I got the call about Randy."

The woman in the white cap had ended her laps and was getting out of the pool.

"Did you see Randy at all here in L.A.?"

Brian shook his head. "Just spoke to him on Friday before he died. That's when I found out that Jiro was right, that Randy was going off the deep end."

"Whatchu mean?" Mas couldn't help but ask.

Brian unconsciously began cradling his bracelet with his left hand. "He started talking about how he'd found our dad. That story again. I told him to forget it. Our dad left us; we've had nothing to do with him for over fifty years. Why start now? 'If Mom was alive now, she would spit on him,' I tell him. But he said that he was going to meet with him on Friday afternoon. What the hell."

"Why didn't you mention it to me?"

"Because I knew that you would make a big deal of it. But it's not. Believe me. I've gone through a lot with Randy over the years. I had warned him not to meet with the guy. He was probably only after his money, I told him. But there was no stopping Randy. Obsessed. Ever since he was a teenager. Obsessed about our dad. Drove our mother crazy with all his questions. I can't tell you how many times she just started crying. My grandfather whipped his *oshiri,* told him that it wasn't worth looking back at the past. You know, all that Japanese shit. *Shikataganai.* What, it cannot be helped. I agreed with Grandpa, actually. Why look at stuff you can't change? But Randy wasn't that type of person. He liked to brood, you know. Wallow in his pain."

"He never mentioned anything to me about his father. I just knew it was an off-limits topic."

"You know how his obsession started? When he was drafted in the seventies. Everyone was messed up. Our mom. Our grandparents. And Randy. He didn't want to go over there and kill people. Or get killed himself. But he said that he wouldn't go to Canada or anything like that. That his number was called, so he had to go. Why should he be any different than any other Buddhahead in Hawaii? But then the army called. Turned out they were doing some checking into our family's background. They started asking Randy if he's a communist. Crazy stuff. He was the tailback for McKinley High School, almost failed civics, eh? What the hell does he know about politics? But they said that our dad was one of them. A commie. A Red. I couldn't

271

believe it. My grandparents were upset. Mom was crying. So the army doesn't want to take Randy, but then he made a fuss. He wanted to see proof about our father, but the army offered nothing. It's all classified, for some reason. Randy said that he'll sign any paper saying that he's a true red, white, and blue. I don't know what he was doing, eh. Because he could have gotten out of the service, you know, but instead he insisted that the army take him."

G. I. sat on the beach chair, his fists clenched so hard that his knuckles stuck out like ridges of a mountain range.

"You didn't know any of this, did you?" Brian smiled again. "Randy was good at keeping secrets. Especially from those he cared the most about. Runs in the family, eh? What can I say?"

There was a high-pitched ringing and G. I. excused himself, pulling his cell phone out of his jacket pocket.

Brian finished the last bit of his drink, even crunching on the celery stick. He must be hungry, thought Mas. Maybe he didn't have money for a decent breakfast.

"What's your name again?"

"Mas. Mas Arai."

"So what do you get out of this?"

"Excuse?"

272

"G. I. pays you?"

Mas shook his head. His relationship to G. I. wasn't Brian's business.

"You related to him or something?"

Did Mas and G. I. look anything alike?

"I get it, I get it. You guys *mahu?* Together, you know, like boyfriend-boyfriend?"

"Juanita his girlfriend," Mas said plainly.

"Oh, she's one good-looking chick." Brian licked tomato juice from the edge of the celery.

G. I. walked back from his phone call and pulled Mas aside. "That was Juanita. That professor, the one you and Juanita met, called her. The Torrance PD contacted her to come in for some academic consultation."

"Whatsu about?"

"I'm not sure. I guess the *shamisen* and something else; I wasn't too clear. I have to go to court, so I told Juanita that you would go over there. That's okay, right? You don't mind meeting with the professor again, do you?"

The Torrance Police Department building looked like it had been constructed during Mas's professional heyday, the 1970s. It was big and blocky, and made up of squares of cement. It wasn't pretty, but it didn't have to be.

The parking lot was in the back, and Mas had no trouble finding a spot for the Ford. Crime was obviously not a big deal in Torrance. Before he got out of his truck, a car — one of the those new VW Bugs, the color as strong as the greenest green tea — parked in the next space. He noticed an orange gerber daisy in a vase on the dashboard. Before he was able to sneer, a familiar figure emerged from the driver's-side door. Genessee Howard.

She was wearing a black suit, appropriately dressed for an official visit with a police detective. Mas suddenly felt self-conscious in his jeans and khaki work shirt.

"Mas," she said as he stepped onto the asphalt. "Juanita told me that you'd be meeting me here. It's good to see you again."

Again, the funny tingle on the base of his neck. *Kuru-kuru-pa,* Mas berated himself. He tried to picture Chizuko, wearing her trademark full-length apron, wagging her finger at him and laughing. But still the tingle did not go away. *Piri-piri, piri-piri.*

Mas didn't bother locking the truck, and even threw the screwdriver underneath the front seat. He didn't need a replay of the L.A. courthouse episode again. For Genes-

274

see, he wanted to look like less of a fool than he normally did.

They were walking together toward the police building when Genessee tripped over a cement bumper block. Mas automatically reached out to her waist to steady her, and then quickly released her once she got back on her feet. Her middle was firm, not at all squishy as he'd expected. She smelled musky, like the first summer thunderstorm on hardened soil.

"Oh, my, must be my nerves. Even though my nephew is on the force, I haven't had good experiences with the police. I'm glad you're here. Strength in numbers, right?"

Mas wasn't familiar with the saying, but understood the part that she was happy he was with her, walking side by side. Mas's back straightened. He didn't mind being a bodyguard, though he didn't know if five feet two inches of anything could do much protecting. But he was willing to try.

"Ready, Mas?" she asked before the glass automatic doors.

He waited for Genessee to take the first step onto the rubber mat. "Ready," he murmured behind her.

Dressed in the same tan sports coat he'd worn at Mahalo, Detective Alo came to the front desk. "Mr. Arai," he commented, "you're everywhere."

Genessee tugged at Mas's elbow. "He's good to have around."

"Well, we're most interested in your expertise," Alo said before leading Mas and Genessee into a windowless room with a dusty vent. They sat in metal chairs around a table. On the table was the broken *shamisen,* and Mas surprised himself by cringing at the sight of it. It wasn't as though the instrument were a human being, but now Mas had experienced its power. Something that evoked such emotion needed to be respected; even Mas knew that much.

"So, Professor, anything distinctive about this *shamisen?* Would it have any value to anyone?"

Genessee lowered her bifocals and carefully looked over the battered *shamisen.*

"May I touch it?"

"Sure." Detective Alo pointed to a pair of nylon gloves on the table that Mas noticed for the first time. "Wear these gloves, just in case. The instrument's been dusted for fingerprints already."

The detective didn't say if the fingerprints matched any criminal's. They must have found the judge's, but Parker claimed to have already spoken to the Torrance PD.

Genessee began with the top of the neck, where three narrow pegs had once held the strings of the instrument. The middle of the neck was broken off from the *shamisen*'s body, and the decaying strings attached to the bone pegs, one of them black, lay limp and useless. The face of the *shamisen* was completely busted, as if a prizefighter had taken a left hook to it. The snakeskin, in fact, was curling up, revealing the *shamisen*'s hollow insides.

She stuck her nose in the broken face of the *shamisen* and then moved it back and forth toward the fluorescent lights. "This *sanshin* is very old, could date back even to the nineteenth century. Could be a *sanshin* that the royal court musicians used. But in terms of monetary value, I don't think it would be worth much even if it weren't damaged."

Detective Alo tapped his fingers against the surface of the metal table. "One reason why I asked you to come, Professor, is that we discovered something in the neck of the instrument." The detective placed a plastic bag on the table. Inside was a yellowed scroll about five inches long. "We thought that you might be able to tell us what this is."

Genessee's eyes grew wide. She waited for Alo to give her the go-ahead.

"Go on — open it up."

Genessee pulled the scroll out slowly, as if it were a vial filled with dangerous contents. The paper was brittle, and Genessee took her time unrolling it. If it had been Mas, he would have torn open the paper; but perhaps that's why Mas dealt with plants, not books. Genessee knew the value of paper — its ability to tell stories and give information through the strokes of a pen. Mas preferred nature. He understood the secrets told on plant leaves — burnt edges, stripes, holes, each imperfection evidence of the sickness that lay inside.

Finally, the paper was completely unrolled, its image fully exposed to the three of them. A grid of brushstrokes.

"What is it?" the detective asked.

Genessee turned to the detective, her eyes filled with tears. "An Okinawan *kunkunshi*. A very old one."

It was if the professor had been landlocked for her whole life and was seeing the ocean for the first time. Her eyes devoured the document. In fact, she got so close to the *kunkunshi* that the detective told her to keep a little distance. "We wouldn't want it damaged in any way, right?" he said.

Her reading glasses were smeared with tears like a windowpane splattered with raindrops. Mas blinked hard. The *kunkunshi* was obviously sacred to the professor.

"What is it, exactly?" The detective had taken out a pad of paper and was writing down notes.

"A musical score for the *sanshin*. The *kunkunshi* system was developed in the sixteen and seventeen hundreds. Before that, the music was just passed down orally. The *kunkunshi* has actual links to the Ryukyu court music. It's like a road map of how our music developed."

Mas noted how the professor used "our" instead of "their." She saw this music as a part of herself — no wonder she was crying.

"How old do you think it is?"

"You would need to have it analyzed in a laboratory. But it is definitely handmade banana paper — that's unique to Okinawa. They developed it in the eighteenth century. This could date back to that time."

"Suppose it's the real deal — how much do you think it's worth?"

"Tens of thousands of dollars," she said. "But it's worth more than the money, when you consider its value to a people. It belongs in a museum in Okinawa."

"So how did it get in there?"

Mas could process the detective's thoughts. If the *kunkunshi* had been hidden in the *shamisen,* it meant the owner probably had placed it there. Kinjo, the man who had been so desperate to have the *shamisen* returned to him?

"I'm not sure. I'll have to spend more time analyzing it. There are more experts you can call in from UCLA and USC. And, of course, the Okinawan Prefectural representative. He has an office in L.A."

Genessee recited names, which Detective Alo scribbled into his notebook. After the fifth one, he stopped her. "I think this may be enough for now. I'll call you if we need further assistance."

Mas could read between the lines. Now that he had what he wanted from Genessee, Detective Alo was trying to get rid of them. He practically pulled the chair out from underneath Mas and opened the door to the hallway. "After you," Alo said to Genessee.

Before they left the building, Genessee gave Detective Alo some final advice: "You'll have to get a special box, acid free, for it. And place it in a temperature-controlled, properly humidified room."

"Yes, yes, don't worry, Professor. We'll

take care of it. You've been a great help." He left them before the automatic doors. Genessee asked for the bathroom, and Alo pointed to a door down the hall.

While Genessee was gone, a woman in a sweater and name badge approached Alo. "We've traced the knife in the Yamashiro case. It was purchased from an army supply store out in Vegas."

Standing by the door, Mas, as usual, was forgotten. "When?" Alo asked the woman.

"A little more than two weeks ago."

"Do they have a record on who purchased it?"

"Cash transaction. But an Asian, the seller said. That's about it."

"Get a better description. Age. Size. Any distinguishing marks. Send over the mug shot of Jiro Hamada. It's twenty years old, but he still looks the same. And we'll have to get a photo of Hasuike. Maybe from one of the local newspapers. And the brother, Brian too."

Alo then turned and finally noticed Mas. "You didn't hear that. Any of it, right? If I hear word that you've leaked this to any of your friends, Mr. Arai, you're going to be in big trouble."

Arai was so surprised that he didn't know how to react. A few minutes later, Genessee reappeared, and together they stepped onto the rubber mat and walked out the door.

"Mas, I don't think that the police department's going to take care of that *kunkunshi* properly. They're just looking at it as evidence in a crime, but it's more than that. It's the legacy of a people. We're going to have to contact the Okinawan Prefectural government and inform them about what's going on."

Mas's head was still full of what Detective Alo had said about the murder weapon. "Betta not *jama*," he said. In case Genessee didn't understand *jama,* Mas repeated, "You knowsu, stick our noses in it."

"Why not? Don't you understand, Mas. This is big news. If it's what I think it is, the *kunkunshi* deserves to be back home. Where scholars can study it and *sanshin* lovers can trace how their music has evolved."

Genessee's mind was now spinning around the *shamisen,* but she had left the main issue behind. Like who had killed Randy, and what might this latest discovery have had to do with it?

Mas walked Genessee back to her car, but her heart was now completely surrendered to the *kunkunshi.* He could tell in the way her eyes moved back and forth, barely focusing on the mundane parking lot before them. Her eyes were instead following her thoughts, which must have been traveling back in time to when the Okinawan court musicians were sitting *seizo,* on their knees, their precious instruments held close to their hearts, the melodies soaking into their skin. Genessee was calculating her next move to save the *kunkunshi,* and Mas knew that it wouldn't be with him. Just as Detective Alo had used them up, Genessee was through with Mas, at least for today.

They stopped in front of Genessee's VW Bug. "Mas, thanks so much. This was an exciting day." Genessee gave Mas a quick squeeze; he kept his arms awkwardly to his sides. This time he felt no tingle, no *piri-piri.*

He waited for her to pull out of her parking space before approaching the Ford. He waved and realized that even after the VW left the parking lot, her musky smell was still on him.

CHAPTER TWELVE

Mas went home and played two rounds of solitaire, losing both times. Bad deck of cards, Mas thought, throwing the whole set in the trash. He didn't know what to do with Alo's information about the knife. He should tell G. I. Because G. I. was innocent, right?

It was only seven o'clock in the evening, but Mas got into bed. He thought of Gushi-mama's roommate, how gray her face had looked from oversleeping. Mas was imagining his own face as a piece of overripe fruit, spoiling on the vine, when the telephone rang.

"Mas, Stinky."

"Unn," Mas grunted, waiting to be either mad or annoyed.

"Wishbone found out that the guy, Saito, has an account with the Japanese Credit Union in Crenshaw. He's been sitting there every day, waiting for Saito to show up. I think something's going to happen tomorrow. It's the last day that the CD matures; he's got to take it out or pay extra. And this guy isn't the type to want to pay extra for anything."

The phone began to crackle, but Mas ignored the noise. Was Homeland Security going to care about the comings and goings of a two-bit hustler like Wishbone? If they did, the country was really in trouble.

"Whatchu want me to do about it?"

"Go over there, huh? Make sure Wishbone's okay."

"Whaddabout you?"

"Bette has me on this painting project. Got out of it today, but don't think my excuses will work tomorrow."

"Well, I gotsu *shigoto,* too, tomorrow."

"Go after work, then. Not working full-time, right?"

What did Stinky take him for? Some lazybones with nothing to do?

"He's getting around with crutches. Even driving around with his bum ankle. He could get hurt, do you know what I mean? Just take a look-see, after your last job."

Mas didn't give a definitive yes or no, but Stinky knew what the answer was.

"Thanks, *ne,* Mas. You're a good guy. Sorry for the stuff I've been saying about you."

Mas didn't care what kind of *warukuchi,* literally "bad mouth," was coming out of Stinky, but he was kind of curious what it could be. Before he could hear any details, however, Stinky had hung up the phone.

Friday mornings were easy. First was a ten-unit condominium complex in Pasadena, not even a "mow and blow," but a "shave and blow." Shave off the ivy along a wall on the walkway and then a good blow from his gasoline-powered machine. Since the condos were in a business zone, it was legal to break out the blower, although some sleepy-heads would sometimes yell out in protest before slamming their windows shut. The next and final job was a small, neat bunga-low in north Pasadena, the home of an emergency room doctor and now his newly-wed wife, also a physician. They liked to keep it simple — a manicured lawn and a passion fruit tree in the corner. Since they were either not home or sleeping during the daylight hours, it didn't make sense to put too much time in the landscaping.

But today Mas spent extra time at the doctors', just to spite Stinky. First of all, he had lunch, which he'd never done before. And then he hand-weeded most of the lawn,

286

resulting in an old lady across the street coming over to ask whether Mas was taking any more new customers. "Gardeners today, all they do is zip in and out, use blowers when they're not supposed to. What happened to a good old rake? Using your hands, not machines," she rattled on and on.

Mas didn't even bother to look at her. If she was so against machines, did she walk instead of drive? Use a washboard instead of the washing machine? Machines were good for the customer, but not the gardener. Besides, Mas knew that she would balk at his rates, even though he hadn't raised them in ten years. If you want hand-weeding, it's going to cost you money, *obasan,* he thought to himself. But these folks who wanted him to work extra never seemed to want to pay extra.

Mas pretended that he couldn't speak English, and eventually the woman retreated into her house, going through her garage and apparently pressing a button to close her automatic garage door.

Mas finally got up, tossed the last of the weeds in his grass catcher, and dumped the contents into the doctors' garbage can. Driving to the Japanese Credit Union in the Crenshaw District in Los Angeles, Mas hoped that the whole thing would be over. That Wishbone had caught his man and retrieved his money. Case closed.

But as he entered the thick of Haruo's neighborhood — his duplex was only three blocks away from the credit union — Mas's temples began to pulse. He parked the Ford on Jefferson Boulevard and saw that the case was indeed not over. Sitting in a lawn chair underneath an umbrella was Wishbone Tanaka. He was looking intently through a pair of binoculars toward the credit union parking lot across the street. He had a thin towel around his neck, a small vinyl cooler at his side. His crutches were leaning against the chair.

"What, you watchin' the horses from here?" Mas asked.

Wishbone lowered his binoculars. "What are you doing here?"

Mas continued walking down the cracked sidewalk toward the bare piece of ground that Wishbone had claimed.

Wishbone moaned. "It's that *bakatare* Stinky, right? I told him that I don't need a damn babysitter. It's because of him I'm out twenty grand."

How about all the others who lost money? Mas thought. Wishbone had gotten a taste of his own medicine, and he obviously wasn't feeling too well afterward.

"Any sign of da guy?"

"Nope. But he'll be here. Believe me. Soon. It's four fifteen, and the credit union closes at five. The guy won't want to lose one bloody cent."

"How much he got in there?"

"He told me fifty grand. And twenty of that is mine. He'll be here; I guarantee it." Wishbone held up the binoculars to his eyes again. Mas noticed a security guard standing in front of the tinted glass door. A couple of black men sitting outside a clothing store pointed fingers Wishbone's way. For a guy trying to be inconspicuous, Wishbone was sure attracting a lot of attention.

"Guard ova there, don't say nutin' about youzu?"

"Came over here once yesterday. Asked me what I was doing. I told him that I was watching birds." Wishbone gestured toward a couple of crows resting on a telephone wire next to a pair of ragged tennis shoes that were hanging by shoestrings that had been tied together. Bird-watching in Crenshaw? Didn't make sense. It was like saying you were collecting butterflies in Watts. It was *kichigai,* or crazy, talk.

"What heezu say?"

"What can he say? Free country. This sidewalk is public. I'm not hurting no one." Wishbone dabbed at his face with the edge of the towel as if he had been in an athletic competition. Obviously spying was taxing on the body. "Waitaminute. I know why you're here. This is about that Sanjo guy you're looking for."

Mas did a double take. Were his ears acting up? Or had Wishbone said Sanjo?

"I heard all about it from Gushi-mama."

"Gushi-mama in hospital."

"Yah, I saw her there. After talking with her, I was able to put two and two together."

Mas waited.

"Saito, this Saito fella I'm waiting for? He's the same guy you want. His real name's Sanjo."

"Sanjo's dead."

"I don't know. That's all Gushi-mama told me. That she saw this Saito come to Keiro once. My Saito. But it turns out she remembers him from way back. Sanjo."

Why hadn't Gushi-mama mentioned this to Mas? Before he could quiz Wishbone more, the old man pointed a crooked finger toward the street. "There — there's that SOB!"

A white car drove into the parking lot. It was one of those cheap soup-can rental cars.

290

A man opened the car door and got out of the driver's seat. He was short, but well built. Strong shoulders. He must have studied karate or judo when he was younger.

"*Chotto,* letsu see." Mas nudged Wishbone for the binoculars. It took a couple of seconds before Mas could find the man through the binocular lenses. The man had puffy bags underneath his eyes, and a face that Mas had seen before. At Mahalo, Mas remembered. The man sitting next to him at the bar, ordering sake on the rocks. Now watching him carefully, Mas could see that the resemblance was unmistakable. Randy's face, aged twenty years. Mas didn't know if this was indeed Randy's father, but it had to be a Sanjo, one way or another.

Wishbone pulled at Mas's sleeve. "Wait until he gets the money out. No sense catching him before that." He reached back for his crutches and hobbled onto his unsteady feet.

Mas was unclear what Wishbone expected them to do. After a couple of cars passed by, Mas helped Wishbone cross to the parking lot. The guard was up from his chair too. He wore a pair of sunglasses. A long club was attached on his belt.

"When he comes out, talk to him," Wishbone said. "Whatever you do, Saito can't get back into his car."

Whatever you do? When did I come into the picture? Mas wondered.

And then, as if he'd heard his name, the man walked out of the credit union. "Go on, Mas, stop him. Stop him." Wishbone practically pushed Mas forward.

Mas almost tripped on the asphalt. "Sanjo," he called out. "We needsu to talk."

Sanjo quickly got into the car, slamming the driver's-side door closed. He revved up the engine, backed out, then sped toward the exit, barely missing Mas's feet.

Wishbone had already positioned himself in front of the exit. "Stop!" he yelled, waving a crutch. Sanjo had no choice but to stop, unless he wanted to add a manslaughter charge to the other crimes he was piling up in L.A.

The guard ran out, his hand on his club.

Wishbone began banging his crutch hard on the rental car's hood and then on the driver's-side window. Bam, bam. The window was close to shattering when the guard pulled Wishbone aside and motioned Sanjo to get out of the car. As soon as Sanjo emerged, Wishbone swatted Sanjo's hand with his crutch, causing him to drop his keys onto the ground.

"Hayaku." Wishbone poked Mas. "Pick up

the keys."

Mas dutifully scooped up the keys without thinking.

A small crowd stood outside the credit union.

"Should I call the police?" a Japanese man in a suit asked the security guard.

"No, no police," Wishbone said.

"No police," Sanjo echoed.

Apparently Wishbone and his partner in crime had something in common: they liked to tell lies, and they were good at it. Both were laying it on thick with the security guard.

"Old friends, we're old friends. Just wanted to get his attention," Wishbone said.

"Yah, big mistake."

The two men hugged each other's head, two coconuts on a tree.

The security guard folded his arms and grunted. More bank employees were now outside, clutching paper bags and briefcases. It was past five, time to go home. A woman with big *chi-chis,* wearing a tiny T-shirt and tinier miniskirt, strutted into the lot and stared at the security guard. "What's going on? You ready to go?"

The security guard looked at the two old men, then at his woman friend, and then back at Wishbone and his partner. "You guys handle your problems off of the bank's property, okay?" he said, shooing them out of the parking lot.

"You drive his car," Wishbone hissed in Mas's ear.

"Where?"

"I don't care. Just take us someplace where I can pummel this guy."

Mas reluctantly got into the driver's seat while Wishbone forced Sanjo into the back. Both Mas and Sanjo were unhappy with this new arrangement. The rental car was filled with rumpled clothes and fast-food containers. The man had clearly been living out of his car.

Sanjo's spirit was now as flat as a pancake, like an old tire that had been punctured by a nail. He was empty of all energy or rebellion. He must have been tired of running.

"Where you taking me," Sanjo said, more than asked.

Mas didn't bother replying. He made a right out of the parking lot and then a left, two blocks down, to Haruo's house.

"Mas, didn't knowsu you gonna come by." A lopsided grin on his face, Haruo held open his security gate. He must have just taken a shower, because his long graying hair was plastered against his keloid scar, resembling wet seaweed over barnacles. Badly equipped with an ancient fake eye, Haruo usually embodied the classic *Ron-Pari* look. That is, one eye focused on London; the other, Paris. Today his fake left was barely visible, as if it had left the map.

Before Mas could enter the duplex, Wishbone nudged his hostage forward with the back of his crutch. "Gotta borrow your house," he said to Haruo.

"Hallo," Haruo said, smiling at the stranger. "Hallo," he said to Wishbone. "Yah, datsu *orai*. But Spoon and her family comin' to pick me up for dinner, so you gotta be out of here by seven."

Mas felt guilty bringing the two criminals to Haruo's one-bedroom apartment, but he didn't know where else to go. Haruo was Mr. Hospitality; he probably thought "borrow" meant "visit."

Haruo had moved his persimmon bags into the house; they were lined up against the walls. "What's this? Trick or treat?" Wishbone hobbled around the duplex with one crutch and peered into a bag. "Ah, trick," he said, almost cackling. "No kid will want *kaki* for Halloween."

"No, from my tree. Take some." Haruo handed a bagful to Wishbone. With Wishbone's hands full of persimmon, Sanjo thought it was an opportune time to make a run for it. He headed for the door, but Wishbone expertly caught the leg of his pants with a crutch. Sanjo fell forward and instinctively tucked his head, turning an ugly yet complete somersault on Haruo's carpet. Mas's hunch had been right. The man had gone through some martial arts training.

"You *orai?*" Haruo asked, helping the man to his feet and into a chair. "Whatchu doin', Wishbone?" Haruo had finally realized that something was amiss.

Wishbone didn't answer. He disappeared into the next room in an attempt to turn Haruo's tiny kitchen into an interrogation room. With one sweep of his crutch, Wishbone cleared the card table of all condiments — soy sauce packages from the local Chinese restaurant, ketchup and mustard packages, salt and pepper shakers. He lifted Haruo's high-powered flashlight on the floor and duct-taped it to the side of his five-foot refrigerator as a spotlight.

"Here, you, Saito, Sanjo — whoever the hell you are — come over here." Wishbone finally directed Sanjo to sit down at the kitchen table.

Haruo walked into the kitchen and stared at his condiments strewn on the floor.

"Whatchu doin'?" he repeated.

"Have to question our man here."

"What kinds of questions?"

Mas finally had to step in when Wishbone tried to duct-tape the man's wrists together. "Listen, Haruo, call G. I., will youzu?"

Thankfully, G. I. was home and available. While they waited for him to arrive, Haruo poured each of them a glass of 7-Up with ice.

"You from here?" he asked the stranger. By this time, Sanjo seemed totally deflated.

"Don't bother asking, Haruo," said Wishbone. "I'll get the truth out of him."

"You knowsu, I don't think I wanna have sumptin' like dis go on my house," Haruo said. Mas was familiar with this tone of voice. Haruo was setting his "boundaries," which Mas previously had connected with property lines, not invisible ones regarding what you want and do not want to do.

"Well, it's too late, Haruo. We're in, and we're not going to leave."

Just in the nick of time, G. I. appeared at the security gate. "What's going on in here?"

Wishbone commanded G. I.'s attention, admitting everything, from first meeting Sanjo at a friend's house, to the hatching of the stock market scam, to the scene at the credit union.

"He's been calling himself Saito, but other people know him from way back as Sanjo."

G. I. rolled up his long sleeves and leaned toward the man sitting at the card table. "What's your real name? Sanjo?"

"*Hai,* Sanjo." There was no doubt that Sanjo's English was poor. It was a wonder that he and Wishbone, whose Japanese was equally bad, could have communicated enough to hatch a scam.

"Mas or Haruo, one of you, get in here," G. I. said.

Haruo pushed Mas into the kitchen.

"Find out who he is —"

"*Namae.* Whatchu name?"

"Saito."

"That's not his real name," Wishbone interjected.

"Real name. *Honto no namae,*" Mas demanded.

The man grimaced as if he were holding something bitter in his mouth. "Sanjo. Anmen Sanjo."

"Live in Rosu, L.A.?"

"Don't live nowhere special," he said. "Just go from town to town."

"Ask him what he did with the rest of the money. We should have thirty grand more," Wishbone spouted out.

"*Okane.* Where's the rest of the *okane?*"

"All gone. I sent to Okinawa."

"Sonofabitch," Wishbone cursed.

Mas had his own line of questions. "How are you connected to Isokichi Sanjo?"

Anmen abruptly looked up, and Mas noticed that whites of his eyes looked yellowish. "My *niisan.*"

"Do you know Randy Yamashiro?"

"My nephew. I know that he's dead. That's why I haven't left. I need to get the one who did it."

"You did it, you double-crossing Jap!"

"Wishbone, *yakamashii.*" Mas tried to shut Wishbone up.

G. I., meanwhile, sat cross-legged on the living room carpet, listening intently to Haruo's shotgun interpretation. With Haruo continuing to whisper in G. I.'s ear, Mas asked, "Why you call Randy?"

Sanjo bent his head down. "I saw the article about him winning the money. I knew who he was. Thought maybe he could help me out."

"By taking his money?"

"The money's not for me. Anyway, I met with him on a Friday, found out he was *kichigai.* Like his head was on fire. He asked me how I could leave the family, abandon them. How I could cause so much trouble?" Anmen looked down at his hands. "Finally,

299

I told him the truth."

Everyone, even Wishbone, stayed quiet. All that they could hear was the hum of the old refrigerator and the ticking of the cheap clock mounted within the stove.

"That I wasn't his father, I'm his uncle. That his father was dead. He wouldn't believe me at first, but I told him the year that he had died. The same year that his mother had taken him and his brother to Hawaii."

"Youzu the one at coroner-*san's*."

Anmen nodded. "I was worried. I went to see Isokichi after he was arrested, and the INS office told me that Isokichi was no longer in the building. The agent who had arrested him was also gone. I knew something had happened. If they had released him, he would have gone straight home. But we had heard nothing. So I went to the Japanese hospital, every place I could think of. When he didn't turn up there, I knew that he might be dead.

"I heard about the Japanese man working at the coroner's office. It had been big news. Just like first Japanese teacher, first Japanese department store worker. It was in the *Rafu,* first Japanese working in the coroner's office.

"So I went there at night. Saw his body.

Who could have done this to Isokichi? That INS agent, Metcalf?" Anmen spat on Haruo's floor. "He was a terrible man, coarse, with a bad mouth. I was at the house when Metcalf and another agent came to arrest Isokichi. Actually, we were in the middle of a fight."

"Kenka?"

Anmen grunted. "It was *baka*. It was about the *sanshin*. Isokichi found out the *sanshin* was special. That there was a special hiding place inside for the *kunkunshi*. He told Kinjo that it belonged to the Okinawan government. And then he stole it."

"Kinjo's *sanshin*."

Anmen nodded.

"Kinjo was always bragging that the *sanshin* had belonged to a court musician who'd performed for an Okinawan king. That his *sanshin* was better than anybody else's. I was sick of it. I was glad that Isokichi took it. Kinjo was so angry; he said that he'd get us. Then, two days later, the immigration officers came to our door."

After a few minutes of listening to Haruo's translation, G. I. spoke up. "You told this to Randy?"

Anmen said in English, "Yes." He let out a deep breath and then resumed speaking in Japanese. "Through the Okinawa Club, I

301

was able to contact those *hakujin* lawyers who were trying to help the Japanese."

"Edwin Parker?"

"He and an older attorney, Delman-*san.* Delman was famous, a good man. But he was involved in too many cases, so he had to pull out. Too bad, because I didn't trust Parker."

"Why?" Mas asked.

"Too young. Too green. Barely graduated from law school. He was one of these types who was just figuring what kind of man he was. He wanted to be an Isaac Delman, but without going through any suffering that made your insides strong. He wanted the title and fame without the work. So I asked him to stop being Isokichi's lawyer."

So, Mas thought. That was the real reason Parker had been released.

"After I saw Isokichi's body, I went back to his wife. Told her that she needed to get out of L.A. — fast. Change her name, go back to her folks in Hawaii. For the good of her boys.

"I left town, too, for a while. But not until I saw Metcalf. I needed to see him, face-to-face. Or maybe I needed him to see me. I packed a baseball bat in my cloth *sanshin* case. What was I going to do with that bat once I saw Metcalf? Self-defense, that's what I called it. My brother couldn't do it, so I would do it for him. I waited for him at the INS office, but he never showed up. The police declared him officially missing. I figured that he was on the run, and the INS and police were covering it all up."

Mas remembered how the police told Hajime Kaku, the coroner's clerk, to keep silent about the G-man he'd encountered.

"So I changed my name too. Didn't need the government keeping tabs on me. But I kept track of my sister-in-law and nephews. Whenever I came into L.A., I would try to look up Agent Metcalf. But nothing. I'm sure the government placed him in another town with another identity."

Anmen's hunch was proven wrong, with the recent discovery of Metcalf's bones. Like Isokichi, he had met an untimely fate. But the question remained, were the deaths related?

G. I. got up from the floor and asked more questions, but Anmen was less coherent, was obviously getting tired.

"I want my money," Wishbone broke in.

"Ah, yes, the money. Where is it?" G. I. asked.

Anmen glanced at G. I. and removed an envelope from his shirt pocket. "I don't have anywhere to go. *Okane nai.*" No money.

"You're staying with me," said G. I., pulling the envelope from Anmen's hands. "And you, too, Mas. I'll need your translation services."

"I want my money," Wishbone repeated.

"I think that we need to find out who's owed what. And as the cofounder of this 'deal,' Wishbone, you will be compensated last. You need to pay back your other investors first. We'll see what's left."

Wishbone was looking mighty defeated now. "I want my money," he whimpered.

After the hour of going back and forth in Japanese, English, and a mishmash of both, everyone was ready to collapse. None of them, except G. I., was the type who could sit through such focused talking. Gossip was one thing. At Wishbone's former lawn mower shop, rumors had flown hard and fast. But it wasn't like you really had to pay attention; you could just reach out for the bits that caught your fancy, like canned goods on a grocery store shelf.

G. I. suggested that they get ready to leave, and Mas thought that suggestion had come an hour too late. Haruo, of course, handed Mas another bag of persimmons; it was no use refusing it. What about my boundary? Mas thought, but with Haruo, boundaries were actually crossed all the time.

Outside they heard the slam of cars doors and voices of women and teenage boys. "Spoon's here." Haruo smiled, sliding a comb down his hair.

It was an army of people. Spoon with three women, most likely her daughters. Two of them resembled Spoon, skinny on top, with a wide behind. The third one was thin, with a sprinkle of freckles, not as intense as Jiro's, but more like chocolate dust on top of a hot drink. Two gangly teenagers stood behind by the van.

"You have guests," said Spoon.

"We're just leaving," G. I. explained. They had decided that Mas would move his truck to Haruo's and then drive Sanjo's rental car to G. I.'s. G. I. offered to drop Mas back at his truck, but Mas opted to walk.

Mas was introduced to the three daughters and watched as the two boys, probably fourteen and sixteen, awkwardly greeted Haruo.

"Hey, Uncle Haruo," they said. Mas was surprised at how Spoon's grandchildren addressed a non-blood relative. Mas wondered what kind of relationship he could cultivate with his own grandson, living so far away.

"I gotsu get goin' to G. I.'s," Mas said,

excusing himself.

"*Orai,* Mas, I be seein' you, soon. Just park the truck in the driveway," Haruo called out, but by the time Mas looked back, his friend's attention had been captured by the two teenagers.

Mas walked down the street. The sun was setting, and a grayness was spreading over the sky. Boys kicked a soccer ball in the street, calling out in Spanish and English. Mothers sat on stoops, taking breathers before dinner, the last peace of mind before sunset.

As it turned out, Mas was the first to arrive back at G. I.'s place. The rental car was a disaster, and he couldn't wait to be rid of it. Mas parked the car outside on the curb. A few minutes later, G. I. and Anmen pulled into the driveway toward G. I.'s one-car garage in the back.

G. I. opened the door, a large bag smelling of garlic in his hands. "Cuban chicken," he said.

Once he was inside, Anmen's eyes didn't seem to register the mess in G. I.'s living room. Like a dog sniffing out a buried bone, he immediately found the *shamisen* hiding in the corner by the bookshelf in the living room.

"Ah, *sanshin*. You play?" G. I. apparently went up several notches in Anmen's estimation.

"No, that's Juanita's grandfather's. She wanted to show me what an intact *shamisen* — I mean *sanshin* — looked like."

G. I. pulled out three Styrofoam containers from his paper bag. Mas opened his container, revealing a chicken leg, roasted brown and simmering in garlic juice, yellow rice, and fried bananas, which G. I. called plantains. And a small container of crushed garlic, more *ninniku*. G. I. turned on the television, which was a relief. No talking; instead, they ate silently while watching car crashes and gang shootings mixed with segments on pig beauty contests and football games.

G. I. then excused himself to take a shower and make phone calls. Anmen circled the living room a couple of times — searching for what, Mas didn't know.

Finally, he stopped at G. I.'s bookcase and picked up a framed photograph. "This man, who is he?" he asked Mas, who was dozing off.

Mas wiped his eyes. There were three men on a fishing trip, and Anmen was pointing to the one on the right. "Thatsu Jiro."

"Jiro?"

"G. I. and Randy's *tomodachi.* From Vietnam. They callsu him Kermit."

"Kermit," Anmen repeated.

"Why, youzu see him at party?"

Anmen didn't answer at first. "Tired," he said. "Very tired." He stretched out on the couch; he didn't have to know that it had been the last resting place of his nephew.

G. I. was supposed to give Mas a lift back to Haruo's, but when Mas peeked into his bedroom, G. I. was fast asleep on his futon, Mu curled up in the crook of his arm. Mas didn't want to wake him, so he figured he might as well stay the night. Mas unrolled Juanita's sleeping bag; he didn't mind sleeping on the floor. It reminded him of camping trips he had taken in Ventura County with Chizuko and Mari; Juanita's bag even had the same smell of charcoal from past campfires, and a pinch of sea salt from the ocean.

After Mas turned out the lights, Anmen began to talk. "You think I'm rotten, *ne.* A *dorobo* who doesn't deserve to live."

Mas wouldn't have gone that far, although folks like Wishbone and Stinky might have other opinions. But he was a *dorobo,* there was no doubt. A thief was a thief was a thief.

"I heard that you are a *hibakusha,*" An-

308

men said. "That you were there in Hiroshima, two kilometers from the epicenter."

"Who say dat?"

"The man with the *kizu*." Scarface Haruo. Mas sneered in the darkness. Why did Haruo have to open his trap to complete strangers — to, in fact, a bona fide criminal?

"I know what it's like, *yo*."

Mas listened.

"During the war, I hid in a cave in Okinawa. I was afraid that the Americans were going to kill me. But they pulled me out and set me free. My legs had been bent in that crowded cave for so many weeks."

Mas had heard of these stories. Of men, women, and children hiding in caves to escape American flamethrowers, gunfire, and grenades during World War II. One of the bloodiest battles ever fought in Japan. Rivaled the Bomb in terms of Japanese casualties, although the Battle of Okinawa occurred over the course of numerous weeks instead of a single minute. Mas had heard of the caves. Described as honeycombs of land next to the shore, they were the final refuge for both soldiers and civilians with nowhere to go. The same Japanese military that had conscripted twenty thousand Okinawans, including boys and girls, was at the last minute only more than willing to kick these same people out of the caves to make room for the "real soldiers." Everyone had heard of the tragic fate of the Himeyuri Corps of schoolgirls, who were forced to be nurses to the Japanese soldiers, only to be forcibly released into gunfire and explosions. One out of eight Okinawan civilians had been killed.

"All during the war, Isokichi was in America. He left Okinawa when he was only fourteen. Was a Christian, *yo.*"

A-ra, Mas thought. Christians in Japan were few and far between at that time. Radicals, soapbox preachers, men and women who didn't mind swimming against the tide.

"He had dream about America. Wanted to see democracy in action. Was tired of seeing Okinawa being pushed around by Japan. He went to Hawaii and then worked on a sugar plantation. Couldn't find democracy there. And then sailed off to California, joined Christian farming communities in the San Joaquin Valley. Made just pennies — where was the Great Democracy? I could tell that his heart was getting hard. His letters seemed bitter at that time; he must have started to go to those political meetings. And then, during the war, nothing, of course. He was worried sick about us, even

310

though he was stuck in a detention center in the middle of nowhere.

"After the war, we were able to find each other. He helped me to come over. I thought this was my chance to make it big. I started a *sanshin* school and was going to send my money to them. I have no children of my own; this was one way I could live on."

Anmen's voice became softer as he went back in time. "Our father was a *sanshin* instructor. That's how we both learned how to play. He even brought a *sanshin* into the cave my mother and he were hiding in. They were the next cave over. I could hear the tinkle of the *sanshin* all night. It's what allowed me to sleep. But one day the mountains shook and the music stopped. My parents were never found."

Mas stayed still and quiet.

Anmen obviously wanted to change the subject, because he started humming and singing an Okinawan song. Mas tried to smother his ears in the sleeping bag, but it was no use. Actually the song wasn't so bad. In the end, Mas even clapped two times. Maybe if he clapped one more time, Anmen would be silenced, like those sound-activated lights.

But before he knew it, Anmen was talking again. "You know, Isokichi was always writing songs. He even sang a song for me at the immigration office when I visited him. He called it 'Sayonara Udui.' "

"Udui?" Mas loosened the sleeping bag from his ears.

"Okinawan for 'dance.' I never forgot it." Anmen stirred from the couch and turned on the lamp. He picked up the *shamisen* and brought it over to the couch. Tightening the pegs, he tuned the three strings, took a deep breath, and began playing the familiar singsong melody. And then he began singing. First a low murmur, and then, with each lyric, Anmen's voice began to rumble like the start of the earthquake. Then, in a flash, the song was over.

Mas only understood half of the words. The song ended with "sayonara"; that much Mas could pick up.

G. I. came stumbling out of the bedroom, in a torn green UC Davis T-shirt, shorts, and black-framed glasses. His hair was in a single braid like the queues of Chinese pioneers during the Gold Rush. Mu slithered in between his legs. He lifted his glasses and wiped some sleep from his eyes. "What's going on?"

"Sanjo's song," Mas said.

"Huh?"

"Isokichi write song before he die."

"No kiddin'." G. I. fell into his purple chair. "Well, play it again. Please."

Anmen did an encore — this time he closed his eyes as if he were trying to better capture his brother's voice.

The melodic song made Mas's ribs hurt and his ears ring. There was something haunting about the words, even though he couldn't quite follow them.

"What's it mean?"

Mas shrugged his shoulders. "Too much Okinawan. Can't understand."

Anmen repeated the lyrics, and Mas tried to throw out the words in English. G. I. then chose prettier words and wrote them down on the back of an envelope.

"Okay, this is what I have," G. I. said finally after five tries.

Tears, the stars I see out the window
Years of struggle, pennies for blood
What hope for my boys?
The door is closed; I cannot breathe
My sons, wife, someday
    must dance again.
Sayonara, sayonara, sayonara.

G. I. and Mas let the words rest in the room before they spoke.

"*Jisatsu,*" Mas whispered.

"This is a suicide song," said G. I.

Anmen looked up, nodded, and Mas noticed the edges of his eyes were wet. "I told Agent Metcalf that my brother was not himself. That he could not be left alone. But he kicked me out of there. He told me to come back the next day. But both of them were gone by then."

Mas remembered what Hajime, the clerk at the coroner's office, had said. Isokichi had been missing his shoelaces. He must have removed them to commit suicide, perhaps hang himself? Mas didn't know how it was possible, but if you were hard-headed and *ganko* enough, you could do most anything.

"What do you think, Mas? Was Isokichi planning to kill himself?"

Mas nodded. But the coroner's assistant said the cause of death was blunt force trauma, not death by hanging. So whether or not Isokichi planned to do himself in, someone else beat him to it.

CHAPTER THIRTEEN

Sleeping on G. I.'s floor, Mas had another nightmare. He and another boy he grew up with, Kenji, were in a rainstorm. The water came down hard and fast, stinging his skin. Then he noticed that the raindrops had turned into small pebbles, and then larger rocks, the smooth kind that Mas used for dry gardens. He felt his head being knocked about, the stones pelting his shoulders, his neck. He fell to his knees — where was Kenji? — and the rocks were beating his thighs and knees. He could not cry out, speak. All he heard was the thunder of rocks cascading around him and then on top of him.

When Mas woke up, he saw that Anmen was gone. The black couch was squished down in the middle, evidence that a human body had been there at one time, but Mas figured that it had not been for long. Anmen had had to cut open his memories. And once he did that, he left.

Mas walked barefoot to the living room window and pulled at the curtain. The sky remained gray, still trying to make up its mind whether to squeeze out rain or clear to blue. A single bundle of the L.A. *Times* had been left on G. I.'s lawn. There were no cars Mas recognized parked outside.

"Mornin', Mas." G. I. came out of his bedroom, wearing the same pair of glasses. He had loosened his braid, and his long hair went past his shoulders. He had a faint smudge of stubble underneath his nose. G. I. was one of those Japanese who couldn't grow much on his face, other than a long mustache and a paintbrush of a beard, just like those Asian villains in black-and-white movies. Those same villains always had strange Scotch-taped, squinty eyes and long, curved fingernails; Mas had never seen any human being, much less an Asian, with that kind of appearance. Mu ran out behind him, his paws swiftly padding on the hard-wood floor. At least one living creature had energy this morning.

"Anmen gone," Mas said.

"What?"

"Heezu gone."

G. I. went to the window and looked at the parked cars. "Dammit," he cursed. He surveyed the living room. He lifted the blanket he had given Anmen and then pulled at piles of dirty clothes and the bags and containers from the Cuban restaurant. "That shithead took Juanita's *shamisen.*"

"*Honto?*" Could it be?

Mas went into the kitchen, just to make sure. But other than the small Formica table, a couple of metal chairs, and a bag of Haruo's persimmons, nothing. But something was on the table. A note. In Japanese.

G. I. joined Mas at the table. His breath smelled awful, like something green, gelatinous, and left out too long, but Mas knew that his own wouldn't be much better. Surely the amount of garlic they had consumed the night before didn't help.

"What's it say?"

Mas had left his reading glasses in the truck, but G. I. handed him a magnifying glass instead. The glass was a heavy-duty one with a rectangular black frame.

G. I. rubbed his mustache stubble. Mas spent a few minutes trying to make out Anmen's writing. He'd obviously been in a hurry and maybe even writing in the dark. "Itsu say heezu sorry. He not a kinda man to stay until the end."

"So, basically, he's a coward."

Mas shook his head. "Heezu used to run-

317

nin'. Can't stop, even if he wants to."

"Did he mention anything about the *shamisen*?"

Mas read the note over again. "Nutin' about *shamisen*."

"Well, he's an asshole, a thief, and maybe a killer."

Mas frowned. "Youzu think he killsu somebody?"

"Maybe. Why has he been incognito for all these years? I'm going to call the rental car company. Maybe they can trace his whereabouts." G. I. then went back to the living room and cursed again.

"Whatsamatta?" Mas asked from the doorway.

"That guy took my address book. Must have thought it was a wallet." G. I. then went on a tear in his closet. More cursing. "He also took my gun."

"Thought police take away."

"They took my knives, but I convinced them to leave my gun."

Mas then recalled what he had overheard at the Torrance Police Department. "Police know where knife sold."

"What?"

Mas repeated the information he had learned. A store in Vegas. Cash. Asian buyer.

"Kermit was looking at knives in Vegas,"

G. I. said softly. His face was pale. "You know, I haven't heard from him in a couple of days. Ever since Randy's death, he'd been calling once, even two times, a day."

G. I. got on the phone in the living room, and Mas heard him leave a message for Jiro and then Detective Alo.

As G. I. made his calls, Mas was feeling damp and sweaty, in need of some heavy-duty cleaning. He also needed a strong cup of coffee to shake up his brain, but he refrained from being a *nezumi,* a rat, scurrying through G. I.'s kitchen cabinets and refrigerator. Something was nagging at him. Didn't he have to go somewhere this morning? And then — *a-ra!* His appointment with Olivia Feinstein. Mas turned the twine on his Casio watch to see its face. The appointment was forty-five minutes from now.

Mas removed the address that he had written on the back of an old receipt in his wallet. The attorney's daughter lived in zip code 90210, Beverly Hills, maybe only five miles away from G. I.'s address.

G. I. apparently struck out on his calls, because he returned to the kitchen table in a bad mood.

"I gotsu to go," Mas told him. "Appointment with dat lawyer's daughter."

G. I. offered Mas his second car, an old

319

Volvo whose muffler was held up by wire. "I wish I could go with you, Mas. But I have to see if I can find Jiro. He's supposed to be at work, but he hasn't come in. And Juanita and I were supposed to go to that concert at the Okinawa Association. Actually you should be there, Mas. I know that Kinjo is involved somehow; I'm sure of it. It all goes back to that *sanshin.* You need to get some straight answers from Kinjo, even if you have to confront him onstage."

"I try to make it," Mas said. In the meantime, he would need to use G. I.'s shower and borrow a clean set of clothes. He was sorry to be such a *meiwaku,* but going to Beverly Hills required being a bother. He couldn't visit a fancy lady in clothes he had just slept in, not to mention the smell of garlic permeating from his mouth and skin.

G. I. was about fifteen pounds lighter and five inches taller than Mas, but he was able to find a loose Hawaiian shirt and a pair of dark pants that Mas could fit into. In the shower, naked, with the water pounding down on him, Mas tried to think.

To use Lil's word, Anmen was most definitely a *yogore.* And there Mas, hearing about caves and explosions, had felt sorry for the man. Why had Anmen Sanjo left in the middle of the night with a stolen gun?

And this Olivia Feinstein, what could she possibly shed light on? What would she know that Edwin Parker hadn't told Mas already?

The shower didn't provide any answers. Mas got out, dried himself off, and got into G. I.'s clothes. He combed his hair back and, for the hell of it, splashed some cologne from the medicine cabinet on his neck for good measure. G. I. gave him a disposable razor and a toothbrush. Mas also requested fizzy water, which he used to soak his dentures for five minutes.

Mas then left the bathroom to put on his socks and loafers in the living room. The legs of the pants were too long, so Mas folded over the cuffs two times. If G. I. was serious about Mas confronting Kinjo, he had to have reinforcements. Mas discussed with G. I. who those people needed to be.

Before he left, Mas asked G. I., "By the way, whysu Kinjo's band at your party?"

"I don't know. I figure the restaurant handled it all."

Mas didn't have many opportunities to go into Beverly Hills. His gardening route was limited to the northeastern side of Los Angeles, so he rarely strayed beyond the west side of downtown. Mas remembered an old-time gardener telling him that during the Great Depression of the thirties, some people in Beverly Hills tried to pass a law that banned all Japanese gardeners from the city. Out-of-work *hakujin* had entered the gardening trade, and they didn't want to face competition in a free enterprise economy. But as it turned out, while a single Japanese gardener might usually be quiet, when you got a thousand of them together, they could make quite a racket. And that's what happened; the gardeners got together and formed a Japanese gardeners' association in response to the proposed ban, and the law was killed.

That was a long time ago, however. Beverly Hills had gotten its *bachi,* or comeuppance, as it was now populated with as many immigrants as *hakujin.* Still, Wilshire Boulevard hadn't changed a whole lot. The ivy-covered Beverly Wilshire Hotel was still there. And sure, fancy stores might have different names, labels, and models, but they were still selling top-of-the-line products.

Mas parked the Volvo on a small street three blocks off Wilshire Boulevard. He had expected a fancy mansion and instead got rows of fourplexes that looked as if they'd been constructed in the forties. The lawns and gardens were immaculate, and Mas knew that the new men and women who tended them weren't Japanese but most likely newcomers from Latin America with their own sets of dreams.

Olivia Feinstein lived in a back unit. The gardener had shaved a boxwood hedge into the shape of a mouse, with another matching one cut like Swiss cheese, holes and all. Very clever, Mas thought disdainfully; he preferred geometric designs over Disneyland in his topiary.

At the first ring of her doorbell, Olivia opened the door. Her bobbed hair was completely white, but with a silvery sheen. Like the hedges outside her door, she looked recently primped and groomed. She smiled widely, and Mas could see the schoolgirl in her. It didn't matter if you were three or ninety — a woman could go a long way with an attractive smile.

"Hello, Mr. Arai." Olivia welcomed Mas inside.

Mas pulled down on G. I.'s Hawaiian shirt. Hawaiian shirts weren't Mas's thing; in fact, he had never worn one in his life Luckily, there weren't any bikini-clad wahines on the shirt. The only remotely Hawaiian touch was a pattern of surfboards that resembled the shape of leaves. Leaves, Mas could deal with.

323

Olivia Feinstein left Mas in the living room, which had rounded corners and alcoves. She had a white carpet, which made Mas nervous. He couldn't remember if he had properly wiped his shoes on the welcome mat. The Japanese had the custom of leaving your shoes at the door, which only made sense. Why bring the dirt and the foreignness of the outside into your home? But the *hakujin* were quite married to their shoes, Mas understood. It was as if the loss of height, style, or status would lessen their power in a room. Shoes, whether they be a man's wingtips or a woman's stilettoes, were like calling cards. Stockinged feet, on the other hand, were too human and vulnerable.

Olivia Feinstein brought a tray of tea and placed it on the table in front of the couch. Mas tried to the refuse the tea, but she still poured him a cup from a flowered teapot. A bowl of sugar cubes and a small pitcher of milk remained on the tray. Mas would have accepted a cup of green tea, which would at least have had some grit to it. But sweet tea and milk — Mas couldn't take that much civility today.

Olivia dropped a sugar cube in her tea with a pair of mini tongs and stirred. "Now, Professor Howard was telling me that you're

324

interested in my father and one of his cases during the 1950s?"

Mas licked his lips. He wasn't quite sure how to begin, so he merely blurted out, "Isokichi Sanjo."

"He's a past client, right? I think I recall his name." Olivia removed a box from the table and thumbed through some index cards. "S-A-N . . ." She waited.

"J-O."

"Yes, yes, here it is — the Sanjo case, one of the Japanese deportees. Now I remember. I'm editing my father's memoirs right now. He regretted not being able to help him more. Didn't Edwin Parker take over the case?"

Mas nodded.

"There was something about this one." Olivia tapped the edge of her three-by-five card. "Was this the one in which the deportee was found dead a few days after being arrested?"

Olivia was a sharp one. Mas felt his pulse quicken. Maybe this trip to 90210 would be worth it.

"They weren't able to locate the INS agent, Henry Metcalf, involved in the arrest, right?" Her face grew more animated. "My father wrote pages and pages about Metcalf. A horrible man. He thought it was his personal mission to get rid of all immigrants, especially those of Mexican, Jewish, and Asian descent. He viewed them to be un-American, and joined the bandwagon to deport those with any connections to the Communist Party. It was the Cold War, of course, and we had to be protective of our national security, but Metcalf took it too far. Even his own agency, the INS office in L.A., was troubled; they didn't know what to do with him. When he disappeared, everyone suspected foul play — that either he had committed a crime or a crime had been committed against him. In terms of the theory that he had been killed, there was a whole line of suspects. My father was even questioned. In private, he said that he would have gladly taken credit for Metcalf's disappearance if only he could have had experienced the pleasure of doing away with him. But no pleasure, no credit."

Mas had trouble following Olivia, but he understood the gist of her comments: that more than one person had wanted this Agent Metcalf dead. And judging from her comments, Mas figured she had not yet heard about Metcalf's bones being unearthed from downtown L.A.

"There was something else," Olivia added. "Wasn't there an informant?"

326

"Man from Sanjo-*san*'s band."

"I remember Edwin talking about this case."

Edwin?

Olivia blushed the slightest shade of pink. "I was seeing Edwin Parker at that time. We dated for a few months until I broke it off. I was very cruel, actually. I told him that he was more enamored with my father than me. I'm still embarrassed when I see Edwin and his wife at social functions."

Olivia crossed her legs, and Mas noticed they were still slim, with only a faint web of varicose veins visible underneath her nylons. "But I remember hearing about this informant. Unreliable, to say the least. I think that he certainly had other motives in cooperating with immigration services. Some of these informants lied. Some were even planted by the INS. It's amazing what some people are willing to do if the price is high enough."

The lawyer's daughter then spent a few minutes reading notes on her index cards. "The informant had made an appointment with my father after the deportee's death. But he then canceled; never gave a reason why."

Mas looked down at his watch. If he wanted to make a stop before the concert, he would have to leave now. "I gotsu to go. Sank you very much."

"You didn't touch your tea." Olivia Feinstein looked disappointed. Unfortunately, Mas had spent his life disappointing women; one more wasn't going to make a whole lot of difference.

Mas went back to the beginning. Where it all started. Mahalo, the Hawaiian restaurant in Torrance.

The hostess — could it be Tiffany? — greeted Mas with a menu in her hand. "Aloha! How many in your party?"

Mas rechecked her name badge. These pretty young girls all looked alike. But sure enough, the badge read TIFFANY. "Youzu the one at G. I.'s party."

"Excuse me?"

"The day the man killed."

Tiffany finally recognized Mas. Her face turned pale in spite of her tan. She looked nervous. "You were the guy outside with the screwdriver. What do you want?" she asked.

A family walked in, and Tiffany took a few steps toward these real customers and then stopped, glancing nervously back at Mas. She was rescued by a young man who had also worked that night at the party, the one whose short black hair was gelled up like porcupine quills. His name was apparently JOSH.

"Is there something I can help you with, sir?"

"The day Randy Yamashiro killed, you have Okinawa band. Whysu you use dat band?"

The young man frowned. "May I ask why you need that information?"

"Just needsu to know why youzu pick them."

"The restaurant had nothing to do with it."

"Youzu sure?"

Josh must have been eager to get rid of Mas, because he finally said, "Look, I'm the one who took the phone call. I remember because it was at the last minute — the night before the event. The guy planning the party — the one who was killed — told us that we had to book that band, that Kinji and Son."

"Kinjo."

"Yeah, Kinjo and Son. I told him that I couldn't promise him anything — not enough advance notice — but he said that he would pay extra. Even double their usual fee. I didn't understand why it was so important, but we did it. You know — the customer is always right."

Josh then turned his attention to another couple who was waiting to be seated. He obviously didn't want to waste any more time with Mas, which was fine, because he was late to the concert.

The Okinawa Association parking lot was full, so Mas parked two blocks away. He didn't know which building to enter, so he first went into the newer one, glossy with a mirrored outside, but the glass door only led to a spiral staircase to the second floor and a long hallway leading to offices. No sign of a concert there. It was also dead quiet, aside from the hum of the air conditioner.

The door to the second was locked, but a door to the third was held open with a metal chair. It went right into a heavy-duty steel kitchen with a professional-looking stove and a springy rubber floor mat. A couple of Japanese women were by the sink, their hands wet and their hair freshly coiffed and sprayed. Seeing Mas, they smiled and nodded as if they knew him. Mas pressed his lips together, managing the best grin he could.

Hearing the music coming from the other side of the kitchen, Mas knew that he was at the right place. He walked into a large hall, which was filled with at least two hundred people seated at long tables assembled in rows in front of a wooden platform. Three *sanshin* players, all middle-aged women in orange and yellow kimonos, stood behind microphones, singing. Each one of them had a black cone-shaped wig attached to the top of her head.

One of the women from the kitchen pushed Mas toward a side counter that was filled with food. She held out a paper plate and motioned for him to serve himself. He was a stranger, yet she wanted to feed him. This much kindness made Mas suspicious, but not suspicious enough to refuse the food.

The line of dishes represented a typical Japanese American potluck, including the Okinawan *dango,* which Chizuko herself used to make on special occasions, dozens of fried round donuts in different trays and pans. Someone had placed the *dango* in a round bowl; they resembled the backs of sparrows huddled together in a nest.

Less familiar to Mas were the trays full of cut-up pork and *goya,* bitter melon. Chizuko had had an Okinawan hairdresser who always gave her bagfuls of *goya.* It was a funny-looking melon, green, bumpy, and long like a cucumber — like something you might find in the toy section of a pet store or perhaps on another planet. But sliced and cooked, the *goya,* which was a brilliant yellow inside, with orange seeds, was pretty, the outside ridged like the petals of a flower. Here the *goya* and pork were stewed together. Mas was in the mood for bitter, so he scooped up a huge spoonful and placed it next to his Okinawan *dango,* macaroni salad, and Spam *musubi.*

The women were still singing, so Mas remained standing on the side.

"Please sit." One of the ladies from the kitchen gestured toward the long tables. But most of the seats were filled.

Mas opted to wait rather than disturb people during the musicians' performance. After ten minutes, he felt the bottom of his paper plate grow soggy and heard his stomach grumble. The song finally ended, releasing Mas to make his move.

As he went down the first row, he was surprised to see Gushi-mama there in a wheelchair, her pigeon-faced roommate beside her. And then, next to her, another familiar face. The professor, Genessee Howard.

"This seat's open, Mas." She gestured to an empty seat beside her.

Mas hesitated and remained standing. "I

dunno youzu gonna be here," he said.

"I always come to the concerts. I'm an adviser for the association."

"You knowsu Gushi-mama?"

"Oh, we're great friends. After my husband died, Gushi-mama was the one who brought *maze-gohan* to my house every week. That's when she was living on her own."

Gushi-mama's dried-out mane was tamed inside a knit hat, and her mouth was filled with a set of perfect teeth. She was looking good. "My *maze-gohan* the best, you know," she said, peering at his plate to see if he had any of the rice-mixed-with-red-bean dish. "None of this stuff any good."

Mas didn't know how to respond. If he agreed, he would be insulting the hands that had made the *ogochiso,* the feast before them. If he disagreed, he would be denigrating Gushi-mama's culinary expertise. He must have had a funny expression, because Gushi-mama then commented to Genessee, "This man, *omoshiroi.*"

Omoshiroi. The word could mean "interesting." But also "peculiar." She then clarified, "He looks like nobody special, but he has a head for things. Smarter than he looks."

If Gushi-mama hadn't been recovering

from a lack of food and fluids in her body, Mas would have had some choice words to throw her way. But he refrained.

"Yes," Genessee said. "I figured that out the first time I saw him."

"*So,*" agreed Gushi-mama's roommate.

Embarrassed by his all-female fan club, Mas almost dropped his plate of bitter melon onto the floor.

"Sit, sit." Genessee pulled at the sleeve of the Hawaiian shirt. Mas finally acquiesced and claimed the folding chair next to her.

An emcee in a suit and tie spoke into the microphone. "More food left, everyone." He then added, "No *enryo,*" before introducing the next performers.

Enryo was the standard Japanese response to any social situation, large or small. Mas and Chizuko would tell Mari not to beg for soft drinks at a friend's house and, in fact, to refuse it when it was first offered. (It could, however, be accepted upon the second offer, and a definite yes by the third.) And of course, no one took the last bit of anything on a plate at a Chinese restaurant. It didn't make sense, really, for that final piece of sweet-and-sour pork or chicken chow mein to end up in the trash rather than someone's stomach, but that's how things were done. Most *hakujin* wouldn't be able to survive living this way; they would probably scream and *monku* until the system was changed. But then that's how the Japanese American had survived this long under bad circumstances. You pushed aside your own wants for the larger good, which in most cases meant some type of unity. Of course, sometimes fights would break out, and people would go off on their own — only to start up another new group. And so the process went on and on. No wonder there were thousands of groups within the Japanese American community.

Mas began eating as a new group positioned themselves on the platform. As he ate and listened, he kept one eye on the door. He hadn't seen Kinjo, Alan, or Halbertson yet — not to mention either G. I. or Juanita.

The emcee returned to the microphone. "Next is Kinjo and Son Band," he said. The audience clapped.

From the kitchen entrance came Kinjo, Alan, Halbertson, the woman with the skunk stripe in her hair, and the young man with the tortured push-lawn-mower hair.

The music was more of the same, but it was good nonetheless. Mas had to disagree with Gushi-mama on this — Kinjo was a good *sanshin* player. Maybe not quite good enough for him to have his nose in the air, but enjoyable nonetheless.

In the middle of the third song, two new guests entered the hall. One was Detective Alo, whose immense size attracted half of the crowd's attention. The other half seemed more interested in his companion, a squat, balding Japanese man wearing a dark, expensive suit revealing his high position.

Genessee whispered in Mas's ear, "Why is Detective Alo with the representative from Okinawa?"

Mas almost cracked a smile. G. I. was to be commended. He had worked his persuasive magic in getting the men to a concert on a Saturday afternoon. Genessee was not a woman who wasted any time. She rose and made her way toward the two men. Whatthehell, thought Mas. Isn't this why I took the trouble to come here in the first place? He got up and joined Genessee by the door.

Alo was in a deep conversation with the suited Japanese man, bending down to his height and periodically pointing to Halbertson and then Kinjo. The singing duo were in trouble and they knew it. Kinjo's voice went flat, while his *hakujin* sidekick looked like he had caught a bad case of the stomach flu. They stopped performing after the third song, prompting hard looks from Alan and the other members of the band. Both Kinjo and Halbertson bowed and quickly left the stage, looking for an alternate door besides the one in the kitchen. There wasn't any.

"Going somewhere?" Detective Alo blocked the exit.

Kinjo hugged his *sanshin* to his chest, while Halbertson's once-perky white mustache dipped down.

"You know that musical instrument that you claim is yours, Mr. Kinjo? Well, we've discovered that it was stolen from the prefecture of Okinawa. And the musical score hidden inside — it happens to be a national treasure, missing since World War Two." Alo gestured toward his balding companion. "This is Mr. Oyadomori, a representative from the Okinawan government. He'd like to discuss how exactly you got your hands on those two items."

By this time, the audience was no longer following the next musical act but the more interesting sideshow that Alo was providing.

"*Soto, soto.*" Kinjo wanted to take his private business outside, away from the curious looks of the Okinawa Association members. "Go outside."

Leaving behind Alan and Halbertson,

Kinjo deftly darted behind Alo and headed toward the wide openness of the parking lot. Only he didn't stop once he was outside. He was moving toward the street.

A black car swung into the lot, preventing his escape. The driver's door opened and Agent Lee, impeccably dressed and groomed as usual, slowly emerged from the car.

"Hello, Mr. Kinjo," he said. It was obvious that the two had met before.

Kinjo blinked furiously — a mouse caught by two, no, three cats. His legs must have been shaking, because his kimono-covered body bobbed back and forth.

Alan, seeing his father in trouble, ran to his defense. "What's going on here?" he said, standing beside Kinjo. "Nothing is going to happen without our lawyer present."

"No, no. Too *takai,* expensive. Pay too much already." Kinjo hung his head. He was giving up.

Mas saw Detective Alo approach Agent Lee. They were also clearly familiar with each other, because they were soon having their own argument about who should be questioning Kinjo first, and where.

"This is a murder case; I think this takes precedence over something that happened fifty years ago," Alo said in his breathless voice, but a little louder than usual.

"But this is murder, too, with larger ramifications. I think that I should have first crack at him."

Finally, Genessee interrupted them, waving a set of keys. "You can meet next door in our office building." Alan continued to try to deter his father from cooperating, with little success. Mas was going to stay behind, but Genessee took hold of his arm. She led them to the modern, mirrored building. They passed the spiral staircase and went down a hall to the first door, which Genessee unlocked with one of her keys.

They all took seats around four tables arranged together in the center of the room. Kinjo, Alan, and Halbertson sat on one side; Oyadomori, Lee, and Alo on the other. Mas stood awkwardly by the door. He felt odd without Juanita and G. I. there. Had G. I.'s business with Jiro taken all day? Genessee, meanwhile, walked back and forth, her arms crossed as if she were a schoolteacher ready to reprimand her students.

Kinjo pointed to Halbertson and blurted to Mr. Oyadomori in Japanese, "This man is the one who stole the *sanshin* and *kunkunshi* from Shuri Castle in Okinawa during World War Two."

Oyadomori's heavy eyebrows went up, and Alo and Lee were eager to know what had been said. Alan looked shocked — it was obvious that he had been unaware of his father's past association with Halbertson and the stolen *shamisen.*

The Okinawan official was apparently fluent in both languages. "He said his friend took the *sanshin* and *kunkunshi* from a very important landmark in Okinawa, which was totally destroyed after the war." Oyadomori spoke slowly and deliberately, with only the slightest of accents. He then scolded Halbertson. "Do you know how valuable the *kunkunshi* is? This is like the Bible for *sanshin* players."

"I didn't know anything about the *kunkunshi*. Yes, I took the *sanshin* as a souvenir. At that time, I didn't know what I had. In fact, I saved it, you could say. If I had left it in the castle, it would have burned, for sure. The neck was loose — in fact, it completely came off — and that's how I found that scroll. When I was working at Jerome, I showed it to Kinjo." Halbertson gestured toward Kinjo. "He said that it was just some scribbling, nothing important. He paid me fifty dollars for it. A lousy fifty dollars. And now you are telling me the score is priceless?"

"You did not tell me you stole," Kinjo shot back.

"You knew where I had taken it from."

Like a married couple on the brink of divorce, the two men continued to shoot accusations at each other.

Alo finally raised his hands. "Is there another room we can use?"

Genessee lifted her set of keys and gestured toward the room across the way.

"Mr. Oyadomori, perhaps it would be better if you interview Mr. Halbertson privately for a little while," Alo said. "I have another investigation to handle here."

"Don't forget mine," asserted Agent Lee.

There was a flicker of annoyance reflected on Alo's face. "And you." He spoke to Alan. "We'll need you to leave the room too."

Alan tried to argue with the detective again, but Kinjo shook his head. *Orai, yo,*" he said. "I'm *orai.*"

Alan did not want to leave his father's side. His handsome face was tight with worry, and Mas realized the son, all this time, had feared that his father had somehow been involved in the death of Randy Yamashiro.

Alo then got on his phone as the Okinawan representative and Halbertson made their way into another room. Alan also reluctantly rose from the table.

"I've asked for a Japanese interpreter to come, so we can wait until she arrives," Alo announced after his phone conversation.

"No." Kinjo's eyes flashed, their intensity matching his brilliant white hair. "I talk now."

Alan tried to talk sense to Kinjo, but he wouldn't budge. The police detective then asked Alan, this time more forcefully, to leave the room. Mas turned toward the hallway, eager to comply. "No, not you, Mr. Arai," said Alo. "I need you here."

It was as Mas feared: Alo was going to use him as a makeshift interpreter. The detective told Mas to sit beside him, across from Kinjo, while Agent Lee reluctantly moved to a side chair. Removing a small tape recorder from his jacket pocket, Alo then addressed Kinjo. "May I?"

"Hai," affirmed Kinjo, his eyes blinking furiously, *pachi-pachi.*

Alo then asked Kinjo perfunctory questions. Name, date of birth, place of birth. Kinjo seemed antsy to jump from the realm of the mundane into the meat of the matter. "I did not do it. I did not kill him," he blurted out in English. "Randy Yamashiro is the one."

Alo exchanged looks with Lee. "What are

you saying?"

"I do not kill Yamashiro; he try to kill me."

The statement was heavy, and it sunk into the silence of the room for a few seconds.

"So what you're saying is that Randy Yamashiro tried to kill you?" Alo repeated.

Kinjo nodded. "With *katana* this size." He raised his hands about a foot apart. He knew that he would need to provide the police with a detailed description of what happened, so he turned to Mas and explained in Japanese, "After the performance, Randy told me to meet him outside so he could pay me. He said that he had to leave right away, so I left Alan to pack up, and I went to the parking lot. I couldn't find him at first; then, there he was behind a van, carrying the *sanshin.* I was so excited to see the *sanshin;* it was like being reunited with an old friend. I thought that Randy was returning the *sanshin* to me, so I rushed over to him.

" 'You recognize this?' he asked, and before I can answer, he breaks the neck from the body, right before my eyes."

Kinjo's cheeks were shiny with tears. Mas took the opportunity to retell as much of Kinjo's story as he could to Alo and Lee.

"Go on," Alo gently prodded Kinjo.

"I yelled out, 'What are you doing?' and

then he brought out a huge knife — more than a foot long. 'This is for my father,' he said. 'Isokichi Sanjo.' He plunged the knife toward my chest. I jumped back, and the layers of my kimono were cut and torn. I tried to yell again, but nothing came out of my throat. And suddenly, before Yamashiro could try again, somebody took a hold of his arm."

Mas knew what was coming next. "It was a short Sansei man with the freckles. Randy's friend. Jiro.

"They are trained fighters, I could see. They were on the ground, wrestling, and finally Jiro was on top, struggling to get the knife out of Randy's hand and then —" Kinjo swallowed. "And then the knife was in Randy's neck. Blood was pouring out. His legs and arms were still moving, as if he were being suffocated. And then his body stopped moving. Still. Jiro and I were in shock, and then he barked at me, 'Get out of here. And say nothing. I saved your life. You owe me.' "

Mas licked his dry lips. Again, *osewaninatta*. It was a curse. Kinjo took a deep breath, and it seemed that he was done talking for a while. Mas did his best to give a summary of Kinjo's testimony.

Alo straightened out a paper clip that had

been on the table. "So you said nothing about what you saw."

Kinjo shook his head. "I say nothing. Not even to my son. I drive away, and Jiro runs away, too, but someone see him."

"Who?"

"Someone I don't see long, long time. But I know. Isokichi's brother, Anmen."

So Anmen had witnessed Jiro fleeing the scene? He had said nothing about this to Mas and G. I.

"He didn't see me, but I recognized him. The same body. The same way of walking."

Mas tried to remember what Anmen had said at Haruo's. That he was going to get the man who did it.

Kinjo's voice was getting hoarse, as raspy as Jiro's even. *"Mizu,"* he finally said.

"He want water," Mas explained.

Alo went to a water cooler in the corner, and Agent Lee followed. They conferred for a minute and returned. Alo, handing both Kinjo and Mas Dixie cups of water, took Lee's seat, while Lee took Alo's place across from Kinjo. The questioning was turning, Mas realized, from the present back to the past.

"So the son knew about you informing on his father in 1953?"

Mas roughly translated the question, and

Kinjo affirmed, "*Hai.* He blamed me for killing his father. I didn't do it. But I know who did."

Mas shivered as if cold water had been poured down his back. He provided a rough translation, and Lee nodded for Kinjo to continue.

"It was fifty years ago in Los Angeles. I couldn't sleep the night of Sanjo's arrest," Kinjo explained. "I could hear the smallest noise. The ticking of the clock. Sirens in the distance. A car backfiring down the street. A part of me despised Sanjo, and yes, that probably all came from jealousy. He was a musical genius. He had a talent that I could never attain. I don't know why I wanted to bring him down rather than be happy to be in his presence. I consoled myself with the fact that I had a royal *sanshin.* And the *kunkunshi.* It gave me special powers, an edge, I thought. When it was stolen one night after a performance, I knew that one of the Sanjo brothers had done it. I had gotten in a terrible fight with Isokichi. He told me that I needed to return the *sanshin* and the *kunkunshi* to the Okinawan government. I told him to mind his own business. The band was breaking up, never to be reunited again."

Kinjo seemed to be in a trance, and Mas

didn't want to interrupt him. Besides, how could he translate all this *komakai,* detailed information? He glanced at Agent Lee, who somehow knew what Kinjo was saying from the tone of his voice. Pointing at the tape recorder, he mouthed, "It's okay," to Mas, and then motioned for him to keep Kinjo talking.

"So I had gone to this Agent Metcalf, and we'd struck a deal. He had been nosing around, making empty threats that he would deport any Okinawans connected with the Communist Party. He was coming up empty, but I was going to give him the biggest fish possible. The beloved Isokichi Sanjo. For my testimony, I would receive immunity from deportation myself, since I had gone to a few *aka* meetings. I was just curious. I didn't really know what they were talking about. I wasn't a political man. Not like Isokichi.

"Anyway, the night they took Isokichi away, I had insomnia, and I felt a demon was dancing in my insides. I had done wrong, I knew it, but I didn't know how to undo it. So I left my wife in the bed and drove down to the INS building. I don't know what I was thinking. They weren't going to let me in. But like a wolf howling at the moon, I was drawn to the place where

Sanjo was caged.

"I passed the parking lot and then I saw it: two men carrying another man on their shoulders. *Yopparrateru,* drunk, I thought. Until one of the men turned and stared at me. He was a hundred yards away, but I knew who it was. The INS agent, Metcalf.

"Suddenly I knew that the third man wasn't drunk. He was dead. And that he was most likely Sanjo. I felt like a starting gun had gone off in my stomach, and I began to run as fast as I could. Back to Little Tokyo. Back to the true drunks in the *nomiya.* But I heard a car's engine rev and follow right behind me, driving on sidewalks and finally following me down an alley. *Shimmata.* A dead end. I thought my fate would be the same as Sanjo's. We would both be gone. Metcalf came out first, and then the other man. Metcalf took out a knife and pressed it against my throat. 'I can make trouble for you, Kinjo,' he said. 'I know that you were at those meetings too. I can get you deported. I can send you back to your own country.'

"I waited for the other man to say something. But he said nothing. The Ford's headlights were on, and all I could see was the black outline of his body. He seemed young, as young as a teenager. Then he moved into the light, and I recognized him too — Sanjo's lawyer, Edwin Parker.

"Afterward, I knew that I probably needed to say something. I even made an appointment with that Isaac Delman, but then Edwin Parker came to my house. He spoke in riddles. He pretty much said that Metcalf was gone now, so there would be no trouble. If I wanted it to stay that way, I would let it go. I remember what he said in English: 'Let sleeping dogs lie.' Then he patted Alan on the head and said that he hoped that we would be together for a very long time. I knew what he was saying. Open my mouth and be sent away. So I canceled my appointment with Delman and shut my mouth. At that point I knew that he had done away with not only Metcalf, but Isokichi. All I could do was watch Edwin Parker become a big shot over the past five decades.

"I couldn't believe it when I saw him at Mahalo. I think he was surprised too. But he still came up to me and said, 'Hello, Kinjo, so good to see you.' Like he was daring me to tell people what I had seen fifty years ago. He couldn't get me now, but he knew that I had stayed silent all these years. Why should I talk now? And who would believe me?"

The door shook with a firm rap. It was a

uniformed officer, his hair the color of newspaper twine. He was young, most likely right out of the police academy, because he reported in a loud voice, "Detective, there's a hostage situation in a town house in Torrance. They say it may be related to this case."

CHAPTER FOURTEEN

Alo went into the hallway with the officer, closing the door behind him. Mas's throat felt so parched, the Dixie cup of water did not do anything to quench his thirst. He walked to the water cooler for more, leaving Agent Lee with Kinjo. What was going on? Hostage situation? Who had kidnaped who? Mas gulped one cupful of water after another.

The door opened, and Alo returned to the table. "I'll have to speak with you more later, Mr. Kinjo," he said, retrieving the tape recorder. "I'm going to have to take care of something right now. Mr. Arai —"

Ready to be excused, Mas wiped the excess water from the edges of his mouth.

"I need you to come with me."

Mas wadded up the paper cup in his fist and threw it into a trash can. Kinjo and Agent Lee looked up, curious.

After Mas followed Alo into the parking

lot, the detective explained, "Anmen Sanjo has taken Jiro Hamada hostage in his town house. He has a gun, and he's asking for you."

Mas nodded. His heart rattled against his old bones, but he still agreed to accompany Alo to the town house.

Genessee ran out from the building. "You don't have to go with him, Mas," she said.

"Izu know," Mas said. "I want to go."

The Torrance Police squad car led the way, its siren blaring and the lights flashing. Alo had a brown sedan with its own flashing light in the rear window above the backseat. He was putting all his energy into steering the car and dodging the *baka* drivers who failed to stop or even slow their cars for the police. Mas knew that this wasn't the time to ask questions; he would find out what was going on, sooner or later.

Jiro lived in one of these gated cookie-cutter complexes where three-story units were slapped right against each other. They all seemed to follow the same floor plan: garage on the first floor, living room and kitchen with adjacent balcony, second; and bedrooms, third. The main gate was propped open, and another squad car was parked there to keep anyone from entering.

A small crowd, including housekeepers and residents, stood outside. Detective Alo slowed his sedan enough to ask an officer, "What's the latest?"

"No shots fired yet. We think he has three hostages in there. Two men, including the resident, and a woman." The officer then gazed into the backseat. "Is that Arai?"

Alo nodded.

A nasty pain shot up Mas's neck. Alo drove through the gates and made a left into a large driveway in between two rows of town houses. About five sheriff's squad cars were scattered haphazardly in the flat space like mixed-up mah-jongg tiles.

Alo and Mas walked around the squad cars like rats in a maze. A group of officers stood clumped together alongside the last garage door. Their attention was fixed on a unit one row away to the right. "It's the middle one," an officer reported to Alo. "The one with the cars parked in front of the garage." The cars confirmed Mas's worst fears.

He saw a filthy car full of junk. Anmen Sanjo's rental. Next to it was a red Toyota truck.

"Juanita," he murmured.

Alo nodded. "We think Miss Gushiken and your friend George Hasuike are being held. Along with Jiro."

Detective Alo picked up a white megaphone from one of the squad cars. He pressed down on a button, and Mas was surprised at how loud and clear his voice sounded. "Mr. Sanjo, this is Detective Alo of the Torrance Department. I'm here with your friend. Mas Arai."

Mas objected to the use of "friend," but it was no use to make a big deal out of words now. Alo handed Mas the megaphone, and he was surprised at how heavy it was. A couple of tries and Mas finally got it to work. "Sanjo-*san,*" Mas called out. His voice, magnified tenfold, echoed down the driveways. He felt like a fool.

"Tell him to give himself up," Detective Alo said in Mas's ear.

Mas held the megaphone with both hands. "No good, *yo. Da-me.* Better give up."

There was a hush over the complex. And then Anmen spoke. "I want to talk to you, Arai," he called out in Japanese from the balcony. "But just you. No one else."

"He saysu he wants me to go ova there. Just me," Mas told the detective.

Alo murmured, "That's unacceptable." The other deputies shook their heads no. They convened again, and Mas heard a deputy say, "There's no telling what he will do."

Mas didn't know what it was. Maybe that Anmen had specifically requested his presence. Or it could have been plain stupidity, or ego. But Mas heard himself volunteer to meet Anmen in the town house.

"I think it's too dangerous, Mr. Arai. Too dangerous," Alo said.

What did Mas care? He was closer to death than the beginning of life, more so than any of the police officers, Juanita, G. I., or Jiro.

"I try. Itsu *orai*. No sue," he told Alo.

Alo smiled briefly. "I'm not worried about you suing us. But it's not normal protocol to send a civilian in full range of a gunman."

"Get him to give up."

"We should just wait him out."

They then heard the motor and blades of a helicopter flying above. Some movement on the balcony. And then a gunshot so loud that it hurt Mas's ears. Silence. And then another voice. Jiro's, his voice sounding sharp and desperate. "Back off," he pleaded. "Please."

The officers spoke into their walkie-talkies, and the helicopter lurched back up into the sky.

The captain said nothing, but Mas heard

others cursing behind him.

"I go," Mas said. "He wantsu me."

Alo's round eyes stared at Mas, measuring whether a seventy-two-year-old man could weather the stress of facing a hostage situation.

"Put a jacket on him," Alo instructed.

Mas felt a heavy weight around his chest and back as a deputy outfitted him in a black bulletproof vest. It was cumbersome and awkward, but Mas wasn't complaining.

Alo picked up the megaphone and aimed his voice toward Anmen. "I'm sending Mr. Arai to you, but he can't go alone. I'm coming with him. Unarmed."

Silence, just the faint drone of traffic in the distance.

"Mas, you better translate."

Mas sent the same message in his broken Japanese.

"Mr. Sanjo, did you hear me?" Alo asked.

"Hai. Orai."

Alo removed a gun and a holster from around his shoulder, but shoved something down in his sock. Mas moistened his lips. He feared that this would end badly, not only for himself but most likely for Anmen.

The garage door then opened, revealing a mess of boxes, multiple packages of toilet paper and paper towels, as well as stacks of

356

bottled water. Jiro was a big-box shopper, stocking up for the big earthquake or another future disaster to befall Los Angeles County.

As they slowly approached the garage, Mas heard the officers position themselves, their rifles cocked and ready. His legs felt so *darui,* weak, that he thought he would collapse in the middle of the driveway.

"Mr. Sanjo —" Alo called as they stepped into garage. He then peered up the stairs leading up to the second floor. "Why don't you come down so we can talk?"

"Arai, come up." Mas could hear Anmen's voice.

Alo led the way, hugging his body against the wall up the stairs. He reached the second floor first, and Mas could see him raising his arms in surrender. Mas then emerged in the doorway. Anmen, still in the same clothes he had slept in, was standing with a gun to Jiro's head. Jiro's lip was swollen as if he had been banged in the face a few times. Mas looked down the hall to the living room, where Juanita and G. I. sat in chairs, duct tape wound around their mouths, arms, and legs. Even from that distance, Mas could see Juanita's eyebrows. They said it all. She was afraid. And also mad as hell.

"I didn't want to kill him," blubbered Jiro. "Mas, tell him in Japanese. I was trying to stop Randy from killing."

"Damare!" Anmen whipped the back of Jiro's head with the gun. He pushed Jiro down to his knees onto the hardwood floor. "I saw this man with my nephew. Lying there in his blood."

Then why didn't you say anything? Mas thought. But he knew the answer. Anmen was a wanted man. *"Honto, yo,"* Mas said to Anmen in Japanese. "He speaking the truth. Randy the one who was going to commit murder." It all made perfect sense to Mas now. The knife. Randy's special request — no, demand — for Kinjo and Son. The premeditated murderer here was not Jiro, but Randy. "He going to kill Kinjo. For getting his father in trouble."

Anmen's eyes remained frozen on Mas's face. He understood Randy's hatred. Because he held the same hatred himself. "He couldn't have done that because of me," Anmen murmured.

"What?" Mas asked.

"I told him that Kinjo had been the one who got his father in trouble."

Mas took a deep breath. By giving his nephew this information, Anmen had launched his revenge. But it had boomeranged, and led instead to his nephew's demise.

"We get you a *bengoshi,* lawyer. Good one. Number one best. *Ichiban,*" Mas added for good measure.

"Why don't you put down your weapon, sir, and we can all talk this out," Alo said in his calm, soothing voice.

Anmen was obviously distressed. His hands were shaking, and the gun along with it. It was only a few inches from Jiro's throat. One slip of his hand, and Jiro's head would be shot off. The detective extended his arm as if to shield Mas from any oncoming gunfire. The arm moved ever so slowly toward the sock with the hidden weapon.

"Sanjo-*san,*" Mas called out loudly. "*Dame.* No more. This has to stop. You have another nephew. *Ikiteru.* He alive. He just lose *oniisan.* You can't do this to him."

Anmen's eyes softened. Perhaps the mention of a big brother made Anmen think of his own. The gun then fell on the hardwood floor, and Anmen hid his eyes in the crook of his arm.

Alo pulled the gun away from Anmen's feet and then quickly secured Anmen's wrists with heavy-duty plastic ties. He pushed Anmen forward to the balcony and waved his arm, signaling that he had caught his man. The police officers then swarmed into the town house like worker ants.

Mas watched as an officer took custody of Anmen. From the balcony, Mas could see Anmen's head being pushed down into the back of a patrol car. A wire cage separated Anmen from the front seat. From this moment on, he would have to get used to looking at the world from barred windows and fences.

Back in the living room, some officers were delicately removing the duct tape from Juanita's and G. I.'s faces, arms, and legs.

Juanita was the first one to be set loose. "Mas, you were unbelievable! You handled it like a pro. Better than a pro, even."

G. I., meanwhile, was more concerned about Jiro, who was being led down the stairs. "Wait, that's my client. I need to talk to him in private."

He called Mas over to stand watch by the bathroom door, which was in the second-floor hallway. "Stay close to the door, Mas. Don't let anyone come near," G. I. said before he and Jiro disappeared inside.

Mas felt silly standing guard. The town house, including the bathroom door, was made of flimsy material. Mas could hear everything, whether he wanted to or not.

"I don't know how all of this happened,

G. I.," Jiro was saying. "I didn't mean for it to happen. It happened so fast. In a split second. I tried to stop him. But he was out of control.

"It all started in Vegas after he won the jackpot. I told him not to buy any knives there. Would only lead to trouble. But he said that he needed self-protection. From what? I was so worried that I called Brian and told him to get to the mainland, fast. I told him that Randy was losing it again.

"And then, when we got back to L.A., Randy got that call from that shithead Anmen, looking to fleece him out of his jackpot money. Goes out. And when he comes back, he's loaded. You were out meeting with a client, but I heard it all. He says his money's finally safe, out of his hands. And then he keeps talking about Kinjo. Kinjo, Kinjo, Kinjo, he says. If Kinjo took his father away from him, he would take him away from his son. I thought I'd talked him out of it, but then at the party, I heard the name of the band, Kinjo and Son. I knew that Randy was up to no good.

"I confronted him in the bathroom at Mahalo's, and that's when I saw the knife poking out of his shirt. I knew what he was up to. I told him that he was crazy, that I was going to tell you what was going on."

"Shit, Kermit, why didn't you?"

"G. I., you're the only one of us who made it, man. Randy looked up to you. He told me if I said anything to you, he would never forgive me. And I couldn't have other people see Randy as being bad or evil. He wasn't, man. Just lost."

Mas didn't hear anything for a while. Just a catch of a throat like a hiccup. And then the door finally opened.

"Remember, let me do all the talking," G. I. whispered to Jiro. "Don't say anything to anyone."

Mas clenched his false teeth. He disagreed with G. I. There had been too much silence. It had to finally stop.

CHAPTER FIFTEEN

Mas couldn't keep his hands from shaking. He tried to breathe deeply. *I can do this. I can do this*, he told himself. And then he knocked on Judge Parker's door.

"Hello, Mas. I've been expecting you."

What does that mean, he's been expecting me?

Judge Parker gestured toward a chair, but Mas wasn't going to fall for that trick again. He pulled at his windbreaker, making sure that it hid the extra weight he was carrying.

"I heard about Anmen Sanjo being arrested." Parker sat in his black leather chair, his back as erect as ever. "Kidnaping and shooting a firearm in a public place. Initiating a ponzi scheme. He's in quite a bit of trouble. I don't know what I can really do to help."

Did Parker really think that Mas had come to beg for his mercy on Anmen? Mas could have handled this a number of ways, but he decided to go for the bull's-eye first. "Whyzu you kill Isokichi? And why youzu following Juanita Gushiken?"

Parker's face visibly darkened and his eyes narrowed like slits. He waited before responding. "Do you know what is the Japanese American's strongest trait?"

Mas wasn't about to fall into the judge's verbal trap.

"Loyalty," Parker answered. "That's why the internment was such an irony: why would these people turn on the U.S.? Most Nisei were true believers, more patriotic than myself. And their parents — it didn't matter whether they were born here or not. Even if secretly, deep down inside, these Issei felt connected to Japan, rooted for them, they wouldn't have done anything. For one thing, they didn't have any power. Even Japan didn't take them seriously. Only the misfits, minor-league men and women, went to America from Japan. And secondly, these misfits felt obligated to America for giving them a second chance in life."

Mas's forehead was wet with sweat. He didn't know where the judge was leading him, but it was too late to break loose now.

"You see, white Americans — *hakujin* Americans like me — we can't see beyond the color of one's skin or hear beyond words and accents. We're stupid, really, if you think of it. We act like we own America. We were the ones who came here first, right, on the *Mayflower.* Forget about the Native Americans who lived here off the land. Forget about all the Mexicans who lived in California and Texas way before the *Mayflower.* Those folks don't count.

"If we say American, we don't mean Native American, Canadian, or South American, or anyone with remotely brown skin and brown eyes. We mean good ole U.S. of A., and only the Caucasian ones and not the blacks. Those same whites could be one degree separated from Germany, Holland, Ireland, and they would still be considered full-fledged American. But not you. Not your friends. And not your children and not your grandchildren."

The judge put his hands together like he was praying and put the tips of his index fingers on his lips. "Anyway, what can you do? You could have Kinjo go after me. Or have your friends in the coroner's department make some accusations. That's not going to get you very far. Who's going to care about your man Isokichi?"

Mas's shoulders sagged as if he were melting right there in Judge Parker's office.

"You think your newspapers will listen to

you? I've been on the board of Japanese American organizations for decades. Spoke out against the internment. Who's going to protest, Mas? The only one these people will go after is you. These people owe me. Their loyalty is unfailing."

Again, *osewaninatta*. Mas didn't realize that Judge Parker was so perceptive. He did understand Japanese Americans; and now he was planning to use that understanding against them, or at least against one dead man, Isokichi Sanjo.

"But you kill him anyways."

"I didn't necessarily want him dead, Mas. I wanted him to go forward with the trial. But he was a coward. And then his brother fired me. Neither of them realized what was at stake. Our government had abandoned the Constitution; his case could have helped others. But he had given up. I was mad — hell, I was mad. I had every right to be. I had spent hours on that case.

"So, Mas, you ask why I killed Isokichi Sanjo. Well, whatever I may have done, I'll have God to contend with. But believe me, Sanjo did much worse. He wasn't thinking beyond himself. If he took a stand, he might have stopped the purging, or at least slowed it down. And Metcalf, he thought he had one over me. What a foolish man. He didn't know who he was dealing with."

Mas felt numb, as if he had just experienced a beating. Only the beating wasn't of his body, but of his mind.

"Mas, I'm happy you stopped by. Feel free to come over anytime. I have a new gardener, you know. He studied horticulture at Cal Poly Pomona. You might learn a thing or two from him."

Mas left Judge Parker's office, feeling sick to his stomach. He feared that he would *haku* right there in the courthouse hallway.

Parker was a man full of ideas and principles. He'd seen Sanjo's case as the fulfillment of those things early in his career. The only thing was, Sanjo wasn't an idea. He was a man, a husband and father. A man who was, yes, Japanese, specifically Okinawan, but who wasn't only defined by his ethnicity. Sanjo hadn't had any fight left in him, which had enraged Parker. And when the attorney had been fired, he must have confronted Sanjo, yelled and screamed at him, and finally killed him.

Mas didn't know if it was intentional or accidental, but what happened next was definitely calculated. Parker spent years, decades, working on behalf of Japanese Americans. Each effort was like a baseball umpire extending his arms out — safe, safe,

safe. Until maybe today.

Mas stumbled down the corridor and then opened the door to the last room. Wearing a pair of earphones, Detective Alo sat with four other men, including Buchanan Lee, and a woman at a low table filled with tape recorders and other high-tech equipment. Alo removed his earphones. "You did good."

"I dunno," Mas said as the woman lifted his shirt and peeled off a microphone taped to his chest. Mas wasn't sure if Judge Parker had actually confessed. But much of what Parker had said was true. "No Japanese goin' to go after him."

Agent Lee stood up. "But you're forgetting, Mr. Arai. We're not Japanese."

After being stripped of his bugging device, Mas went to his next destination with good news. Antonio Gushiken would be released immediately from his holding cell on Terminal Island, according to Agent Lee. "The Department of Justice is only happy to drop it," he told Mas. Apparently some politicians with close connections to Judge Parker had been the ones putting pressure on certain Homeland Security administrators to go after Antonio, in an attempt to squash Juanita's investigation of the Sanjo case. Lee suspected that the judge himself had been the one who had planted that antiquated tracking device in Juanita's wheel well.

That piece of news at least took some of the bite away from what Mas would be experiencing next. Another commemoration of a dead man's life. He went to more funerals these days than weddings, holiday parties, and anniversary celebrations combined. This one, however, would be new in that they would be gathering at the Los Angeles County Cemetery. As he drove through Evergreen's entrance, Mas felt a wash of sadness. He had been better about visiting Chizuko's grave site lately — coming on her birthday, Memorial Day (well, actually, the day before, to beat the crowds), the anniversary of her death, and New Year's Day (again, one day afterward, to beat the crowds). But still not enough.

The memorial service was actually Itchy Iwasaki's idea. He thought every death needed to be remembered formally at least once. And, of course, these remembrances would, conveniently, be good for his business.

Although the Los Angeles County Cemetery was only accessible through Evergreen, Mas had never been there before. He drove down a sloping path to a simple chain-link fence. A huge pile of reddish dirt, crisscrossed with the tracks of a forklift, sat inside. On one side of the fence were the collapsed wooden frames of old floral arrangements. A granite Japanese headstone lay abandoned next to a stack of white caskets. Mas's gut felt queasy. Surely Isokichi Sanjo, master *sanshin* player, had not been in such a place for fifty years.

After Mas passed the first metal gate, he entered a grassy area shaded by a massive pine, a willow, a eucalyptus, and even a couple of fruit trees next to a white wood-framed chapel. Itchy was there, wearing a suit and white gloves. It was a small crowd — the son, Brian Yamashiro; G. I.; Juanita; and himself. Gushi-mama would have made it if she could have, but she'd said that she would send a representative. No such representative had arrived.

Little round cement markers the circumference of soup cans pockmarked the Bermuda grass. They each had two numbers designating row and column, a grave site graph. The small party stood underneath the pine tree, where Isokichi's ashes were apparently buried underneath 5/2.

Itchy read a short biography on Isokichi Sanjo. Date of birth and date of death. And not much else.

"Does someone want to say something?"

Brian kept his eyes on the numbered marker.

"Mas? You know something about him," G. I. said.

Mas looked around. Strange thing was, he did know more about Sanjo than anyone else there. "Heezu a man who loved *shamisen* — well, *sanshin*. He care about his wife. His boysu. He care about America. He fight so hard, in the end, all fight gone."

Mas heard sobbing beside him. Brian's shoulders were shaking. Monster tears dropped down the sides of his face. Itchy was right. It was ones you least expected to crack that did so at times like this.

Brian would now have to go back to Hawaii and have a funeral for his brother. Sorrow on two sides of the Pacific.

G. I. looked distressed. He began to curve his arm around Brian's back and then thought better of it, and returned this arm to his own side. Mas bit down in agreement. Right now, Brian didn't need anyone's sympathy. He had to learn to hang on to his dignity. He needed to find that hard place inside that would center him like the middle of a compass. Throughout his life, the needle would point in various directions, but he would have to know where he stood. Brian Yamashiro now had an uncle that he had never known existed, but for all intents and purposes, he would still be alone.

Making arrangements to meet later at a restaurant in Chinatown, they walked toward their cars.

"My father is going to be released tomorrow," Juanita said. "I owe you so much, Mas."

Mas shuddered, hearing those words. "No, no. But I gotsu a favor — don't say no more Izu some kind of detective." He said this loud enough for G. I.'s benefit. "I gotsu a bad *hyoban* to begin with. If people thinkin' Izu some kind of spy, I keep gettin' into trouble."

Before leaving the cemetery, Mas had something to do, namely to make sure Chizuko's resting place was free of dead leaves and dirt. And also to think about whether he missed his wife so much that he was seeing her face everywhere, even in an African Okinawan American professor.

Mas was a few steps away from the Ford when he saw a lone figure by the cemetery's chapel.

"Hallo, Kinjo-*san*."

"Gushi-mama told me to come."

Mas nodded. The old lady was conniving, yet she knew what she was doing. The Uchinanchu needed to come together. G. I. and

372

Brian had already recognized that, as they had agreed to donate Randy's Las Vegas winnings to the Okinawa Association to begin a center for the study of the *sanshin* in the United States.

"I didn't want to *jama* and disturb the service. I'm sure Isokichi's son doesn't want to see me."

Mas was glad that Kinjo had exercised discretion. Gushi-mama might have expected an immediate reconciliation, but people's feelings weren't like wooden blocks you nailed together.

"If I had known what would happen, I would have never gone to Metcalf."

Kinjo didn't have to explain anything to Mas. Mas had made his share of mistakes and knew that it didn't help airing them to either friend or foe.

"What can I do? I've already agreed to testify against Parker. Send money to Isokichi's son? Donate money in memory of Isokichi's name to the Okinawa Association?"

There was also explaining himself to Isokichi's brother, Anmen. But the hope of that conversation was slim to none. Some relationships were so severed that no intervention — even that of a 106-year-old matriarch — could rectify them.

Mas looked beyond Kinjo to the chapel, whose doors were ajar. "Sing his songs."

"What songs? The songs he wrote in the band?"

Mas shook his head. He didn't literally mean Isokichi's songs, but the subjects he wrote about. The fallen tears while earning pennies in the fields. The love for his sons. Isokichi's last song had been a farewell, but they needed a new song that would bridge the past to the present.

Mas tried to explain as best he could, when Kinjo interrupted. "Do you know what's strange, Arai-*san?*"

A breeze blew through the cemetery, causing brown pine needles to drop on the Ford.

"I miss him. I never let myself miss him before."

The following week went fast, because there was nothing to look forward to. Mas stopped by Eaton's Nursery: Mr. Patel had recently heard of the feng shui merits of an indoor money tree, the small tabletop plants with multiple trunks twisted together, and seeking good luck, he wanted a few for his restaurants. Eaton's wasn't the cheapest, but it was the closest, and these days convenience was worth more than it used to be.

It was a half hour before closing time. Mas

wasn't surprised to see the gang of five beginning to unearth their Budweisers from the bottom of their coolers. What did surprise him was that behind the counter, instead of the kind, welcoming face of Kammy, was a craggy, shrunken fellow with a limp. Wishbone Tanaka.

Wishbone saw Mas's surprise in his eyes. "I broke out of Keiro," he said, grinning. "Nah, my doctors figured out that causing trouble is good for my health. But it's bad for everyone else. So they kicked me out."

"You workin' here now?"

"Have to, to pay off my investors." Wishbone leaned on his good foot. "Yup, that's the deal we're trying to make. No one wants to get involved with a lawsuit, anyhows. It's the lawyers that always win."

Mas couldn't argue with that.

"Saw Anmen in the slammer this week."

"Oh, yah?"

"He'll be out once he makes bail. All these musicians in Okinawa are sending money to him — he's going to get the best lawyer in L.A. If he only had known, huh? This could have been his best scam yet."

So the gears of the legal system were slowly turning. Mas had heard from G. I. that Jiro was already out on bail. Hopefully, with Kinjo's testimony, Jiro wouldn't have to do any jail time. But, as with anything involving lawyers and judges, you couldn't take anything for granted.

Mas walked over to a display and selected the six money trees with the healthiest leaves and most beautiful braided trunks.

"Everybody is going wild over these," Wishbone said, helping Mas carry them to the counter. "I guess everyone wants to be rich."

Mas grunted, opening up his wallet. He knew the real reason for the plant's popularity. It was no muss, no fuss. No fertilizer, and just a sprinkle of water a week. It was plain easy to keep them alive.

The following Monday night meant dinner at the Yamadas', and this time Mas did not come empty-handed. He drove all the way down to a Hawaiian restaurant in Monterey Park to bring back a set of eight Spam *musubi,* all wrapped in cellophane.

Lil had said that the dinner would be a celebration in his honor, so she had invited G. I. and Juanita, Haruo and Spoon. That made three couples, six people, plus Mas to make it an odd seven, but Mas figured he could always eat two people's worth of *musubi.*

He was the last to arrive. He recognized

Haruo's mini Honda, the red Toyota truck, but *a-ra* — a green-tea-colored VW Bug? Mas looked into the window, and instead of an orange gerber daisy in the vase holder on the dashboard, he saw a white stephanotis. Stephanotis — fragrant, star-shaped blooms — were popular for weddings, Haruo had told Mas.

The cellophane-wrapped *musubi* were slippery in Mas's hands. He rang the doorbell and Tug answered, a sloppy grin on his face. Everyone, except Lil and Tug, was already seated at the Yamadas' dinner table. G. I., Juanita, Haruo, Spoon, and, yes, Genessee.

"Hello, Mas." Everybody seemed to talk at once; they were so happy to see him. As if he were a hero of some kind.

Lil appeared, wiping her hands on a kitchen towel. "We were waiting for you. Have a seat." She gestured toward an empty seat between Genessee and Haruo. Tug returned to his place at the table while Mas presented the Spam *musubi* before sitting. He should have noticed a little bit of hesitancy on Lil's part as she accepted his gift. He soon discovered what the problem was when she tentatively set out each *musubi* on its own plate at each seat.

"What's this, Mom?" Tug grimaced, creating an ugly face that Mas was not used to seeing on his friend.

"Spam *musubi*," she said, presenting a fake smile. "Mas brought it."

"Sorry, ole man. I'm just not a fan of Spam. We had it all the time in the army. Just seeing it gives me a stomachache."

"Tug!"

"Orai, orai." Mas almost started to laugh. Chizuko always said that Mas had a healthy dose of *shitsurei,* rudeness, and, in contrast, held up Tug as a modicum of gentility. To see Tug mixed up with *shitsurei* amused Mas to no end.

"Here, you have mine, okay, Mas?" Tug nudged the plate over to Mas's side of the table.

No problem on Mas's part. He knew enough to wait before he started. "*Bikuri,* surprise," he commented to Genessee beside him. She was wearing a soft white eyelet blouse, which made her skin look luminous, like a fresh-roasted chestnut. "Didn't expect to see youzu."

"Well, hope it's a good *bikuri.*"

Mas was too embarrassed to nod yes.

Tug then called for his ritual of grace, and each person opened their hands to their neighbors. Mas quickly wiped his right palm on his jeans before he extended it to Genessee. Her hand was as smooth as an ocean stone polished by thousands of waves. Tug ended his prayer with an amen, which Mas could hear Genessee repeating under her breath.

"Ittakimasu," G. I., the latent Buddhist, then announced. It was now officially time to eat.

Lil had made roast beef and potatoes, but Mas chose to start his meal off with his appetizer. He unwrapped the cellophane from the *musubi* and then opened his mouth wide, letting his dentures squeeze down on the grilled Spam, soft vinegared rice, and strip of black seaweed. The salty firmness of the processed meat, sweet tang of the soft rice, and dryness of the nori all merged together in a great taste symphony, signaling that for a moment, everything was all right.

ABOUT THE AUTHOR

Naomi Hirahara is the Macavity Award nominated author of two previous Mas Arai mysteries, *Summer of the Big Bachi* and *Gasa-Gasa Girl.* A writer, editor, and publisher of nonfiction books, she previously worked as an editor of *The Rafu Shimpo,* a bilingual Japanese American daily newspaper in Los Angeles. She earned her B.A. in international relations and spent a year at the Inter-University Center for Advanced Japanese Studies in Tokyo. She and her husband reside in her birthplace, Southern California. For more information and reading group guides, visit her Web site at www. naomihirahara.com.

The employees of Thorndike Press hope you have enjoyed this Large Print book. All our Thorndike and Wheeler Large Print titles are designed for easy reading, and all our books are made to last. Other Thorndike Press Large Print books are available at your library, through selected bookstores, or directly from us.

For information about titles, please call:
  (800) 223-1244

or visit our Web site at:
  www.gale.com/thorndike
  www.gale.com/wheeler

To share your comments, please write:
  Publisher
  Thorndike Press
  295 Kennedy Memorial Drive
  Waterville, ME 04901